CHICAGO FIX

CHICAGO FIX

FIX

GREGORY C. RANDALL

This story is dedicated to
my grandfathers,
Harold Struble and Howard Smith

1

THEY WEIGHED EIGHT OUNCES—SEPARATELY.
Each glove laced tight to the tape-wrapped fists of the fighter's abused hands. In sum, they added a pound of weight—sixteen ounces of death-dispensing leather and horsehair. The gloves were there to defend the boxer and prolong the battle. Men died wearing them, and men killed using them.

The empty ready room reeked of sweat, liniment, alcohol, ammonia, and leftover fear. Three incandescent light bulbs, in wire mesh enclosures secured to taut electrical cords, hung from the ceiling in a line directly over a training table; the middle bulb was out. Above the caged lights, a fan slowly spun; one of its three wide blades was cracked and, during each revolution, clicked loudly. In one corner, a white trash can with a red X painted on its side sat full to overflowing with bloody strips of cloth and gauze. Piles of clean white towels filled the shelves on the opposite side of the room. Of the used and bloodstained towels, half had found the laundry basket, half lay strewn on the floor. White cloth tape, twisted, torn, and speckled with blood, was strewn across the black-and-white tile floor. It looked like bleached-out dead minnows had washed up on one of Chicago's famous beaches.

Beyond the steel door, out in the hallway, buzzed a crazed,

almost electrical crowd noise: the palpable static of inhuman passion. As if pushed by the sound, four men burst into the room. Two of the men, in white shirts and white slacks, supported a man between them. He was in boxing livery, his arms over the shoulders of the other two, his toes dragging. Blood dripped from splits just below each of his eyes; it dribbled down his chest and spotted the floor. The fourth man, in the lead, was a short, bald, narrow, rat-faced fellow carrying a well-worn and stained leather satchel. On his white T-shirt and arms, blood had left a betraying history of cuts, gore, and spit.

In one well-practiced and sweeping move, the two carrying the unconscious man pitched him onto the table. Their companion retrieved a finger-sized glass vial from the bag and, after snapping off its top, released a cloud of smelling salts that he thrust under the boxer's bloody and broken nose. The boxer did not react. The rat-faced man lifted the boxer's right, swollen eyelid and looked at the pupil.

He turned to the other two men.

"Get the fucking doctor. Get the son of bitch, and get him here now."

The doctor arrived. For an hour they worked industriously on the fighter; this wretched labor was more diligent and longer than the fight itself. When they were done, there were more broken ribs and bloody injection sites in the boxer's arms and chest. The fighter never opened his eyes.

"Get him to the hospital," a man in a striped suit—and late to the sad work—said most officiously from the corner. "I don't want him dying here, got it? Get him in the meat wagon, then to Cook County. He's not their first. Just get him the hell out of here."

When they didn't move quickly enough, he added, "We need the room for the eighth bout, so clean it up. Get it ready. I want no word of any of this—you guys get it? No word. One word, one hint, and I'll make sure the commission knows it was your fucking ineptitude, got it? Get him out of here. Use the back stair."

The suit looked around the room.

"Where's his gloves, dammit. Where's his gloves?"

Once the doctor had entered, Rat Face had held back, slouching near the door. He lit a cigarette and answered, "They's under the towels in the corner. Over there."

He pointed.

"Get 'em."

"You fucken' get 'em yourself. I'm done with this shit—done, Mr. Stingly. Done."

Rat Face turned and walked out of the room.

"What about the kid's old lady?" one of the other men said. "She's been at her wit's end and pestering me since we brought Benny down here. For Christ's sake, Mr. Stingly, you have to tell his mother."

"Do I look like her fucking rabbi?" Stingly snapped. "Tell her he's going to the hospital. Get the word to Rabbi Harris, so he knows you're coming. He'll be ready."

Five minutes later, the training room was cleared of the bloody towels, the dead minnows on the floor were gone, and the white can with the red X was empty. Two black attendants used clean towels to quickly wipe down the table and other surfaces; the unmistakable smell of antiseptic alcohol filled the air. The room, again vacant, waited for the ringside bell that signaled the end of the next fight.

* * *

For Tommy O'Shea—'Flying O'Shea' on promotional posters and handouts—the fight had been tough and bloody, ten rounds, neither fighter had backed down. He had bite marks in his shoulder from the clinches to prove it. His right side felt like it had been stove-in. Every breath hurt to Jesus. He showered and with the help of the cut man, an Irish boxing fixture named Kibbie Kimble, he dressed. A knock on the door startled them. O'Shea's manager and promoter, Duffy McGoin, left for twenty seconds, and then returned.

"How's Benny?" O'Shea asked.

"Haven't heard—was still out cold. We need to get going."

"What's the hurry?"

"Some of the boys are celebrating at Schaller's," McGoin said. "They want to shake your hand. It was a good fight, damn good."

"And help beer sales, I'm sure. Shit, Duffy, I'm beat and my head hurts like a fucking vice is squeezing it—"

"Just a short stop, that's all," McGoin promised.

"Like it'll pop," O'Shea continued, as if McGoin hadn't spoken.

McGoin gave him an appraising glance.

"The Sox played this afternoon, beat Detroit two to nothing, and the place will be full," he told the fighter. "Just a handshake or two. Then you can go home."

O'Shea's dressing room was on the opposite side of the Chicago Stadium from Benny's. The promoters and the stadium officials split the fighters to reduce potential pre- and post-fight clashes. Sometimes the fighter's camp-followers got into it. There had been more than one shooting in the bowels of the Stadium since it opened four years earlier.

McGoin rushed O'Shea to a side door that led to the Madison Street parking lot. He looked for reporters and, seeing none, he threw a towel over the fighter's head and pushed him into the waiting massive Buick sedan.

"Hey! My head hurts enough," O'Shea said, pulling away the towel. "Hey, did you see Daisy? She said she was gonna be here."

"No, I didn't see her, kid. She's probably at home taking care of the little one. We gotta go. You know the press—they will hound you over the fight, the same old crap about what punch and when. Saving you from them, m'boy. Daisy will find you."

They took Ashland Avenue south, over and under the railroad tracks that extended out from Chicago like an iron spiderweb spread across America. Eventually, they crossed the Chicago River. At 37th Street, they turned east to South Halsted; two blocks later, they pulled to the curb under the neon sign of one of the city's oldest taverns. Schaller's was the political and cultural heart of Bridgeport, a sprawling Irish neighborhood and also home neighborhood of the city's current mayor, His Honor Edward Joseph Kelly.

A lanky Irish kid, wearing a silver-buttoned valet uniform, opened the door of the Buick. McGoin stepped out and then turned back to reach in and pull O'Shea out to the curb. Once on the sidewalk, he grasped the prizefighter by the shoulders and pivoted him toward the crowd.

"Smile, Tommy. Smile, m'boy. Your public wants to see the best Irish middleweight fighter that Bridgeport has ever produced."

A dozen kids held out handbills, clamoring for O'Shea's autograph.

"Tommy, Tommy, here, here," they yelled, waving the papers. Newsmen were on hand, and two photographers from the *Tribune* and the *Daily News* stood on stepladders behind the crowd—it all had been orchestrated by McGoin.

The explosions of flashbulbs startled O'Shea. He recovered and turned to the first waiting boy.

"What's your name, kid?" he asked, reaching for the boy's handbill.

"Bill, sir."

"Well, Bill, let me sign that thing. Duffy, you got a pen or something?"

The manager produced a pen from his coat pocket and held it out to O'Shea. As the fighter reached for it, he suddenly looked confused, his eyes unfocused.

"You okay, Tommy?" asked McGoin.

"Huh, what?" O'Shea muttered.

"Tommy!" McGoin yelled. "Give him room."

O'Shea collapsed, driving his already battered face into the concrete sidewalk.

"Tommy," McGoin said again. He knelt at the side of his boxer. "Get some water, someone."

The kids formed a dense circle around the two men, the silence broken only by the driver of the Buick demanding that everyone get out of his way. The man, a giant of an Irish kid who'd played football for Notre Dame until his knee failed him, picked up O'Shea and carried him to the back of the automobile.

"Mr. McGoin, we gots to go, now," the driver said. "Mercy Hospital is just a few blocks. We gots to go. I've seen this before. Every minute makes a difference."

McGoin leapt into the back seat with O'Shea, and the Buick squealed out onto Halsted Street. The neighborhood boys with their handbills fluttering in the night breeze, and the newsmen with their notebooks, and the photographers with their cameras, watched, not understanding what just had happened.

2

HYMEN ROSENBERG sat in the back seat of his Cadillac and watched through the opening in the shrubbery, as the two men rolled the body into the hole. Their last act was tossing in the man's hat. Twenty minutes later, after throwing shovels in the trunk, the driver slipped into the front seat and his partner took a seat next to him.

"That son of a bitch won't be causing trouble no more, Mr. Rosenberg."

"Well done and efficient, Ziggy. It's always good to be prepared. When did you dig the hole?" Rosenberg asked.

"Two days ago. We needed some exercise—you never know when you need a hole in the ground," Ziggy Feldstein said with a snort.

"Where to, Mr. Rosenberg?" Gus Teitlebaum, the driver, asked.

"Take the long way home, through the preserve. Maybe stop while I enjoy a cigar on this fine Sunday morning."

"Yes, sir. The Forest Preserve it is."

Hymen Rosenberg's rap sheet was long and sordid, but he'd managed to stay out of jail and avoid the assassin's bullet more than once during his days with the Outfit. Rosie had been born to a prostitute in the stink of a barn a hundred

miles south of Warsaw, Poland. He managed to scrape together—steal would be the more correct term—money to flee the
pogroms in Poland. This was just before the start of the Great
War. He reached Chicago where a half cousin gave him a bed
and a job. What saved the twenty-two-year-old Polish Jew was
Prohibition. First, he started bringing in liquor from Canada in his own truck, and when Capone made him an offer to
buy his gas if he went to work for him, he shrugged and said,
"Why not?" For twelve years he'd reported to Capone's fixer
and political muscle, Jake Guzik. Now with Capone in prison,
and the Outfit searching for a new leader, Rosenberg had gone
back to what he knew best: murder for hire. Meanwhile, his
wife and two children lived in a nice home in a respectable
neighborhood of Oak Park.

Rosenberg leaned over the back of the front seat and handed envelopes to the men. They never questioned what was giv-
en, never questioned what was asked.

"This would be a good spot," Rosenberg told the driver.

Teitlebaum pulled to the side of the road; a trail led off into
the thick forest of oak and beech trees.

"You want us to wait?"

"Please, I'd rather not walk home."

"Oh, yeah, right. Sorry, boss."

Rosenberg took a cigar from a case in his breast pocket
and lit it. The smoke hung in the August morning air; hardly
a breeze rustled the trees. He walked up the trail and disappeared from the view of his crew.

The walks were a routine that Rosenberg would not give
up; the exercise cleared his head and gave him time to think.
And, the timing being random and unpredictable, he felt safe
from those who would like to put him into one of those holes
in the Forest Preserve. The cigar was Cuban; he ordered them
by the hundreds from a friend who ran a casino in Havana.
The earthy smell permeated the woods; he inhaled deeply as

he turned his mind to examining the problem. Someone had seriously fucked up Friday night.

Rosenberg's bets had been placed in four books: twenty-five grand in Cicero, twenty-five in Berwyn, thirty thousand with a bookie connected to the Russians, and twenty with a small joint a block from the Hide Away run by the cheap bookie who now rested uncomfortably in a hole a few miles back. Rosenberg had put all the money on Schwartz. He'd seen the kid fight; he was good, damn good, and when he'd gotten confirmation that the O'Shea kid would drop, Rosenberg had put down the bets. The odds were 3:1 because the Irish kid hadn't lost a fight. O'Shea was 12–0. It would have made for a good evening, but now Rosenberg was out a hundred thousand, not chicken feed, even for the depression. He'd paid McGoin ten grand for the setup. O'Shea's manager said he'd make sure the kid got five thousand, a fortune to a Mick fighting for a two-hundred-dollar purse. The bookie now in the hole had pleaded that he didn't know anything; he offered to give Rosenberg all the money he made. He begged for his life.

"No one screws with me, kid, no one," Rosenberg had said.

Ziggy had grabbed the bookie by the shoulders, and Gus threw a heavy black bag over the man's head and pulled the cord tight around his neck. Thirty seconds later, as the man twisted and gagged violently under the bag, Rosenberg casually had drawn his Colt revolver and put two bullets into the bookie's head.

No one fucks with me, he thought now, as the smoke drifted along with his walk.

He could count on one hand the men he'd killed for personal reasons; the rest were for money. He never asked why. Four of the contracts had been women, some from the sordid and very uncomfortable businesses that Jake Guzik's brother, Harry, ran. Rosenberg didn't abide white slavery and the brothels; they brought too much heat from the churches and other do-gooders, whereas no one cared about gambling, the track, and the fights. Nonetheless, a contract was a contract.

His own story was like many who fled Europe. His business now was a bullet for a buck. He thought about a business card with that inscription—then again, that would be pretentious. He'd recently turned down a few jobs that were too complicated and, in his opinion, resolutions to personal problems. He'd like to think he didn't pander to vendettas, but if the money was right, he'd find the right bullet.

When Rosenberg returned, Gus and Ziggy were standing next to the Cadillac. They said nothing as he approached, crushed out their own cigarettes, and opened the rear door for their boss.

"Lunch?" Gus asked.

"Not today. Take me home, Gus. Keep the car. Ziggy, I'll see you in the morning. Mrs. Rosenberg says that Sarah and David want to go to the fair tonight, a special event in the lagoons, a show, or something. I can't disappoint them. Gus, go get a bite, and then pick us up at six o'clock."

"Yes, sir."

Rosenberg lit another cigar, cracked the window an inch, and sat back and watched the Forest Preserve change from woodland to farms to houses. To the north, on the near horizon as they turned north onto Cicero Avenue, the skyline of Chicago spread majestically. He could think of no other place to live.

"And don't forget to clean and wash the shovels."

"Yes, sir," Ziggy answered.

3

DETECTIVE TONY ALFANO strolled into the Racine Street police station, and placed a large box of warm donuts on the desk of Sergeant McDunnah.

"I suppose you now want me to make fresh coffee?" McDunnah asked.

"Can't eat these things without something to flush them down," Tony said. "And besides, you could say thanks."

"Thanks. And thanks also for the two extra pounds. The wife will kill me."

"I thought you were getting a little too thin for your position."

"And that's what? Your—growing fatter by the donut—babysitter."

"I do not need a babysitter."

Pulling a cruller out of the box and tapping it against the side to knock off the excess powdered sugar, Alfano asked, "Messages?"

Sergeant McDunnah paged through the stack of pink notes on his desk.

"Two. His Honor wants to see you when you have a minute, no hurry. The second is from Dr. Abrahamson."

"Did the doc say anything?"

"He has two stiffs that you might be interested in."

"Really? And I was hoping for a slow day. I'm going to my desk, finish this cruller, and drink this cold cup of your crud. I'll call him then—don't think the bodies are going anywhere."

"My hero."

"Coffee, Sergeant. Please."

"Now that you asked nicely."

Alfano wove his way through the desks to his small fiefdom in a back corner of the kingdom of the detectives. Behind him, a high window showed a cloudless sky. A vertical four-drawer steel file cabinet stood against the wall, and next to the cabinet a corkboard on a movable frame and wheels. It was one of two he used. A calendar from the Swift Meat Company was pinned to the cork; all the dates before Monday, August 14, 1933, were X'ed out with a pencil. His massive oak desk, manufactured sometime in the final decade of the last century by a defunct Grand Rapids, Michigan, furniture company, took up most of the remaining real estate. He'd found the label on the underside of the right bottom drawer during one of his biannual purges. He'd wondered how many other cops had pulled themselves up to this desk over the last forty years. He picked up the handset and dialed a familiar number.

"Mayor Kelly, please. This is Detective Alfano, returning his call."

"The mayor is awfully busy."

"Look, I'm returning his call. Tell him to call me—I'll mention how helpful you are."

"No need to be so rude, Detective," the secretary responded. "I'll put you through."

"Wise girl."

Alfano waited as the call was routed.

The thick, full-throated voice of the mayor of Chicago punched him in the ear.

"Detective Alfano, thanks for the return call. Goddamn, what a weekend. The fair was crazy. More than half a million people came through the turnstile."

"Yes, sir. Quite a weekend, Mayor," Alfano said.

Late Friday afternoon, after his shift, Alfano had climbed into his Packard and driven to Racine, Wisconsin. Rented a cabin on the shore of Lake Michigan, ate a cold meatball sandwich, and drank until the bottle was empty. Then fell blissfully to sleep. That was the first full night of sleep he'd had in a month.

There was a pause on the line.

"You still there, Detective?"

"Yes, sir. Sorry, a bit distracted this morning."

"Hungover, right?"

"What can I do for you, sir?"

"Stop by later. There's things in Bridgeport we need to discuss."

"Like what?"

"Later—can you be here at three o'clock?"

"Yes, sir. Three o'clock."

The line went dead.

Alfano's relationship with the mayor was like that of a mongoose and a cobra. In fact, more like one mongoose and a box of cobras. He did not like the mayor or his friends. Edward Kelly was the current face of complacent Chicago corruption. The man could woo the press, kiss babies, open world's fairs, and speechify to women's clubs and ethnic organizations, seemingly all at the same time. While not exactly filling his own pockets, Alfano was damn sure that the mayor's friends' pockets were not getting lighter.

Kelly had been handed the job, not five months earlier, after the February assassination of the then Chicago mayor, Anton Cermak, in Miami. Cermak was declared a martyr and patriot for coming between a bullet and the newly elected president, Franklin D. Roosevelt. The press rumors concerning Cermak's alleged assassination filled every discussion of Illinois and Chicago politics. Was he the martyred savior, a target of Al Capone's old Outfit, or the retaliation by current gangland thugs? No one knew, or more importantly, no one wanted to know. Most citizens thought little about the loss of one more corrupt politician. Not when their greatest concern, during the "great depression," as Hoover had termed it, was putting food on the table.

As for Kelly, "handed" was not exactly the right word, Alfano thought. It was more like political manipulation on a scale previously unseen in American politics. All neat, legal, and proper, but the elevation of Chicago's chief sanitation engineer to mayor just stunk.

"Coroner Abrahamson, please. Detective Alfano here," Alfano said after he'd dialed the next number on McDunnah's list. He waited.

"Tony, how are you?"

"Good, Doc. Never better."

"I know you; it's Monday. Take some aspirin."

"Thanks, Doctor. What's up?"

"I've got two bodies in the morgue, both brought in Saturday morning. You may know them: Tommy O'Shea and Benny Schwartz."

Alfano paused. "Good God, not the fighters?"

"Yes. I saw them Friday night at the Stadium. It was a good fight, in fact, maybe a great fight. O'Shea won in the last minute of the tenth, a knockout. Six hours later, they both were delivered here."

"Shit. Tough luck. Why the call?"

"You need to see the bodies, and we need to talk. And the press does not know yet."

Alfano never questioned Abrahamson's requests for a meeting. Usually it was something well beyond the obvious.

The doc knew his way around a dead body better than any coroner Tony had known; especially a murdered body.

"One hour?"

"See you then."

McDunnah placed a fresh cup of coffee and another cruller on Alfano's desk.

"You've had your breakfast, now eat your lunch," the desk sergeant said.

"Thanks. Do you know Tommy O'Shea or Benny Schwartz?"

"Yeah, I know Tommy, good Bridgeport kid—grew up a few blocks from us. He's a scrapper, fought in the Golden Gloves, came in second three years ago. Went pro and shifted up to middleweight. He fought last Friday. Why?"

"Doc Abrahamson has him on a slab."

"God, no. This will break his wife's heart. What happened?"

"Don't know, but I'll find out in an hour. Schwartz?"

"He also fought his way up the ladder in Golden Gloves. Missed out being champion each year by a technical knockout. Many said it was his being Jewish. I saw him box a few times, fast hands, could take a punch. Biggest problem was that he'd cut easy, bled everywhere. He's not the other body?"

"Yes, both died after the fight."

McDunnah, crestfallen, said, "Jesus, Mary, and Joseph; there's going to be some sad families after this. Both kids were well liked."

Alfano hated coincidences, in fact, did not believe in them. One death was a tragic result of a fight; it happened before and would happen again. But both fighters, same match—that was different. Something else had gone on. He looked over at Detective Dooley's desk, where a stack of *Tribunes* sat on the left side. Dooley worked the weekend; the Saturday and Sunday papers were at the top of the stack. Retrieving the Sunday issue,

Alfano opened the sports section. Center page was a photo of Tommy O'Shea standing next to a massive car, surrounded by a dozen kids waving programs, looking for an autograph. A man in a pinstripe suit stood behind Tommy, a cigar stuck in his mouth, watching. The photo caption read:

Tommy 'The Flying O'Shea,' mysteriously disappears
after KO win at the Stadium.

Alfano scanned the article. It reported that O'Shea collapsed to the sidewalk in front of Schaller's a minute after leaving the car. He was carried back into the car by the driver and they left. At the time of the article, the beat writer didn't know where or what happened afterward. Duffy McGoin, the man with the cigar and O'Shea's manager, would not elaborate when asked on Saturday about the fighter's condition. "He is in an undisclosed location recovering from the fight," was all that was quoted.

"Now he's on a marble slab in the morgue," Alfano said aloud, to no one.

He'd met many boxers over the years, even shook Max Baer's hand when the fighter—who'd knocked Max Schmeling on his ass in Madison Square Garden—came through Chicago the year before. He'd also read about boxers killed in the ring, or dying days later from a punch. Amateur fights, like the Golden Gloves, were different. Specifically, they were between smaller and younger boys, shorter fights of three two-minute rounds for specific weight classes. It was the pros who died because of longer fights. Alfano didn't mind the contests fought by bigger and faster men; he understood. A man does what he does to survive these days. But there also was the avarice, the gambling, the desperation, and the manly bravado that led to punch-drunk men sitting along the curb, clanking their tin cans on the bricks for coins, waiting for their heads to explode.

He still wasn't sure what drew him to the sport.

Doctor Abrahamson met Alfano outside his office in the morgue. Tony looked down the hallway. Beyond, sheets covered bodies on a dozen gurneys.

"A man or woman's last indignity," the coroner said as he ushered Alfano into his office.

The doctor sat and lit a cigarette. He nodded to Tony, who also lit up.

"Some days I just have to shake my head over the vulgarity of humans and their total disrespect for each other. More often than not, I see only the questionable and felonious deaths. It's the car accidents, heart attacks, and drownings that seldom come down these halls, unless there's a reason—a reason that involves you."

"Bad day?"

"One of the worst. Tommy and Benny fought for three years—in their late teens—in the Golden Gloves."

The pair had boxed each other five or six times in different weight classes, the doctor told Alfano. Abrahamson had been on the medical staff at the Chicago Stadium for the Gloves.

"I won't do the pro fights," he said. "Too much bullshit and politics. Since the return of the Golden Gloves in '27, I've seen a lot of young men make their bones and move on to become decent men. My guess? After another year or two, these two would have pulled out of the game and gotten real jobs. Now they're dead"—the doctor inclined his head toward the autopsy room—"and on the face of it, they died because somebody wasn't doing their job, maybe the referee."

Alfano nodded but said nothing.

"I was there. I saw the fight," continued Abrahamson. "It looked clean, well refereed, nothing that told the crowd there was a fix or something."

"So why me?" Alfano asked.

In reply, the doctor stood and hooked his thumb over his

shoulder toward the doors at the end of the hallway. Alfano followed. After walking through a warren of hallways, the coroner used his shoulder to push open the double doors to the autopsy room. Inside, the temperature dropped twenty degrees. From high overhead, incandescent lamps filled the tiled walls and floor with harsh, antiseptic light, revealing a row of marble-slabbed tables aligned in the center of the room. A lamp with a large white porcelain shade hung over every table. The opposite wall was paneled with dozens of white enameled doors that always reminded Alfano of small icebox doors. The aroma was alcohol sharp with a sweet, heavy smell that he knew all too well: the stench of death.

The men walked up to the two marble slabs in the middle of the room to where two bodies lay.

"Tommy is on the left, Benny on the right," the coroner said. "We've been through this a number of times, Tony—what do you see?"

Alfano slowly walked around and studied the gray-white bodies. He noticed first the bruising; both had numerous bruises, and some of the dark marks overlapped. Both faces displayed swelling, more so on Tommy O'Shea.

"Why is his face more swollen?" Alfano asked.

"Benny's death stopped the swelling. Tommy lived longer."

Alfano continued to look. Benny, true to his reputation, showed the signs of split skin and wounds that had bled. Tommy had bite marks on his shoulder.

"These?"

"My assumption is that Benny's mouthpiece fell out during a clutch, and his teeth were jammed into Tommy's skin. There are three of those marks, all on the same side."

"The bruising, all pre-mortem?"

"Yes, fight related. Look closer."

Both bodies showed the oval shapes of well-thrown punches. The bruises revealed themselves even more after death: the blood caught in the surface skin of the body as the rest pooled away.

"Some of these have a lighter shade around the wound, much darker toward the middle," Alfano said, pointing to a large bruise on Schwartz's body.

"Good call," the coroner said. "The boxer's glove may leave a bruise, but these are different. I've seen them before. The darker area shows that a denser object hit the body at the same time as the rest of the glove. Something heavier and harder left a fiercer bruise."

"Spiked gloves?"

"Probably."

Alfano nodded thoughtfully. Someone had hidden a pad of heavy metal powder or fine lead balls under the face of O'Shea's gloves. The weight added considerable force to the punch, but would not be seen for days in the bruise. Whereas a bloodless, dead body might reveal the gradations of a bruise from loaded gloves.

"But both fighters?" he asked the doctor.

"Neither probably knew. With all the chaos of the fight, the extra weight might not be noticed. Both these fellows may have trained with heavy gloves to add strength."

He told Alfano that the Romans had used something called a ceastus in their gladiatorial fights—"those weighted gloves were made to severely maim or kill the opponent. They fought to the death then."

"My ancestors, what can I say?"

Abrahamson looked at Alfano over the rims of his glasses.

"I fluoroscoped their heads and upper bodies. I'll do a full cranial exam later, but so far it's clear that Benny's jaw and cheekbones are broken, the cartilage of his left ear mangled, and even his left shoulder bone is cracked in two places. Some of the breaks may be a result of trying to revive him—so are the injection sites. But in my opinion, he was beaten to death."

"Jesus."

"Tommy's face also was busted, but not as severely. Subdural hemorrhaging likely caused him to collapse, and then the bleeding into the brain effectively killed him, six hours later. I'll know more later."

"You are saying what?"

"I'm saying that these two boys beat each other to death, and there's a damn good chance that they didn't know it was going to happen. Someone knew about the gloves, someone put them on these boys, someone knew this might happen."

Alfano again walked around the bodies, looking at their hands and the bruises.

"Send me the photos when you get the time."

The doctor nodded.

"You know the fight game here, Doc. Where do you think I should start?"

"Start with the priest and the rabbi. They know everyone and everything."

4

DAISY O'SHEA STOOD in the vestibule of St. Mary of Perpetual Help church in Bridgeport. Father Dominic held her hand as he told the pregnant nineteen-year-old that her husband was dead. Daisy's two-year-old daughter stood next to her, looking up and not understanding. Daisy's friend, Emma Gill, caught the young woman as she fainted, preventing her from collapsing onto the unforgiving marble floor. The priest and Emma lifted and gently sat Daisy in the back pew of the church. The redheaded child, little Mary, crawled up next to her mother on the hard oak bench. As Daisy regained her senses, she began to cry.

"Father, I got no one. Me seven months along, and I got no one."

She rubbed her right hand over her belly.

"What am I going to do? I told Tommy to stop, to get out. 'Just one more. There's a bundle to be made, Daisy,' he says. He didn't say he would die."

"I know, my child," Father Dominic said. "It's not a lot, but Mr. McGoin wanted to make sure you got the prize money from the fight."

The priest removed an envelope from inside his jacket and placed it in the right hand of the girl.

"It's two hundred dollars, a good sum."

"A man's life is worth more than two hundred dollars," Daisy answered. "That will be gone in a month. Who's going to buy his casket? Who's going to buy the hole in the ground? He only had me and Mary and the baby. Now, the Lord takes 'em—why would He let this happen?"

"Father Dominic is just trying to help, Daisy," Emma said. "The church is here to help."

"Then the church should get out of fighting," Daisy said.

She didn't need to explain to the two listening. The Catholic Church ran the CYO—the Catholic Youth Organization that sponsored amateur boxing matches—and helped with Golden Gloves. Some thought the church gave too much hope to the kids, meaning those with troubled families and no jobs, especially in Bridgeport.

"They end up punch-drunk, ears like a monkey's, bulldog face, damaged," people said.

Now, embracing her daughter, Daisy said, "Tommy was lucky. Now he's dead."

"Now, my child, you don't mean that," Father Dominic said.

"Father, I surely do mean it. There's a mother somewhere hearing the same thing about Benny. I knew Benny. He was a good kid—for a Jew—and a friend of Tommy's. He didn't need to be dead. And now they'll say my Tommy was a killer."

Mary tugged at her mother's skirt.

"When's Daddy coming home?"

Daisy pulled her daughter in close with her left hand and with her other hand, still clutching the envelope, covered her swollen tummy, as if trying to shield herself and her offspring from the priest, the church, and the world.

"I'll be going home, Father," she said, sounding decisive. "Emma, can you take Mary? I got to tell Tommy's da. Tommy was all he had, but the stroke left him slow. I'll tell him in my time."

Daisy stood, fingering the envelope.

"Father, that two hundred must take care of three people now. After that's gone, I'm not even sure God knows what will happen."

"God knows all," Father Dominic said.

"Then He should have stopped the fight after the third round."

Daisy and Emma walked through the vestibule. Mary held both their hands as they walked out the massive doors and into the morning sunshine.

* * *

Alfano, in a gray fedora and dark suit, stood in the shadows of the vestibule, watching and listening. He did not approach the two women; there would be time for that. His heart went out to the young widow. He'd given bad news far too often during his twenty years on the force. During the Capone years it had been the worst, sometimes two or three times a day. He was there when his squad broke the back of the Outfit and the word got out to the other bootleg gangs that they would not be tolerated. Sure the Feds took the credit, but it was the police, his people, that cut the gangs down to manageable size. Now that Prohibition was over, or would be at the end of the year, he wondered what would follow. More prostitution, drugs, protection rackets, gambling? Chicago had all of them, especially with the Century of Progress World's Fair not two and a half miles away from where he stood. Every day, two hundred thousand people came into the city to see the wonders of technology and the world, all packed into the wondrous fair built on the shore of Lake Michigan. Just as the mayor had said, the weekend crowds were often twice or more that number. After what the park offered to the people for daily entertainment, the city's underbelly and gangs offered what they wanted the rest of the evening. The ballparks were full, the beaches were packed, and at night, the boxing venues were crammed.

"Father Dominic, do you have a minute?" Alfano asked as he stepped into the nave. He dipped his fingers in the basin of Holy Water and crossed himself. Then, fedora in his hand, he walked down the center aisle to where the priest stood, half-turned toward him.

The priest studied the detective.

"I know you, give me a second . . . Alfano, Detective Anthony Alfano, of course. How are you, m'boy?"

"Fine, sir, just fine. And thank you for remembering."

"Was a sad day, Sergeant McDunnah and his wife, Moira, burying her brother, not eight weeks ago it was, very sad. How are they doing? Not seen the sergeant recently."

"They're good. The sergeant says Mrs. McDunnah is doing okay."

"Good," Father Dominic said. "Is there something I can do for you?"

"Those women, was one of them Tommy O'Shea's wife?"

"Yes. Tommy's death hit her hard. I do the best I can, but these days the world is troubled, and for some people it doesn't give them a break. Through the church, I'll do what I can to help her, but it will be a hard road. Tommy was a good lad—did all he could to help—but boxing was in his blood. He thought he could be a middleweight contender."

"Could he have made it?"

"Maybe, but not with that McGoin character as his manager."

Alfano half-smiled. Beneath his cassock, the priest was a local man, Bridgeport Irish, in his day as good a fighter as any that lived in the neighborhood. Alfano remembered fast hands, machine-gun jabs.

"McGoin is old-school," Father Dominic said. "Heavy punches, in close, wear the man out, but you need a strong body to take the shots. Tommy was quick with both his feet and hands; with the right training, he could have come in fast and taken the match with points. But the pros want knockouts. Reputations are made on KOs not TKOs."

"Did you see the fight Friday night?"

"No, I was here with one of my groups," the priest said. "Rabbi Harris called after midnight to say they took Benny to the hospital. He was there at the hospital, helping Mrs. Schwartz, waiting to hear on Benny's condition. He hadn't heard anything about Tommy but was certain he wasn't at Cook County. I finally got the news about Tommy late on Saturday. It took me all day to find his wife. She'd been looking for Tommy when he didn't return."

"Damn. What a way to find out."

"There's never a good one. Sadly, this isn't the first time a fighter has died, but this one is bizarre. Both fighters? That's very strange—is that why you are here? Was it more than just an accident?"

"When two men die in the ring from the same fight, we take interest."

"So, this is an investigation?"

Alfano nodded. "What do you know about spiked or loaded gloves?" he asked the priest.

"It's been tried—sadly, too often. Sometimes the fighter doesn't even know. It's the managers and the promoters. Detective, you know it takes a lot of money to train a fighter, especially the good ones with promise. The backers want their money back, and they can become impatient. Unfortunately, these fights happen, not for the prize money but the wagers. Do you think that this might be the reason?"

"Too early to tell, but the damage to the fighters was considerable. The coroner said it's more than these two middleweights could have accomplished with their own fists and normal gloves."

"Find the gloves," the priest said.

"That's where I was just an hour ago, but the rooms at the Stadium are empty. There's nothing. Whoever was behind this probably took them and probably tossed them in some incinerator."

"Most probably. The Lord knows I've tried my best to keep these people away from the amateurs, but there's big money out there even chasing the Golden Gloves. Capone was rumored to have bet more than fifty thousand on Dempsey winning the Tunney fight. That's six years back, but there probably were millions bet around the country. Even with these small fights, thousands are bet."

"I was at Soldier Field for the Tunney-Dempsey fight. It was quite a night. Almost thought the place would explode over the count. But Tunney won."

"And I lost five bucks, so you see, Detective, we all aren't saints."

"And I don't think you'd want a man to die for five bucks, either."

"Assuredly not," Father Dominic said.

"Father, I need to find the men who would."

5

DUFFY MCGOIN sat nursing a beer in the last booth of the Green Mill Tavern on North Broadway. The Green Mill because the chance of being seen by someone from the old Southside neighborhood was slim. Bridgeport was all of eight miles and eighty blocks south of where he sat. He pulled out his watch and checked the time; the man was late. McGoin hated late people—he took it personally.

A combo played on the small stage behind him; the tune was "It Don't Mean a Thing." The piano player was good. The kid could play anything; he had a touch of Art Tatum about his tickling. McGoin remembered the night Capone sat in the same booth he was in now, and the same kid was playing a Gershwin piece, and two thugs wanted to settle their differences right there that night. Capone walked up to the boys—both had their pistols pulled—and put his hand up. Both men recognized Big Al and stopped. Capone waved them over and said something only they could hear. The men slipped their guns back into their holsters and shook hands. It was rumored that Capone had told them that if they continued to ruin his evening they both would be dead before closing. Reality was a hard mistress.

The front door opened and a brilliant shaft of light lit up

the speakeasy like a flashbulb. The door closed, and darkness regained the room. Eggie Stingly walked through the bar, threw his hat on the bench seat, and dropped his ample ass across from McGoin.

"What the fuck happened?" McGoin asked.

"You tell me!" Stingly answered. "Your guy was supposed to take the dive in the third. Shit, there he was, dancing around in the fourth like some fucking ballerina. Obviously, Tommy, your Tommy, didn't know what was going on—or wasn't told—and so he kept fighting."

"Wait just a goddamn second. My guy? You telling me that it was O'Shea who was going down? Who the hell told you that?"

"Can't say, but that's what I was told."

"Well, you were told wrong—and why the hell can't you say?" McGoin said. "This town only has so many promoters, and you and I are two of the best. Now we each have a dead fighter on our hands. The commission will be asking questions. I heard that the bodies were taken to the morgue for autopsies. We're going to be fucked over bad, I'll tell you that."

Stingly waved to a cute thing in a short skirt and even shorter top. He pointed to the beer in front of McGoin. She nodded.

"The coroner, that's news to me. I left Tommy in the hospital," McGoin said. "Then I went to that priest at St. Mary's—he said he'd talk to the wife. I want no part of any investigation."

"Whether you want it or not, you're in—like me. The gloves, what did you do with 'em?"

"They were in the training room when we got there. When I went back, they were gone. Yours?"

Stingly paused, and then said, "Gone, too. I left them on the floor, but they weren't there when I sent that fucking cut man back to get 'em. I'll kill him when I find him."

He stopped talking as the waitress approached with his beer.

"Without the gloves, nothing can be confirmed, only speculated," Stingly said after the girl had left. "Jesus, did your boy have to kill him?"

"He didn't know. It was all an accident," McGoin said. "O'Shea was a good fighter—he could have contended. I didn't want him down any more than you did. I didn't fuck with his gloves; they were clean and to Hoyle. Somebody had to load 'em; I sure as hell didn't."

"Okay, okay!" Stingly said. "My guy says ours were new and identical to Benny's usual pair. He didn't notice any difference. They was in the room when we got there, too."

"Something is happening, and we're caught in the middle. If the cops find something or someone talks, we could get charged with manslaughter—or worse."

"They get that close, I'm on the first train to Miami, and a boat to Cuba. There's hundreds of fighters down there—and I'm tired of these cold winters. I'm only staying here because of the fair. We've tripled the gate since that fucking thing opened, and there are rumors it will reopen next year. There's good money to be made."

"Yeah, but only if our fighters stay alive."

6

ALFANO LEANED back in his chair and looked at the preliminary coroner's report that a patrolman had dropped off. There were two envelopes, one for each of the deceased fighters. He read the one for Benjamin Schwartz first. Benny had died from a massive hemorrhage that had formed inside the right side of his brain; it was as if the major blood vessel on that side had split open. The effect was catastrophic and instantly caused unconsciousness; death quickly followed. The rest of the report noted the bruises and broken bones, especially to the face and ribs. If Alfano didn't know better, what he read was more like a report of a fatal gang beating than the outcome of a professional boxing match.

Thomas O'Shea's report was not much different, though no bones were broken. The coroner had detailed an extensive and widespread display of severe bruises over Tommy's upper body. The kid's death also was from an internal brain hemorrhage, but on Tommy's left side. It made sense. Benny was known for his strong right hand. Tommy was a southpaw, and his roundhouse left hand had put many in the Golden Gloves to the canvas.

"Coroner's report on the dead fighters?" Sergeant McDunnah asked.

"Yeah, preliminary. Both died as a result of the fight, or that's what I see here. No drugs that the doc could find, nothing other than the effects of a tough fight. We talked about the possibility that both fighters' gloves were loaded, but after going through the training rooms and talking with some of the custodial staff, nothing turned up. In fact, everything dealing with the two fighters was gone, cleared out. One of the staff said that when they cleaned and prepared the room for the next boxer, one of the fighter's trainers was carrying out a large duffel bag. The cleaner didn't pay it much mind, didn't know the guy. He assumed it was the usual stuff the managers and the fighters always have—"

He nodded as McDunnah finished what he'd been going to say: "Medical supplies, liniments, and pre- and post-fight preparation."

"The bloody towels, they went to the laundry," he told McDunnah.

"Those places are a mess," said McDunnah. "A couple of my cousins fought in the CYO and the preliminaries to the Golden Gloves. Lasted a couple of years, and then they got smart and got out. They hated the training and the swelling and the pain. I'll tell you, their mothers were as happy as saints in heaven when they put down the gloves."

McDunnah asked if he had talked to Father Dominic. Alfano told the sergeant about the conversation and what he overheard.

"Father Dom is a good man," the sergeant said. "I've known him a long time; he believes that the ring is a good place for men to learn discipline and develop a work ethic. He's also the first to help a boy or a man out of the game. Would never think of pushing the fighter if he didn't want to fight."

"Duffy McGoin was O'Shea's manager and promoter, and some guy named Eggie Stingly was Benny Schwartz's. Can you see what you can find about these two, arrest records, their locations, gyms, anything that pops up?"

"And you?" McDunnah wanted to know.

"Off to see a man about a bet. Somewhere, there's a loser and a winner. I want to find out who won big or lost big."

"Don't forget the mayor," McDunnah admonished.

"Wouldn't think of it. I'll stop on my way north."

"I'll say a prayer for you."

"Thanks. And say a novena or two for the kids."

* * *

Alfano drove the Packard east on Washington Street toward City Hall. He hated driving but gave in when the car was offered by his, recently murdered, captain. The gift was given after the department—a few weeks after a raid on a brewery—unofficially claimed the car.

"With the end of Prohibition, we're not going to get these gifts too often, Alfano. You deserve it," the captain said.

"I don't want it in my name," Alfano said.

"Wouldn't think of it," was the answer.

Two weeks later, the captain was shot dead on the Wabash Avenue Bridge by a bomber terrorizing the city. After cornering the killer at the World's Fair, Alfano watched the killer jump to his death from the Sky Ride on the opening day of the fair.

Alfano wasn't sure if the automobile was a good thing or a bad thing. It was powerful and, at times, more than he could handle. On the plus side, he felt he could drive over or through anything that got in his way. The rumor was the windows were bulletproofed, something he didn't want to find out.

He slipped into a parking stall on Clark Street, put the official placard in the window announcing "Police Business," and walked up the steps to city hall.

The mayor's anteroom was empty except for a new secretary.

"Not seen you here before," Alfano said to the young blonde, her hair all up in curls that framed a pair of dangling silver earrings. She was cute.

"His Honor in?" he asked her.

"And you are?" she said with an official air.

"His number-one police detective, Anthony Alfano."

"Huh?"

"Just tell him that Detective Alfano is here. He asked for the meeting. Your name?"

"Lucille Devereux."

"Nice name. They call you Lucy?"

"Only my friends, my close friends. And, Detective, my friends in the secretarial pool have mentioned your name. They said to be careful."

"And why is that?"

"They never really said, even when I pressed them."

All Alfano could do was smile as he lit a cigarette and took a seat. Never once had he been immediately allowed in. Mayor Kelly always had someone or something going on in his office. Of course, Alfano didn't count the few times he'd barged through the doors to confront the new mayor. However, by his count, he'd saved the mayor a couple of times from certain political disaster, so in the back of his mind he felt a smidge of power over the politician. A power he cared little for.

The mayor's door buzzed.

"He'll see you now," Lucille said pointing with a pencil.

For once, the mayor was alone. Alfano was used to seeing at least one or two other people in the room, an alderman, a commissioner, or the mayor's political puppet master, Patrick Nash. Alfano looked around the room, half expecting someone to jump out from behind a closed door or a curtain.

"Spooky, isn't it? Me being alone," Mayor Kelly said.

"Spooky is not the word I was thinking."

"Shocked comes to mind."

"Yeah, that's closer. What can I do for you, Mayor?"

"The one thing I like about you, amongst many, is that you are straight to the point. Refreshing, as I've found out after the last two months. I understand that you are investigating the deaths of the two boxers at the Stadium last Friday."

"Word does get around."

"My job to know, especially when there may be some politics associated with it."

"Politics?"

"Give me a minute, I'll explain. We are like sandpaper and wood, Detective."

"Like as in, I rub you wrong?"

Mayor Kelly grinned a political grin, one that he might use at a women's social club.

"Not sure who's rubbing who," he said jokingly. "In this case, I'm the sandpaper, you're the wood. I need to mold you to fit my needs, and right now I have a big problem. For ten years, you helped clean up Chicago's swamp of gangs, and the federal stupidity of Prohibition in this town. Now that that unfortunate period is passing, the gangs are moving into the next area of profit, gambling."

The mayor lowered his voice slightly.

"I have a few aldermen on the take, or at least they're turning an eye away from the problem, and there are cops and their districts under the control of the bookmakers. Hell, I probably have city employees carrying the numbers and gaming sheets from bar to bar."

"And the fighters?"

"A bird told me that a lot of money was won and lost last Friday night, and there's rumbling on the street about a fix. I saw Father Dominic on Sunday evening, and he mentioned something about the fight and the impact on a couple of the families in my parish. That's getting too close to home, my home. Then Father Dom called today to tell me that he'd talked with you—as always, I can count on you to be two steps ahead."

"Thanks, I guess. There's two dead men in the morgue. Both may have been on the wrong end of a fix. All I care about is finding who set this up and why. Maybe we can stop it from happening again."

"You have my complete cooperation. Tony, this is just between you and me. Pat Nash is out of this. I want to know what the hell happened and why."

"And your interest?"

"Personal, very personal. Tommy O'Shea was my godchild."

* * *

The Hide Away Tavern—one of the more popular illegal casinos and speakeasies on the northwest side—was at the corner of Devon Avenue and Lincoln Avenue in the Tessville neighborhood. It had figured prominently in the gangster wars nine years earlier, during the murderous Al Capone and Dean O'Banion days. Unlike Capone—now ensconced in a federal prison—O'Banion died young at age thirty-two, shot in his flower shop. Alfano remembered the day. All hell broke out for five years between the North Side Gang and Capone's Chicago Outfit. The effects still roiled the alleys and speakeasies of Chicago.

The Hide Away was outside Alfano's district, but if there was a better bookmaking operation in the city he didn't know about it. It focused on the horses, and right now, the season was underway at Hawthorne Racetrack. Alfano also knew that if there was a book on the horses, there also would be one on the fights. Every night there were matches at the boxing venues—Chicago Stadium, Marigold Gardens, Rainbow Fronton, Ashland Arena—and every night thousands of dollars were laid down at the Hide Away.

Lincoln Avenue was busy, far busier than he thought it

should be for an afternoon. Two men stood outside the Hide Away, both straight off the cover of the Police Gazette for their bad suits and one-sided, bulging chests. Two valets ran back and forth, parking cars.

"This must be the church. The choir boys are out front," Alfano said to no one as he climbed out of the Packard.

One of the boys ran up to the car, an admiring look on his face. "Park it, sir?"

"Yeah, kid. But close, I won't be long."

He handed the valet a buck.

The kid took the keys and pulled the car into the front slot of the adjacent parking lot.

Alfano looked at the two bouncers working the door, smiled, and opened his jacket, revealing his shield clipped to his suspenders. They just grimaced and opened the door for him. Inside, the din was deafening. Hundreds of people lined the bar, sat around the roulette tables, and the ring-a-ring of the slots could be heard off to the left.

Another mountain of a man stood in Alfano's path. Much nicer suit, no bulge. His flattened nose and fully cauliflowered ears attested to a past profession.

"Help you, sir?" he asked, his voice gravelly from too many jabs to the throat.

"Looking for Tim Johnson—he in?"

"Now who would be asking?"

"Tell him that Detective Tony Alfano wants a few minutes."

The man seemed about to say something, and then paused. "Yes, sir. I'll tell him."

Looking about the casino, Alfano could not see one legal activity, just the liquor, the slots, and the gaming tables. He didn't want to think about what was going on upstairs, even in midafternoon. Sadly, half the room was full of little old ladies on stools, busily pulling handles, and the other half with young, unemployed men dropping their last dime on a toss of the little red ball. The usual painted women made up the color and plumage. The place stank of stale cigarettes and false hope.

Led by the flat-nosed greeter, a tall, thin man, with an even thinner mustache, came out of an office across the room. His double-breasted pinstripe suit only made him look taller, like he'd been pulled taut from each end.

"What'cha want, Detective?"

"Information, Johnson—and this time I'll not put up with your bullshit. Somewhere we can talk? I don't like the ears out here."

"Sure, always here to help. This way."

Alfano followed in Johnson's wake through the crowd; those who knew the manager got out of the way, others were nudged aside. When they entered Johnson's office, Alfano looked at the ape and shook his head, nodded toward the door. He waited to speak until the man turned and stood guard outside the office.

"I see you've done well, Tim. Really well. It's nice to have friends."

"Yeah, but most of them are in the joint. Me? . . . I'm a survivor. Then again, so are you."

Johnson pulled a bottle from the shelf and poured a finger of bourbon into a crystal tumbler. He offered it to Alfano, who paused and then shook his head.

"As always, the righteous cop," Johnson said.

"In this town, someone has to be. What happened last Friday night?"

"Where, at the fair? At the clubs on State? At the Stadium? The shooting at the Marigold?"

"Where else—the Stadium. I've two dead fighters in the morgue, and the rumor of a lot of money won and lost, probably some right here. All I want to know is where the fix came from."

"I didn't know you were in the gambling and rackets business, Alfano. Thought you was homicide."

"I move around, diverse interests. The mayor sees me as his very special detective."

"A fixer?"

"No, just a little closer to the top than I was before. Less paperwork and bureaucracy. But it has its bad side, too."

"And that's what?"

"Dealing with losers like you."

Johnson lit a cigarette and then finished off his bourbon.

"I'll be straight, Alfano. It took us all by surprise. O'Shea was the favorite to knock out Schwartz before the fifth; he won anyway, but ten rounds. A birdy told me there was big money on the Jew, and I mean big, a hundred large. It wasn't here, thank God. I was told someone put four big bets around town on Benny, to win in six. Someone knew something, and it sure wasn't me."

"Any ideas who?"

"None, but the fact that both boys died makes it even sadder. I liked them both, good kids. I even made a few bucks off them during the Gloves—like I said, good kids."

"Do you know their managers, McGoin and Stingly?"

"Unfortunately, I do. Tommy could have gone on to big things, but not with McGoin. Schwartz, I heard, was going to quit. This was going to be his last fight."

"Hadn't heard that. And this Stingly guy?"

"Eggie Stingly, now that man is a piece of work. He has a couple of other fighters out of the club on Roosevelt, all Jews. Promises the moon to his fighters, gives them shit, and little training. I think he's had one win in his last six or eight fights. The rumor was that O'Shea was to take a dive."

"Fun sport."

"That's why I like the horses. Cleaner and certainly more

interesting."

"Yeah, and if they break their leg, you shoot 'em."

Johnson poured another shot.

"Alfano, why are you here?"

"Tim, we go back a few years. I know you. As you said, you're a survivor. I want to know who set these kids up, and I also want to make sure it doesn't happen again. I want to know who was behind this, who dropped the hundred thousand, and who is pissed off enough to want it back."

"Give me a few days, I'll make some calls. Can't promise anything. But you might check two places: Danny O'Malley's bar on Wabash—it's run by your favorite Outfit business manager, Jake Guzik. And, the Alabaster Lounge on South State."

"The man and his brother are pigs. Why would I waste my time? And you need to get with the times—a fire gutted the Alabaster a week ago, something about beer I was told."

"With Capone gone, Guzik filled the hole. These Yids all try to one-up the dagos—well, they just fall short. Guzik is lying low right now, but one of his men is Hymen Rosenberg. They call him Rosie; he's hardly that. The guy was a gunzel and enforcer for the Outfit when Capone was around. Rumor is, he's personally put two dozen in the ground, and those are the ones they found. He might have put down the bet, maybe."

"Yeah, you Micks are such saints."

"And thanks for the info on the Alabaster—one less competitor." Johnson smiled and lit another cigarette. "Yes, saints and sinners." He crossed his fingers.

When Alfano walked out of the casino, his car was waiting at the curb. He slipped the kid a five, climbed in, and pulled out onto Devon and headed east toward Wrigley Field.

7

THE NEXT MORNING ALFANO parked in front
of the block-long façade of the Marigold Gardens. The club
was the most recent incarnation of a complex of beer gardens,
nightclubs, dance halls, and fight venues, all built on the same
chunk of Chicago real estate at Grace Street and Broadway.
Just a few blocks from Wrigley Field, the entertainment venue had become one of Chicago's premier boxing arenas. Alfano remembered coming here as a young cop with a date and
drinking beer late into the night back when the place was still
called Bismarck Gardens. Anti-German sentiment during the
war and the sale to new owners brought the updated name.
Prohibition had done more to knock out the beer garden than
anything else. Now it was reincarnated, and a thousand boxing
fans could sit and watch in elegant style. To Alfano, the Grace
Street façade now looked tired and old in the morning light; he
wasn't sure what he'd find inside. He tried the front doors and
was surprised when they opened. He strolled into the lobby,
where a small sign with an arrow said "Restrooms/Office." A
massive oak-trimmed door marked the end of the lobby. The
restrooms were to the left.

He knocked on the door's smoked-glass window.

"What'cha want?" a voice demanded.

"Police. A moment of your time, Eddie—it's Tony Alfano."

There was a pause behind the door, and then: "One minute, Detective."

Alfano heard the scraping of chairs and drawers slamming. Shadows appeared on the glass, the door opened, and two men emerged from the office. Neither made eye contact as they put on their hats and squeezed past Alfano, who intentionally stood in the middle of the tight hallway. To his surprise, he didn't recognize either of the men.

"Come on in, Detective."

Alfano strolled into Eddie Dietrich's office. The club owner sat behind a large desk the same color as the oak door. A haze of cigar smoke filled the room. One high but small window offered barely enough light to make its presence worth the effort. Two overhead lamps hung from the ceiling, trying to make up for the lack of sunlight. Alfano had known the nightclub promoter for more than ten years. If he recalled correctly, this was Dietrich's fourth attempt at making a go of the club scene. The others had been shut down for reasons that ran from being a public health nuisance to criminal activities—and the last to a suspicious fire. Dietrich always came away on top, especially after the fire. Now, under its new moniker, he ran what was left of the old Bismarck Gardens. Alfano had heard that the fight game was making him money.

Dietrich stood. He was nattily dressed in a shiny suit and flashy striped tie that helped to take one's eye off the pink scar on his left cheek and the black patch over his left eye. There were rumors about how it happened; the most preferred and retold tale included a woman, a bottle of Canadian rye, and a horse. Eddie Dietrich would never confirm any of them. The promoter walked straight to Alfano and shook his hand.

"Sit, Tony. God, what's it been, two years? Last time was up in Tessville, that hole-in-the-wall speak I ran. Damn, Tony,

I'll tell you this joint is a hell of a lot better—classier people and better hours, and between us, more money."

"You're looking swell, Eddie. Seems that the times are helping. Place looks good, too." Alfano nodded back over his shoulder to the club beyond the oak door.

"We're open seven nights a week, boxing on Friday and Saturday—that's when the big money comes in. Now that we legally can serve beer, it makes it easier and more profitable."

Even though Prohibition was still in effect, in Chicago and at the World's Fair, clubs and taverns were permitted to serve beer, and the Feds were taking a less authoritative stand on liquor of any kind. During the last thirteen years in Cook County, the whole concept of Prohibition had been taken more as a suggestion than law, hence the growth of the mobs and rampant crime and murder in the city. When political and federal pressure rose in Chicago against the gangs, they moved their operations across city boundaries. Some said it was a matter of convenience and practicality.

"So, you finally grabbed the gold ring?" Alfano said, lighting a cigarette.

"Maybe yes, maybe no. I still deal with some of the old characters . . . as they say, scratch mine, I'll scratch yours. So, what can I do for you, Tony? It's a little early in the morning for anything else other than an official inquiry."

"Two kids died last Friday after the fights at the Stadium, both local."

"Tommy O'Shea and Benny Schwartz," Dietrich said immediately. "Damn fucking shame. Good kids. I liked them both."

"Anyone lay down some bets, big bets?"

Dietrich rolled a Havana in his fingers.

"Don't know how to answer that, Detective. Every fight has wagers. I'm not telling you something you don't know."

"Something big enough to set up the fighters and, when it

went south, kill them for it?"

"You thinking that the boys were killed for not rolling over?"

"No. The unfortunate thing here is that these two probably killed each other not knowing their gloves were—"

"Loaded? Shit, Tony, that's old-school. No one does that nowadays. It's too easy to spot, and then the fighter and the manager would go before the boxing commission. They might never fight or manage again. If it happened here, shit, I'd be up before the commission, too. If that's what happened, somebody was stupid or greedy or worse—damn."

"Rumors of big bets or big losses?"

Dietrich put a torch to his cigar and took a long pull. He blew a cloud into the vortex created by the ceiling fan.

"I shouldn't say this, but the word on the street is that four bookies took big wagers, some more than twenty-five grand. All were on Schwartz in less than six rounds. O'Shea was good; the books took the bets."

"All placed by the same guy?" Alfano asked.

"Can't tell. No one knows who placed the bets."

"Or will tell. Can you get me the names of the bookies?"

"Tony, you know I can't," Dietrich said.

"Or won't?"

"Maybe . . . but I can tell you that a bookie near the Green Mill on Broadway disappeared Sunday morning. According to some kids who saw it happen, he was nabbed as he walked home from church. Two guys paced him along the sidewalk, grabbed him, and then threw him in the back of a black car. A few other guys are looking for him, too; they say he owes them money."

"Name?" Alfano said, taking out a small notebook.

Dietrich looked at Alfano and shrugged. "Iggy Jones. Nice guy, been working the rackets for more than a decade. Made his bones during the Capone years. Legit, as far as the racket he's in. Always paid."

"Was he one of the four?"

"That, Detective, I do not know. There aren't many who would take such a big bet—but Iggy was one who would."

"The others, they know?"

"I hope to Jesus they do, and are on a train to Miami or the Coast right now. I also wouldn't give a plug nickel for either of the two managers. Somebody seriously fucked up."

* * *

"This has got to end," Alderman Isaac Solomon said looking at the newspaper. "I will not allow another of our children to be beaten to death for the sport of a few. I can't allow it. It must be stopped."

Deborah Tillerman, a widow of the Great War and daughter of Alderman Solomon, looked up from her desk in her father's front office and sighed—from worry for his health, not in disagreement with his sentiment. Her father hated boxing and took every opportunity to fight those who promoted the entertainment. He particularly contended with those who pushed the sport on the young boys of Chicago, especially the young sons of Jewish immigrants. However, he also knew it was hard to change the mind of a kid with fifty bucks in his hand after a four-round fight. Not when the boy's father made the twenty-five cent an hour minimum wage. Fifty bucks for a night's work versus forty dollars for a month's labor was hard to compete with.

"They sucker in the boys, show them heroes like Max Baer, Barney Ross, and 'King' Levinsky, and then they end up punch-drunk, broken, or, as in the case of the Schwartz boy, beaten to death. There has to be an end to all of this," Solomon told his daughter.

Deborah strongly agreed but also knew that it would be an impossible battle.

"Father, just calm down, and you know what the doctor

says. You'll get your nerves all in a frazzle and then your heart starts fluttering. You promised me that you would follow my orders after mother died."

"Yes, dear. We know Benny's mother and father. They have that newsstand and candy store on Maxwell Street. Benny was their oldest boy, and his brother, Samuel, is just eighteen. They tell me Samuel fought in the Gloves last season."

"So please calm down," Deborah pleaded, tamping down her own thoughts on the matter in favor of her father's health.

Alderman Solomon took in a deep breath and slowly let it out, and then continued perusing the story.

"The *Tribune* says the other boy also died. Thomas O'Shea—and neither of them were twenty-one years old. Thomas left a wife and little girl. This all has to stop."

Deborah knew the pain that a death could cause; she had lost her husband in the war. Her grandparents had come from Ukraine in the 1870s with two small children, Anna and Isaac. Now her father, a pillar of the Jewish community, was the alderman for the 24th Ward, a collection of neighborhoods that included many of the older immigrant communities in Chicago.

"What would you like me to do, Father?"

"Call a meeting, that's what we Jews do. Get Rabbi Harris on the phone. I want to talk to him. He's involved with Father Dominic and the CYO and the Golden Gloves. If there is any impact I can have, it will have to start there."

"Yes, Father."

She dialed, waited, and then said, "Rabbi Harris, please hold for Alderman Solomon," before handing her father the receiver.

"Jacob, did you see what happened Friday? The Schwartz boy . . . Yes, I know it's sad, beyond sad . . . I want to see you and the other committeemen, and especially those fellows you have doing the boxing and training at the Hebrew Institute . .

. I don't care, Jacob. You set it up. Wherever it is, I'll be there
... Yes, I understand, but right now if I can prevent one more
senseless death, God will look down on all of us with approval."

Deborah stood, leaning against the doorframe, and smiled
at her father. "Better?"

"Some, but it is not going to be easy. I know what I'm up
against. There's the Catholics, the Irish, the Italians, the mob,
the politicians, the gamblers, even the fair has weekly fights—
none of them are going to be on my side."

"Our side, Father. Our side," Deborah added.

8

STOPPING AT THE sergeant's desk before heading to his own, Alfano asked, "Calls?"

McDunnah tapped a pencil on his steel desk. "No calls. Did you have fun?"

"Dance halls and casinos just don't seem to have that special look about them in the mornings. The mayor, he's concerned about the deaths. Seems that O'Shea was his godson."

"Damn. That hits close to home."

Alfano told McDunnah about his conversations with Tim Johnson and Eddie Dietrich.

"They's all just nests of snakes. They'd sell their sisters if they could," the sergeant said. "No idea about the guy who laid down the bets? And this Iggy Jones, possible retribution?"

"That's what I'm thinking."

McDunnah already had set up the crime board, as Tony called it, meaning a three-by-eight-foot corkboard that held visual clues related to the case. Over the years, the sergeant had jury-rigged a system of legs and wheels that made it easier to move the board around. Now, centered at its top were large photos of Benny Schwartz and Tommy O'Shea, promotion photos cut from posters. Hand-lettered slips of paper with the fighters' names were pinned below the photos. On the left side was a postcard of the Chicago Stadium and room to add others when needed. On the right side were photos of Duffy McGoin, Eggie Stingly, and, surprisingly for Alfano, pictures of Father Dominic and Rabbi Harris.

"These two?" he asked McDunnah.

"All the players go on the board. We always can take them down, but right now some of this revolves around the two of them. I can get mug shots of Johnson and Dietrich—you want those pinned?"

"If you can put a priest and rabbi on the board, you can at least put up two criminals to balance the display."

McDunnah stuck a postcard of the Marigold Gardens next to the one of the Chicago Stadium.

"Where you get that?" Alfano asked.

"Had it in the drawer, don't ask why."

"Wouldn't think of it."

"Anything else?"

"Can you find a picture of Iggy Jones?"

"The name rings a bell; I'll look into him," McDunnah said.

The afternoon dragged on. About three o'clock, McDunnah walked back to Alfano's desk.

"We have a body," McDunnah announced, as if the note in his hand were a winning ticket at Hawthorne racetrack.

"Where?"

"Cook County Forest Preserve. Seems a man was out for a walk, and his dog picked up the scent and started digging in some newly turned dirt. When a hat appeared during the burrowing, the man pulled his dog away, went home, and called it in. A couple of Park Rangers dug a little deeper. When they caught the sight of a bloody shirt, they stopped. The sheriff's men and the county coroner finished the job. Male, about forty, black bag over the head, two bullet holes."

"And you are telling me this, why?"

"The man's wallet, full of twenties and fifties, was still in his pocket. The man's driver's license says he is your missing man, one bookie named Ignacio Jones."

"And we got lucky, why?"

"All to wreck your week, Detective."

* * *

Alfano drove to the Cook County sheriff's office and parked the Packard in the open lot behind the building; the Chicago coroner's wagon also was parked there. Alfano went through the rear door and walked the corridor until he found Doc Abrahamson talking to a uniformed deputy sheriff. A gurney sat to one side, a white sheet draped over what Alfano assumed to be the body of Ignacio Jones.

"One and the same," replied the coroner, when Alfano asked if the body under the sheet was that of Jones.

"Detective, this is Deputy Milo," Abrahamson said. "He was first on the scene after the call. He opened the hole enough to determine it was a body."

"You get all the fun jobs, Deputy." Alfano extended his hand; the deputy took it. "Anything I need to look at?"

"A few things, Detective," Milo answered. "There were footprints and car treads in the dirt—they were the only tracks by a vehicle since the rain a week ago. The grave was about two-dozen yards off the trail, a little hidden; only a dog would have caught the scent. We got lucky there. I'd guess the scene is maybe only a few days old."

Alfano looked at Abrahamson, who nodded.

"About right," the coroner said. "Best I can tell, he's been dead less than two, maybe three days. I'll know more when I get him to autopsy."

"Preliminaries?"

"Two bullets to the head, from the front," the doc said. "They'd pulled a bag over his head, and then shot him. There's no other damage that I can see. Classic hit. Remember that fellow that floated up in the Chicago River a couple years ago? Bag over his head, two shots. We never did identify him; the body was too decomposed. I'll see if the bullets match; there might be something there."

Alfano asked the deputy if other bodies had shown up in the Forest Preserve.

"We get them occasionally, usually just dumped along the road. Most don't have identification, or money, or anything; sometimes, we can match them through fingerprints. Sometimes, we don't. I've got a book full of photos if someone is looking for a missing person. Sometimes, we get lucky. If you're asking about graves and buried bodies"—the deputy swept his arm wide, as if to indicate the tens of thousands of acres that wound through the county—"we only know what we find. There could be dozens buried out there. Won't know till we know."

"Profound," Alfano said. "Doc, let me know about the slugs. Deputy, can you mark up a map and show me where the body was found? I also want a copy of the photos that you took of the footprints and tire tracks."

"Why the hell would I do that, Alfano? This is our case," Milo said, suddenly defensive.

"You found the body, but somewhere this poor fella got iced, and it's a good bet it wasn't in the county. You play your jurisdictional Dick Tracy games, talk to the sheriff, or get all righteous, I don't care. Right now, mark a map. I'm going to the body dump."

* * *

One deputy stood on the dirt road next to his prowler, there to tell people that the trail was closed and to move along. He was smoking a cigarette and talking with a young woman when Alfano walked up from the main highway a quarter-mile away. The detective opened his jacket and flashed his badge.

The deputy dropped the cigarette. The young lady smiled,

handed him a piece of paper.

"The number is real, sweetie," she said to the deputy. "Anytime," she called over her shoulder as she walked away.

"Perk of the job, right, Deputy?" Alfano said.

"Don't know what you mean, sir."

"Never mind. Deputy Milo said that you were to give me everything I need," Alfano fibbed. "So, let's start with the hole in the ground."

The deputy and Alfano walked through the low scrub toward a grove of trees. The distance was maybe fifty feet, but the shrubbery obscured the site from most of the trail. Alfano noticed only one view opening from the trail. Like Milo had said, only a dog could find it. The hole was neat, like a cemetery grave, with vertical sides, maybe three feet deep. Alfano guessed it took someone maybe a few hours to dig. From the gravesite, he looked back toward the trail. There was enough cover to hide a man if someone walked by. Alfano thought that he'd have gone deeper into the forest, but then there would be bigger roots to deal with. He shrugged.

"Were you here when they removed the body?" he asked.

"No, I came in a few hours ago. There was another deputy here all night. He went home."

The deputy told Alfano what he already knew, that the body had been found the night before and removed early in the morning. Around the hole, the scene was a mess, dirt and rocks strewn over everything. Any important footprints were now obliterated by the dirt removed from the hole. The footprints and tire tracks that Milo had mentioned, according to the deputy at the scene, were along the trail where the police cruiser now was parked. The deputy said that when he arrived, the coroner was backing down the trail.

Alfano sighed. If he had been on-site, he would have frozen the location until everything was photographed. Jones wasn't going anywhere.

"How long are you supposed to stay here?" he asked the deputy.

"'Til nighttime. Then I'm off."

"And the hole?"

"The hole?"

"Yes, who's going to fill this in?"

"Not me—I ain't got no shovel."

AROUND THE LONG TABLE in the conference room of Alderman Solomon's office sat six people: Rabbi Jacob Harris, Father Theo Dominic, Tobias Wertz, Dr. Albert Carson, Deborah Tillerman, and the alderman. The early evening sun streamed through the Venetian blinds casting a bizarre pattern over the group.

Wertz was an Illinois boxing commissioner and was asked as a courtesy by the alderman to attend. A well-known and avid supporter of both amateur and professional boxing, the commissioner agreed. Dr. Carson, on the other hand, had dealt with the physical effects of boxing on the fighters. He thought it a barbaric sport; his leanings personally and professionally were aligned with the alderman. Deborah was there to act as referee.

"Thank you all for coming at such short notice," Solomon began. "I've known all of you for a long time and respect your views, but now something must be done. We cannot allow more of our young men to die in the ring."

Surprisingly, Wertz said, "I could not agree more. Something must be done to better protect and oversee the bouts, and reduce the chances of the fighters being severely injured."

Solomon looked at Wertz.

"That's not what I meant, Tobias. We need to find a way to outlaw boxing in this state. It was illegal for almost twenty years here in Chicago. We can roll back the clock and protect our youth again."

"Isaac, I understand your passionate concern," Rabbi Harris said. "But there are hundreds of people whose livelihoods come from boxing. Our young men are learning discipline, and families depend on the money from the sport. Our volunteers do a wonderful job helping the men, working with the gyms, making sure that they train safely."

"Maybe so, but then why do they change their names so that their own mothers don't know that they are boxing? Why is it that some of the worst elements of the Chicago underworld run these venues? Why isn't there better control over the referees? They should have stopped the fight last Friday night. If they had, two young men would not be dead."

"Alderman, I talked with the O'Shea family," Father Dominic said. "They are heartbroken, and I can't agree more with what you are saying. But these boys and young men need a place to blow off steam. If not, who knows what kind of mischief they will get into? They were easy pickings for the O'Banions and the Capones. You don't want to go back to those days?"

"Of course he doesn't, Father," Deborah Tillerman said, her voice rising as she defended her father. "It's just that this has become more than a contest between young men. It has become a blood sport where money changes hands. Our youth are nothing but pawns, to be discarded like so much—"

"Deborah, please," the alderman said softly.

"Father, I do not apologize for my beliefs," she said, more impassioned than even he had been earlier. She had abandoned her role as meeting referee before she'd begun it.

"These gentlemen are the fourth and fifth young men in the last year to die in the boxing rings here in Chicago," she said. "How many others have been injured or damaged, we just don't know."

"Mrs. Tillerman," Dr. Carson said. "I understand your concern and fully support your hope that we can ban this sport from our city and county. However, please understand that it will just move across the county line. We need to make it state-wide."

"There is no need to go to that extreme," Father Dominic said. "I believe we can make it safer. We can work with the commission and the other organizations to prevent these deaths."

"I understand that you can make things happen in the youth leagues, Father," Alderman Solomon said. "But it's the professional bouts that are the problem, and that's why I've asked Tobias to be a part of this discussion."

"Thank you, Isaac," Wertz said. "We are doing what we can. It's difficult."

"Only because you need the CYO and others to train these young men to be fighters," Deborah said. "Without the amateurs, there would be no professionals. We need to stop this at the source."

"Mrs. Tillerman, this is something that men with experience should deal with," Wertz said.

"Excuse me? Are you saying that a woman's point of view is unimportant? Tell that to Mrs. Schwartz, who waited in the Stadium for hours when her son's body already had been taken to the hospital. He was her oldest son—she's a broken woman."

Deborah sharply reminded her listeners that two other fighters had suffered serious injuries that night; one was still in the hospital.

"Is that the kind of sport that you want our youth to aspire to? Your children to be a part of?" she said.

"There has been boxing for more than two millennia,

from the days of the Greeks," Wertz said.

"Which only shows that we haven't gotten any smarter as a species. This must stop now!"

"Alderman Solomon, I will not be lectured," Wertz said. "If you will excuse me, I am leaving. I suggest that you gentlemen talk some sense into this woman; she is misinformed. What we do at the commission is to protect our sport from those who would turn it into what Mrs. Tillerman believes that it is. We are not what you think we are."

"Mr. Wertz," Deborah said, unfazed, "I believe that right now you are the one who is ill-informed. I suggest that you get your own house in order."

Wertz stood and stared long and hard at Deborah Tillerman, and then at Dr. Carson. He then turned and walked out of the conference room.

"Obviously, we can't rely on his support," Dr. Carson said.

"He is only stating what we will hear from everyone else," Rabbi Harris said. "While I understand Deborah's zeal and commitment, it is important to see the whole picture—"

"The deaths and the injuries?" Deborah was quick to interject. "What else is there? These are the critical things to understand."

"Deborah," her father said. "May I suggest that we defer this conversation? We are now only talking to ourselves. Rabbi Harris and Father Dominic know our positions. We need to have others join our side. There's the newspapers, the radio, even some of the local monthlies. They all can help. There may be some who will side with us and give us a stronger and louder voice."

"Alderman, I like that idea," Dr. Carson said. "I'll make a few contacts. There has to be someone in the press who is sympathetic."

"Thank you, Albert. That's a good suggestion," the alderman said.

With that, the meeting broke. The priest and the rabbi left

together. Dr. Carson strolled down the steps to his car. Deborah stood in the office lobby, watching the others leave.

"I wasn't too strident, was I, Father?"

"Just strident enough, my dear. I believe Mr. Wertz understands that he is at the start of a serious fight, one that he might possibly lose."

* * *

Alfano pulled to a stop in front of the small deli three blocks from his apartment. Two or three times a week he'd buy his dinner from Harvey, the deli owner. The deli also had been one of the most reliable sources of booze—in almost any form and quality—during the previous ten years of Prohibition. In four months, the most bizarre American experiment in social management would be over. What it would bring in its aftermath, Alfano wasn't sure. Unfortunately, as for the gangs, even after all the culling by the government of Al Capone and a hundred other less colorful gangsters, little had changed. Any arrest of a capo, a leader, was an employment opportunity for another ambitious gangster. Alfano knew the wheel would just keep rolling.

"What will you have, Detective?" Harvey asked. "Some fresh corn beef, potato salad? Yvette made a cherry pie—fresh Michigan cherries. What do you think?"

Alfano looked down the counter. The smells and cornucopia of delights made his mouth water, and for a moment the pain in the back of his head disappeared.

"Too much, as usual, to pick from," he told Harvey. "But I'll go with your suggestions. Won't have to turn on the burner. I'm sure the apartment is all the oven I need tonight."

"I'll throw some ice in a carton; should keep your usual a little cooler."

Harvey winked at Alfano. The usual was a bottle of Canadian Club.

While Alfano was waiting for Harvey to put everything together, two teenagers came into the deli, pushing and kidding each other. Alfano stepped back to let them study the deli case. He looked toward the door and saw another kid, younger than the two inside, nervously smoking a cigarette and taking quick glances up and down the street. *Not good.*

As Harvey turned back toward Alfano, one of the kids pulled a pistol from his pocket. The other did the same and pointed it at Alfano.

"No's body fucken' move," the teen with his gun on Harvey said. He had to hold the pistol above shoulder height to aim it over the glass front of the deli case.

"Jesus Christ," Harvey said. "Just be cool. What do you want?"

"The cash in the register and that package you was making up." The boy turned to Alfano. "And you empty your pockets and wallet, grandpa. Now."

The other teen echoed, "Now, gramps!"

Alfano wasn't sure whether it was the robbery or being called gramps that pissed him off more.

"Be cool, Harvey," he said. "Just give them what they want."

The chrome .38 police special in the hand of the second teen was shaking. *Not good*, Alfano thought again. The kid facing Harvey screamed, "God dammit. Now, or I'll shoot you in the fucking face."

Harvey dropped like a rag doll thrown to the floor, knocking pans and trays all over the aisle behind the counter. Stunned, both teens turned and looked to where Harvey had been standing. Alfano, taking the cue, pulled his Smith and Wesson from his shoulder harness and, belying the remark about his age, tapped the second kid on the back of the head with the barrel, knocking him to the tiled floor. Then, in one motion, he put the business end of the revolver to the shocked face of the first teen.

"Think, kid. Is this where you want to end your short fucking life? Drop the gun, or you will die right here," Alfano calmly said.

The kid blinked. Alfano heard the pistol drop and thud against the linoleum floor.

"On your knees," Alfano said.

The kid did as ordered.

An explosion came from behind Alfano. He was positive that he heard the bullet zip past his ear. He'd forgotten the lookout. He spun to the door, fired, and the boy fell, screaming and clutching his leg. His revolver, a match to his companion's .38, skidded across the floor.

"You okay, Harvey?"

Alfano heard a yes, and Harvey reappeared from behind the counter.

"Call the police, and tell them we need an ambulance," Alfano told him.

Harvey looked at the boy on the floor near the door. He was crying. Blood oozed between his hands as he tried to stop the bleeding in his leg.

"Did you have to shoot the kid?" Harvey said.

"Sorry, had to, he shot first. He's lucky. He could be dead."

Alfano looked at the two near the counter. The one he'd pistol-whipped was moving; blood ran down the side of his head. The other sat, stunned, looking at Alfano.

"It was nothing, mister. We'd have been out of here in a minute. You didn't have to get into this, Jesus," the kid said looking at his friend and the blood.

"I'm a cop. There's rules, kid, and you broke one. Now you'll pay for it," Alfano said. He heard sirens echoing in the streets.

Later, as he climbed the stairs to his apartment, his dinner in a bag under his arm, he felt the cool pressure of the ice-filled container against his ribs. The Canadian Club would be especially welcome.

10

ALFANO FOUND THAT, to his surprise, McDunnah was not at his usual seat at the front desk. The crime board had three new pictures; one was a pastoral shot in the Forest Preserve that displayed an open grave and Deputy Milo standing next to it, pointing. There was a police mug shot of Ignacio Jones. The last was of footprints and tire treads, possibly those of the car that was used to carry the body. The soft dirt had captured a good impression of the tire marks. Alfano wished there were catalogs of tires and their tread patterns. He placed a note on McDunnah's desk to contact the Federal Bureau of Investigation to see what they had, and that took time. He also sensed that the sheriff's department was not going to be all that helpful.

An hour later, McDunnah walked up as Alfano smoked a cigarette and was studying the board.

"I thought some of these would be helpful," the sergeant said, sticking more photos on the board. "I had the sheriff rush the photos over; they may not be that forthcoming again. What is it with those guys?"

He added a handwritten card to the board, placing it directly under the mug shot.

"Ignacio Jones's last known address. He was doing okay for

himself, all things considered," he told Alfano, as they looked at the three lines of text written on the card. "It's a suite in the Blackstone Hotel on South Michigan. I called; they gave me his room number. Do you want me to send over a uniform?"

"No, I'll take it," Alfano said. "If what I'm thinking happened, I'd like to be the first to walk the room. Do you need a break? You sound like you have a cold."

"Can't. There's a week of paperwork backed up on my desk. Besides, it's more fun here with the board. Bring me something useful."

* * *

As Alfano pushed his way through the midmorning traffic over the Chicago River, he recalled the sordid biography of Ignacio Jones. He was called Iggy by both his friends—such as they were—and his enemies. Those enemies included those he owed money and those that owed him. McDunnah had added a bit of recent history to the story: "Ignacio Jones, forty-one years old, Irish father and Puerto Rican mother. His file says he was born in Miami, but a note in the file says it may have been Havana. He was orphaned at thirteen, or ran away from home, unclear here also. Came up to Chicago with a couple of Cubans from Miami who were taking wagers on the Florida races, both horses and dogs. When the two Cubans—one cold winter morning—were found dead in the Chicago River locked together with a heavy chain, Iggy filled the economic void by taking on small bets."

Alfano had arrested the two-bit punk a couple of times for running numbers, a relatively harmless racket that involved old ladies and shop owners. Jones unfortunately crossed a line when he pistol-whipped a sixty-year-old woman who was screaming on the street that Jones had stolen her money and not paid up. Alfano was a beat cop at the time, and made sure that Jones got six months in jail. The woman still wasn't paid and Jones, when he got out, was still a punk. Now, somebody had made sure that he'd never reach his forty-second birthday.

Alfano parked the Packard in the valet slot in front of the Blackstone. The stately hotel was on the south side of the Loop and faced Michigan Avenue and Grant Park. It straddled an imaginary line between the city's business core and the start of the less-than-tony Southside neighborhoods. Down the block, the near Southside had its Congress Hotel, where politicians and gangsters coexisted with their sumptuous personal suites on its floors; Mayor Cermak had rented a suite, as had Alphonse Capone—strange bedfellows, Alfano thought.

The parking valet came around to his window and was going to say something, but Alfano cut him off by showing his badge. He handed the kid a five.

"Leave it right here. Anyone ask, tell them it's city business."

"Yes, sir," the kid said as Alfano threw him the keys.

Alfano walked to the front desk, where he found a distinguished gentleman in tails. He held up his star and leaned in to the man.

"I need the key to room six-one-four, Ignacio Jones, city business."

The clerk puffed up and tapped the counter annoyingly with his silver pen.

"Not without a warrant, Detective. We do things according to the law here. That is Mr. Jones's residence. He is a very good guest, and we respect his privacy."

"I understand," Alfano said and took out his notebook. "First, your name?"

"Robert Schiller. I've been the head clerk here at the Blackstone for the past ten years."

"When was the last time you saw Mr. Jones?"

The clerk continued to look at Alfano, and then folded.

"I can't remember the last time I saw Mr. Jones."

Alfano removed a photo from his pocket and placed it on the counter in front of Schiller.

"I assume that he did not look like this."

Schiller blanched and Alfano took a step back, thinking the man might lose his breakfast. The photo was of Jones ten minutes after he'd been pulled from the hole and the bag around his head removed. Two black spots, one over each wide-open eye, dotted the man's forehead.

"Oh, my Lord," Schiller said. "Is that Mr. Jones?"

"In his current glory. Now I can assure you that he won't give a rat fuck over who goes into his room today. So, Mr. Schiller, his key, and some privacy. I do not want anyone to bother me. If by chance, though, I get a phone call, please forward it to me. In fact, if there are any calls for Mr. Jones, forward them on as well."

Alfano looked at the stacked cubbyholes behind Schiller. A brass room number was affixed to the bottom center of each.

"Any messages for Mr. Jones?" he said with a smile.

Schiller paused again, apparently to wonder how long he could hold out—about three seconds. He turned to the wall, reached into a cubby on the sixth level, and removed a stack of papers. Without saying anything, he handed them to Alfano along with the room key.

"I hope you find our cooperation satisfactory," Schiller added.

"More than I expected," Alfano answered truthfully.

He crossed the carpeted lobby to the two gilded elevators. A young boy, who could have been the brother of the valet, stood just outside the doors.

"Sixth floor, sonny."

"Yes, Detective."

As the elevator slowly climbed, Alfano turned to the operator. "How did you guess?"

"Mr. Schiller takes nothing from anyone, so I guessed

you's either a thug or a cop. Weren't dressed nice enough to be a thug, so's I thought you gotta be a cop. You looking for Mr. Jones?"

"Yes. Good guess."

"Nah, he's the only one on six that would get a personal visit from the cops. The rest is quiet, rich, and old."

"Anyone else looking for him?"

"Can't say. I'm on from eight to six, Monday through Saturday. Not exactly Mr. Jones's hours. He tended to late nights and early mornings. Haven't seen him for more than a week."

The elevator stopped. The boy opened the double doors.

"He dead?"

"Yes."

"I did a few errands for him, but my dad, when he found out, thrashed me good. I need this job, so I politely refused to help him again. Mr. Jones said he understood and didn't ask anymore. I liked him—too bad he's dead."

Alfano left the boy at the elevator and walked the long, empty hallway with its oriental carpet that stretched from one end to the other. At number 614, he looked closely at the frame for scratches or jimmy marks. Seeing none, he inserted the key and unlocked the door. He removed his handkerchief from his breast pocket, and after gently wrapping the door handle, opened the door. He glanced around to check that the hallway was still empty, and then closed the door behind him, relocked it with the key, and walked into the suite.

The main parlor was a disaster. The couch and all the upholstered chairs were shredded, as were the cushions. The carpet had been rolled to the wall, exposing the oak flooring. The few books that Jones owned had been pulled from the shelves and ripped apart. Every cupboard in the small kitchen was open, and all the pots spread across the countertops. Even boxes of cereal and other food had been opened and dumped.

The bedroom was not a surprise. The bed looked like a

jealous husband had ripped it apart after finding out he'd been cuckolded by his wife. Paintings were off the walls, and the closet and dresser had been emptied. Every suit was turned inside out, undergarments and other clothing were strewn about the floor. Here again, the carpet had been lifted.

Alfano had to admit it was a very good and thorough search. If they'd found something, they had continued until they were sure they had everything. And since there was no hint of this search from Mr. Schiller or even the boy at the elevator, they also must have been very quiet. He found that interesting.

Alfano was certain that Iggy's killers were the ones who ransacked the suite. They would have used Jones's key to enter and then took their time. Most probably slipped down the back stair or—after Alfano looked out the side window of the corner of the suite—he guessed, used the fire escape. He looked closely; the window was closed but unlocked. Yes, the fire escape. He'd have the forensic boys check for prints here and on any other smooth surface. He'd also have them look at the underside of the open toilet seat. If they took this long, one of them would have to take a leak. A man usually didn't leave his gloves on to pee.

Alfano took the long iron poker from the fireplace set and used it to search through the chaos. He lifted this and that, moved a few things that wouldn't matter, and further satisfied himself that the job had been thoroughly done. He looked at the fireplace; no need for it this time of the year, that was for sure. The gilded chain fireplace screen sat unmolested.

Using the iron poker, he slid back the screen and, after removing his suit jacket and rolling up one shirt sleeve, reached up into the maw of the flue. He tickled around until his fingers found a smooth surface; he traced it from one edge to the other. Then, with his finger and thumb squeezed around the carton, he withdrew it from the chimney and held it in both hands. It was about three bills wide, the height about four inches, and it was heavy.

Alfano smiled.

"Well, good for you, Ignacio Jones. This is as good a place as any."

The lights went out.

11

ALFANO ROLLED onto his back and tried to focus on the detail of the intricate plaster ceiling above him. The throbbing pain in his head made that difficult. He closed his eyes and passed out again.

The next time he awoke, Schiller and the elevator kid were standing over him. Schiller bent down and passed a vial of smelling salts under his nose—the pungent mix cleared the flog from his head enough that he rolled to his side and read the clock on the fireplace mantle. An hour and a half had passed since he'd removed Jones's stash from the chimney.

"Are you okay, Detective?" the kid asked. "You okay?"

Alfano pushed himself to a sitting position and steadied himself with his right hand on the arm of the couch. He ran his left hand through the hair on the back of his head. When he looked at his palm, it was red with blood.

"Jesus Christ, what the hell happened?" the kid asked.

Alfano glanced around, knowing that the package would not be there. He wasn't pleased that he was right.

"Detective Alfano, are you okay? Is there anyone I should call?" Schiller asked.

Still gripping the sofa arm, Alfano got to his feet. He looked down at the fireplace prod and then at the fireplace.

The screen was still open. He turned to the boy.

"Did you bring anyone else up to this floor after I left the elevator?"

"No, no one. It was real quiet. Not seeing you come back had me worried. Thought you might have gone down the fire escape. I called Mr. Schiller; he said to check the room. The door was open a little ways. I pushed it in and called out. When I didn't hear nothin', I walked in, and there you was. I called Mr. Schiller, and he came right up."

Alfano gingerly touched the back of his head again, looked at Schiller. "What's your story?"

"After David called, I immediately came up and found you. I brought along a medical satchel we keep at the front desk. You were still breathing, so I used the smelling salts. It's good to see you standing."

"Did you call anyone?"

"Not yet. I haven't been here more than five minutes. Should I call someone, an ambulance, a doctor?"

Alfano took a step, braced himself on the back of the couch. He took a few deep breaths.

"So, David, I assume that's your name."

The kid nodded.

"You saw no one else?"

"I brought no one to this floor after I dropped you off. But the stair is unlocked from the lobby, so someone could have climbed up."

"You said the apartment door was left open?"

"Yeah, an inch or so."

"Why did you come and look for me?"

"Actually, like I said. Mr. Schiller asked if I'd seen you leave. I said no. So, he told me to check. That's when I found you."

"Thanks for the concern," Alfano said to Schiller.

"My pleasure."

"I also assume that you saw no one in the lobby who was

suspicious?"

"Other than yourself, no."

Alfano wanted to punch the manager in the nose; he let the feeling fade.

"How many keys can open this apartment's door?" he asked.

Schiller thought for a moment.

"As far as I know, there are four. Mr. Jones had one; he kept the spare in the mailbox. That's the one I gave you. There's also the house key and the one the cleaning staff uses."

Schiller finally looked at the destruction to the room.

"I assume that the city will pay for all this damage that you did?"

"It was done before I got here, bub. Obviously, the cleaning staff doesn't come every day?"

"For our long-term residents, they come when they are requested. Mr. Jones had not asked to have the room cleaned. The last time was two weeks ago. I checked."

"You can go now, David. We'll talk later," Schiller said, pointing at the hallway.

"Wait a minute, I'll tell him when he can leave. David, you said there's a stairway?"

"Yes, sir. At the end of the hall."

"Where does it exit?"

"Really two exits, one into the lobby near the rear service area and the other out the back door. That one's locked from the inside. Fire regulations, I'm told."

"Thanks. If you think of anything, let me know."

Alfano handed the kid a business card and then nodded his head toward the hallway. The kid did not need to be told twice.

"What do I need to do to get an outside line?" Alfano asked Schiller as he picked up the phone.

"Our switchboard will connect you."

Alfano spent less than two minutes talking to McDunnah. Told him what happened and when. He told the sergeant to get the forensics team to the hotel and to print the room and the stairway. He also mentioned the toilet. Schiller's eyebrows rose when he heard the request. Alfano ignored the manager.

"Send a patrolman over to secure the room. I'll be back at the station in an hour . . . McDunnah, I'm fine. Just a bump. If they'd wanted me dead, I'd be dead . . ."

Alfano fought the temptation to sit down.

"Have the patrolman report to the hotel desk manager," he told McDunnah. "His name's—"

He looked at Schiller.

"Robert Schiller, Detective," he answered, sounding annoyed that Alfano didn't remember his name.

"Schiller. The guy's name is Schiller. Tell the patrolman to let no one in unless it's the forensics people. And that means no one from the hotel either."

Alfano hung up and walked into the bathroom and removed a towel from the rack, which he soaked in the sink and then applied to the back of his head. It stung. He watched Schiller blanch when he pulled the bloody towel away.

"Are you sure you don't want me to get you a doctor, Detective?"

"I've had far worse, I can tell you that. But let me borrow this towel."

"Why don't you just keep it."

With the towel pressed to the back of his head, Alfano sat for ten minutes in the Packard, going over everything. Obviously, someone with a key had slipped into the hotel room while he was engrossed in retrieving the bundle from the fireplace—a bundle he was sure was a heavy stack of money. Then they clubbed him with a blackjack and took the bundle. He still had his gun, so either the guy didn't know he was a cop or didn't care. All the asshole had wanted was the bundle.

Alfano threw the towel into the footwell on the passenger's side and pulled away from the curb, pissed that whoever it was got the drop on him. He hoped that the forensics people would add even more to the mess that was Iggy Jones's hotel room.

12

ZIGGY FELDSTEIN dropped a package on the desk of Hymen Rosenberg.

"A gift, complements of the Chicago police department."

"How so?" Rosenberg asked as he rolled the package around in his hands.

"There's this detective. His name's Alfano. I've run into him a few times back in the day. So's I'm watching Jones's hotel, like you ask, and I see's Alfano park out front and walk in. He's got to be there to look through Jones's room. So's I sneak around to the side and go up the back stair. Long story short, I zapped him when his back was turned. He'll be all right. No beef against him, guy doing his job. He had that bundle in his hands. I went out the same way. No one saw me."

Rosenberg took up the stiletto he used as a letter opener. Using the tip, he drew a sharp line over the corners; the tape gave way. In less than a minute, bundles of money sat on the desk. On top of each was the face of Ulysses S. Grant.

"So, they found the body. Not good," Rosenberg said, as much to himself as to Ziggy. "Now we've got to find a better place to get rid of them. However, the prick was holding out on us. All he had to do was tell us and I'd have gone easier on him."

He flared the bills and saw they all were fifties, meaning the three stacks totaled about one hundred thousand dollars.

"Where was it?" he asked.

Feldstein told him.

"I'm surprised you didn't look there. You must be more careful, Ziggy. Did you wait around?"

"For almost two hours. I was beginning to think that my tap to his head killed him. He then walks out of the hotel, and I watch him climb into his car. Some beat cop showed up, they talked, the cop left. I followed Alfano crosstown; he stopped at the Racine police station. Then I came here."

"So, the famous Tony Alfano is on the case. That will make this all the more interesting. Where's that creep Kozlov?"

"Gus has him, at the barn in Whiting. You want to talk with him?"

"Not right now. Let him stew."

Kozlov had come out of Russia after the war. He was a lot tougher than Jones, Rosenberg told Ziggy.

"It will take time, and right now we have a few days to get it right," he said. "He'll tell us who set up the fighters, and when I have that, I'll get even. Jones's bundle sets me right; everything else is gravy."

Ziggy eyed the stacks of money, said nothing.

* * *

McDunnah looked at the wound on the back of Alfano's head. "You'll live."

"Thanks, but you don't sound too confident."

"I don't know many who have a harder and thicker head, so count your blessings. It's a half-inch nick; you don't need stitches. Wash it later and put some Mercurochrome on it."

Alfano held a fresh towel against the nick and looked at the corkboard. A few new names and a photo had been added. "What's this?"

"A bookie I know called in. It seems that another bookie,

Igor Koslov, is missing. Kozlov's a big-timer who has some connections to the Russians, the Bolshevik kind. I understand he is the connection and the clearinghouse for money coming in for refugees from Stalin and his boys. He acts like an unofficial banker for the immigrants that arrive. He has one of the biggest books in Chicago."

"Great, now the Ruskies are involved. And this guy is missing?"

"That's why I got the call," McDunnah replied. "All the bookies are scared after word got out about Jones. This guy wanted us to know that Koslov has disappeared."

"So, a few of your well-placed bits of information about the dear departed Mr. Jones paid off."

"Quicker than I thought they would. That tells me the bookmakers are on edge."

"Good." Alfano pointed at one of the cards, which had a Blue Island Avenue address written on it. "And this one?"

"That is Benny Schwartz's mother's address. She was there that night. She called here looking for you."

"She saw her son get beat to death?" Alfano asked.

"That I don't know, but she said she wants to talk to you and only you—in person. Father Dominic called her and said you were on the case. She said she also talked to Rabbi Harris."

The Schwartz address was a block off the west end of Maxwell Street.

"That's not far from here," Alfano said. "Did she say when she would be in?"

"She said, 'I got nowhere to go, with Benjamin gone. I have to take care of Samuel. He's all I got left.' Samuel's the other son. The lady's got it tough. She has a newspaper and magazine stall on Maxwell. However, she said she would be at her house today."

"Would you call her and tell her that I'll see her this afternoon? I'm bushed, my head hurts, and I'm hungry. I'm going to lie down in the back for an hour. I promise you, Sergeant, that when I find the mug that clubbed me, I'll make sure that he feels a lot fucking worse than I do."

13

ALFANO DROVE the Packard the twenty blocks to Maxwell Street and pulled to the curb a half block from Mrs. Schwartz's *World News* newsstand. The street had seen better days. As recently as ten years earlier, it had been a vibrant commercial and social hub of the latest wave of European immigrants, the Jews. The six blocks were changing; the more successful Jews had moved farther west, leaving only their stores and businesses behind. The new tenants were from the south and the rural areas, pushed into the neighborhoods of Chicago by circumstances and the depression. The neighborhood's religion was changing as well as its color. The address on Blue Island Avenue, a few blocks from the newsstand, was a ramshackle two-floor tenement in desperate need of replacement. A woman sat smoking a cigarette in the shade of the porch of the ground floor flat; another woman sat next to her. Alfano walked slowly up the sidewalk to the steps.

"Mrs. Schwartz, I'm Detective Tony Alfano. You asked to talk with me?"

The first woman looked to be in her late forties or early fifties. Her face showed the pain she'd been through the past days. Her eyes were puffy, and she wore little or no makeup. Her hair was in a tangle, partially held in place with a silk scarf tied under her chin. The other woman was younger, no more than twenty-five. She sipped what looked like iced tea.

"Did you call the police, Mother?" the younger woman asked.

"That's all right, Linda," Ruth Schwartz said. "Yes, I called. I want to know what's happening. Please, Detective, sit here." Mrs. Schwartz patted a chair next to her. "Care for some iced tea? It's fresh."

Alfano looked at the pitcher and the dark brown color of the liquid inside. Condensation dripped and ran down the sides. He hadn't realized how warm the day had gotten. He also was parched.

"I would love a glass, Mrs. Schwartz. Thank you."

Mrs. Schwartz nodded to her daughter, who poured Alfano a glass and handed it to him. He took a long sip.

"Delicious."

"Good. Detective, this is my daughter, Linda Gottschalk. She is Benjamin's older sister. She is staying with me for a few days. She lives with her husband in Skokie; he's in real estate."

Alfano studied the daughter. She was well dressed, and her hairstyle matched the times. He read successful.

"Linda left the neighborhood when you could," Mrs. Schwartz said. "Me? I can't. Too many roots, and I have to watch the store."

"Mother, the store can take care of itself."

"I'm not sure that's true, and your father would not approve. I must watch."

"Mrs. Schwartz, I'm sorry for your loss," Alfano interjected. "I saw Benny fight a few times. He was good, in fact, very good."

The daughter turned a glare on Alfano.

"Did you know that he boxed and fought for three years before my mother found out? He even fought under an Irish name so she wouldn't learn the truth, like he was ashamed at being a Jew. He never should have been fighting."

"That's all right, Linda. Benjamin loved what he did. He told me. He also said he was going to quit. Just a few more bouts, and then he was through. That's why I was there, hoping it was his last fight."

Mrs. Schwartz took a small white handkerchief from her sleeve and dabbed the corners of her eyes.

"He should never have been fighting," the daughter said again. "It's all Rabbi Harris's fault, and the whole CYO thing, and that fool Stingly. They filled Benny's head with dreams that never would have come to anything. Dreams that got him killed."

She presented Alfano with another glare. "Now Samuel is fighting in the Golden Gloves," she said.

Alfano could see that this was just one more installment in a long conversation between the two women. Unfortunately, the story now had a fatal end.

"Samuel?" he prompted.

"He's just turned seventeen," Linda answered. "We haven't heard from him since Sunday morning. Mother says he ran out of the house at the news."

Alfano made a mental note to find out what the boy knew.

"You said that Benjamin was going to get out of the fights. Did he tell this to anyone else?"

"As far as I know, no one," Mrs. Schwartz said. "We talked last week when he was here for Sunday dinner. You remember, Linda? He was tired and had lost interest, and he had been asked to work at one of the breweries that was reopening on the West Side. Good job, too. The owner, Jules Lauder, been a friend of our family for a long time. He knew Benjamin worked hard and wanted him in his operation. Benny was excited about it."

"This guy Stingly, he was Benjamin's trainer?"

"No, Stingly was his agent or manager," Linda said. "The

trainer was a strange man"—she stared over Alfano's shoulder for a moment and then looked back at him—"small, narrow, long nose, bald," she added, punctuating each word firmly. "Benny called him his trainer and cut man, whatever that is."

Alfano was sure that this was not the time to explain to Benny's sister and mother the role of the cut man in the ring.

"Has this Stingly fellow stopped by since the fight?" he asked the women.

Mrs. Schwartz looked at her daughter. "Yes, he came by to say he was sorry, and gave me an envelope with money. To help make things a little better, he said."

"You told me that asshole never came by," Linda said.

"Your language, young lady," Mrs. Schwartz said. "It didn't concern you, and we needed the money to bury Benjamin. It was a thousand dollars."

"A thousand dollars? Why would he give you a thousand dollars?" Alfano asked.

"He said he was heartbroken over Benny's death. He hoped that this could help a little."

"More likely, it was guilt over what happened," her daughter added. "He would never have let Benny out of the ring. My brother was too good; he had too good a record. He was doing well."

"You like the fights, Mrs. Gottschalk?" Alfano asked.

A woman inside the house came to the screen door, and both women turned toward her. Alfano could just make out the woman's shape through the screen. A teenage girl stood next to her.

"I'm sorry, Mrs. Schwartz. I don't mean to intrude," the woman said.

"Please come out, Deborah. I want you to meet Detective Tony Alfano. I guess he's investigating Benjamin's death."

Alfano watched the woman push open the flimsy screen door. It screeched just a little, which did not detract from the immediate impression she made. Alfano stood.

"Detective," said Mrs. Schwartz, "this is Deborah Tillerman. She is the daughter of Alderman Solomon of the 24th Ward. She is here to offer her father's condolences. And the child is my youngest, Rebecca."

Alfano extended his hand; Deborah's grip was soft, yet firm. Her dark eyes were intriguing; when she smiled, her lips were soft and smooth.

Alfano turned to the girl.

"Mother still thinks I'm a child; I'm fifteen," Rebecca said, holding out her hand.

"You are still fourteen, Becca," Linda said, correcting.

"A pleasure, Detective," Deborah said, studying him. "Are you the detective who stopped the assassination of that fascist Balbo at the Congress Hotel?"

"Yes."

"I, for one, would have let the woman kill him. These fascists, whether Italian or German, are nothing but murderers. I would have—"

"Please, Debbie, not now," Linda interrupted. She turned to Alfano. "Debbie is very passionate about the things going on in Germany and Italy. Then again, she is passionate about a lot of things."

"Like the fights and the need to outlaw them," Deborah said.

Linda raised her palms upward toward her friend.

"Detective, like I said, however, Debbie and I are of like mind. So, to answer your question, no, I do not like the fights. A lot of Jewish kids from around here have been busted up and damaged by this so-called sport. They hide it from their parents until it's too late, or they get so busted up that it's obvious it was more than some street gang fight."

"There are good fighters that have come out of this neighborhood," Alfano said. "Fighters like King Levinsky and Barney Ross."

"And both good boys, but I didn't like my own boys fighting," Mrs. Schwartz said, looking in turn at Deborah and then at her daughter. "I had enough of it when your father was boxing."

That had been soon after Mrs. Schwartz and her husband came from Russia, she went on to say. Then it had been a tougher and meaner sport—"if you can call it that." Her husband had made enough, got out, and started their business.

Mrs. Schwartz's eyes grew wet.

"God rest his soul," she said. "When Benny said he was quitting, I was happy. I blame Stingly."

"Did this guy Stingly say anything about gambling?"

"Detective, I know where you are going with this," Mrs. Schwartz said. "We own a newsstand, two doors down from Barney Ross's parents' vegetable market. Did you know Ross's real family name is Rosofsky? Good family, religious family, his father is a rabbi. Barney sparred with Benny. They were friends."

Mrs. Schwartz stopped and thought for a moment.

"I read everything. I know about the betting, the odds out there, even that sometimes fights are thrown. Benjamin never would have done that, never."

"You see, that's why boxing must be made illegal," Deborah added. "Even the Golden Gloves—a misnomer if I've ever heard one—is caught up in the gambling rackets."

"Benny's heart was not in it anymore. He wanted out," Linda said. "I think someone wanted him to fight one more time and throw the fight—not die, but take a fall. Now he's dead."

She looked fiercely at Alfano.

"Find Stingly, and you will find my brother's killer."

"The coroner says that Benny died as a result of the fight. Right now, he is saying it may have been—"

"Fixed? I know damn well that it was fixed," Deborah said. "They put two children in the ring and gave them tools that would kill each other. Now you have to find out who did this. They may not have hit Benny, but they sure as hell killed him and that other boy as well. It was murder, plain and simple."

Deborah Tillerman intrigued Alfano. In fact, he was surprised at his reaction to her comments; he was agreeing with her. He had been to fights off and on for years, enjoyed the sporting aspect of the game, the friends from the station house he'd go with. But right now, he was agreeing with the alderman's outspoken daughter.

"Isn't your father against fights in Cook County?" he asked her.

"Yes, in fact, we are leading a group that is trying to make fighting illegal again, this time across the state. It is barbaric and inhumane. We have known the Schwartzes a long time."

She looked at the small gold watch on her wrist and then gently touched Mrs. Schwartz's hand.

"My father intends to stop by when he can. I'm sorry, Mrs. Schwartz, Linda, but I must go. It will take some time to get back to the office on the trolley."

"I know the 24th Ward office, Mrs. Tillerman. May I give you lift?" Alfano asked.

His own boldness shocked him but didn't seem to perturb Tillerman. She looked at him for a brief moment, and then said, "Sure."

14

ALFANO SAID, "It's almost two o'clock, and I'm starving," as he pulled away from the curb. "My sergeant seems to think that donuts are the only food a cop should eat. Me, I need something more substantial. So, Mrs. Tillerman, may I buy you lunch? That is, if you don't think I'm being a little too forward."

"Please call me Debbie. Only my father calls me Deborah. And do not worry about any stories; I'm a widow. I lost my husband fifteen years ago. He died in France."

"Sorry, I didn't know."

"How could you? It's been a long time. Lunch would be a delight, a change from the usual chicken salad I get from the deli. How about a picnic?"

"Really?"

"There's a deli on Roosevelt near Douglas Park. I suggest potato salad and a sandwich. It's a nice day; wouldn't want to spoil it by being indoors. Besides, you look like a man who has not been on a picnic for a long time."

Like years, Alfano thought. "Tell me which way to go."

He made a left turn after passing Garfield Park and began to double back to Douglas Park.

"I've seen a few matches there," Alfano said as they passed

the 24th Ward Club. "If your father is so much against boxing, why does he permit it at the club?"

"He doesn't control the club; the party does, and it's been a battle since the day he was elected. But he won't give up."

"Bad things have happened in this part of Chicago over the last thirty years. Politics in this town can, how do I put this delicately . . ."

"You mean elections through intimidation, voting fraud, and murder? Is that what you were going to say?"

"Yes, but you put it a lot nicer."

"Stop here. I'll be right back."

Five minutes later, Debbie climbed back into the car. A tall young man followed, a white cardboard box in his hands. She took it and placed it on her lap. The man nodded and went back into the deli.

"I've known them, the Levis, my whole life. Their deli has been here for almost forty years. Did you know, Detective, that they have been robbed more than thirty times during that period? Luckily, neither of the Levis nor their children have been hurt."

"It's a tough neighborhood," Alfano said and pulled away from the curb.

What he didn't tell his lunch date was that four times he'd come to this deli and had to remove the body of a thug who thought he could rob the place. Each time Julius Levi, a Jew from Warsaw, had put a bullet through the heart of the robber. Mr. Levi had fought in the late-nineteenth century wars in Europe and fully understood what was required to protect his family and his business. Owning a deli was a tough job in Chicago.

At Douglas Park, Alfano and Debbie walked a hundred yards in and found an empty picnic table. She opened the box like she was unveiling ancient mysteries and spread a wondrous assembly of cartons and packages across the included tablecloth. She set out silverware and napkins that, she explained, would be returned later. Two bottles of cold beer also were extracted. Alfano's stomach growled.

"I'm glad you're hungry. I'm famished, too. Sit, before it gets warm."

It had been a long time since Alfano had enjoyed such a meal. The sandwich meat, a thinly sliced corned beef, was righteously piled high on thick egg bread; a touch of coleslaw was added for crunch. The potato salad was cold and the beer even colder.

"Wonderful," Alfano said as he chewed.

"It was your idea, and a nice change from my desk."

She sipped her beer and looked at him.

"You know my story. Is there a Mrs. Alfano?"

"Got close, too close recently, but it didn't work out. No, been married to the job, as they say."

"They say a lot, I'm told—your whole life?"

"Since I was twenty-two, and that was twenty years ago. Patrolman, beat cop, detective the last ten years." He half grinned. "One of the first in the department to drive a car, and I hate to drive."

"That's a very nice car you have."

"It's the department's; I sort of use it on an as-needed basis. I won't own one of the damn things."

"They can be convenient."

"An indoor bathroom is convenient; an automobile is just a damn . . . I'm sorry, didn't mean to go off like that—delicious sandwich."

"Yes, it is."

They both tried to avoid the real subject at the table. Alfano jumped in.

"What your father is trying to do is going to be very difficult in this town," he said. "He's up against powerful and important people, including the mayor."

"It's the CYO and the Jewish gyms that must understand the damage they are causing. It's the gamblers and the politicians—all of them have blood on their hands. I don't understand the appeal, especially to young boys. Is it the glory and the money? Not that most of them ever will make a dollar."

She voiced her fear that old men still saw boxing as a noble sport, a gladiatorial exhibition—somewhere young men could prove themselves. It was an allure hard to overcome.

"Detective, this change must come from the top, not from the bottom. These men must understand what happens to a boy who is hammered in the head for thirty minutes. It doesn't happen in one fight, but over many fights and hours in the gym. When they realize and see the damage, it is too late."

"At a picnic, please call me Tony. And I understand, though I believe with better supervision and qualified referees it can be much safer."

"Not when a two-hundred-pound young man, with all the force he can gather, smashes in the side of the head of another. Tony, I believe that those two young men died, not because of a boxing match, but the insatiable need for money. Gambling, promoters, seconds, cut men, stadiums, clubs, and back halls, that's where the money is. The kids get nothing; the old men make the money. They don't give a shit, plain and simple."

The "old men" also supported dogfights, cockfights, and even horse racing—all to make a buck off the suffering and death of someone or something else, she reminded Alfano. "It's intolerable and, in these days of enlightenment, just wrong."

Alfano sipped his beer. "You and your father have a lot to overcome."

"We Jews always have had a lot to overcome, and we will 'til the end of time. But it's not just us. There are others in the Catholic Church, and even some of the Protestants—our children have to stop being made nothing more than dogs in a ring, ripping each other's throats out for the thrill of the crowds."

"I have a friend; he's the coroner. He loves the sport, yet sees the damage that happens in the ring almost every day. He's one of the men you have to change. He's a Jew, a good man."

"Yes, I understand. Since my husband's death in man's greatest and murderous sport of all, I've learned that there is much to do. In this wicked and corrupt town, it will be hard. Hell, we murder those that seem a threat to politics; they die by the whims of a few. I hate to think what their reaction will be when we try to stop their detestable income."

"You and your father are in danger. You know that."

She nodded impatiently.

"Taunts, notes, death threats seem to be the rule—but we must make a stand."

She began to gather up the lunch rubbish and place the papers and silverware back in the carton.

"I'm sorry, I didn't mean to get on my high horse," she said, offering a smile. "It's just that we have to begin somewhere."

"I admire your passion," Alfano said truthfully.

He carried the deli box to the car.

"After I leave you at your office, I'll drop these off at the Levis. It will be good to see them again."

"I didn't know that you knew them."

"I've been a cop in this town a long time. I'm amazed at how many people I do know—and the circumstances of how we met."

"Is this one of those . . . circumstances?"

"Yes, I think it might be. Are you available to go to the movies on Friday? I haven't been to a good flick in a long time. There's a Gable and Harlow movie . . ."

"*Hold Your Man.* I would love to. There is a little of Clark

Gable in you, Detective."

* * *

Alfano walked into the station house. McDunnah was eating a sandwich at his desk.

"Have you had lunch?" the Irishman asked.

"Yes, and a lecture. Sergeant, this case is getting stranger and stranger. You know that 24th Ward alderman, Isaac Solomon?"

"The anti-boxing one?"

"The same. It seems he's wrapped up in this along with his daughter. She was at the Schwartzes, offering condolences and help."

The sergeant looked at Alfano.

"I assume you then had to have lunch with the daughter?" McDunnah said, the corners of his mouth noticeably turning upward.

"See what you can find out about their anti-boxing league, or whatever they call it. The daughter is Deborah Tillerman. A widow. And not one to keep a low profile."

"And is she cute?"

Alfano ignored the comment, turned, and looked past the desks scattered around the room to where the crime board sat, behind his desk, in the far corner. Most of the others were populated with suited men in hats and holding cigarettes. In the corner, the newly assigned captain's door was open.

"I knew it. She is cute. Dammit, Detective, when are you going to find a girlfriend?"

"Don't I have enough on my plate with you?"

McDunnah went back to his sandwich. Alfano started toward his own desk and then stopped.

"See what pops up about a kid named Samuel Schwartz. He's Benny's brother. And there's an older sister—Linda Gottschalk. She said her brother took Benny's death hard. He's also in the Golden Gloves. The family hasn't seen him for a few days."

"Will do."

Dammit, she was cute, but in a womanly way, he admitted to himself. Nice figure, sure of herself, and smart. Those dark eyes just drew you in. He was a young guy. McDunnah smiled and waved. Alfano sat down at his desk.

* * *

"The Russian says he'll pay you anything you want, boss," Gus Teitlebaum said over the telephone. "In fact, he's begging now. God-awful thing when they beg."

Rosenberg twirled bourbon around in the tumbler he held and watched his two children climb the stair to their bedrooms. They were followed by the nanny. Until Gus's call, it had been a nice evening. Now the mood was broken. The vision of Igor Koslov trussed up and sitting in a bathtub in a barn just ruined it.

"Get him to tell you where the money is first, got it? Then do what you have to."

"Yes, boss, got it."

Rosenberg placed the telephone receiver on its cradle and walked through the house to the front room of his Oak Park home. His wife looked up from the newspaper and smiled.

"Thank you for the nice afternoon. The children are happy, I'm happy, all's well," Agnes Rosenberg said. She asked who he'd been speaking with on the phone.

"It was Gus, asking what time he was to pick me up in the morning. I told him I'm going to sleep in late. What do you think?"

Agnes blushed a little. "That would be nice."

She was from a reasonably well-off Jewish family. Both her father and mother were born in Kiev, Ukraine, and fled with their parents to the United States after the 1882 pogrom. Eventually, in 1895, their families made it to Chicago, where Agnes was born and raised with her three sisters. Always rebellious, Agnes challenged her businessman father on most everything and eventually fled the house when she was twenty.

Hymen Rosenberg was the strong man she always wanted. Decisive and direct, she knew that he would do whatever was necessary to protect their family. Over the last ten years, due to his business connections, they had moved in some of the more powerful circles in the Chicago community. Circles that did not take her anywhere near her three annoying sisters and mother. She did not care what her husband did for a living. She found an occasional bloodstain on a sleeve and once a pocketful of bullets, but never a gun. She left the bullets in the pocket and never mentioned them to him. She made sure the house, with the help of the nanny, cook, and housemaid, was well kept. She did not want to disappoint her husband. She had learned from other relatives—those who also fled the Ukraine—that she never would allow her family to be victims again.

15

THE NEXT MORNING, Rosenberg walked down the front steps of his house and climbed into the back seat behind Teitlebaum and Ziggy Feldstein. Ruth waved from the porch as the car pulled away. Rosenberg rolled down the window and waved back.

"Kozlov?" he asked as he lit a cigar.

"We took the launch out late last night," Gus said. "He's in a hundred feet of water somewhere off the city's intake plant. We searched his house, and the idiot had hidden the stash in a vent shaft in the parlor."

"I bet you've never said parlor in your life," Ziggy offered.

"I'll have you knows I have. I was talking to this nice little piece the other evening: 'You want to play a little parlor game?' See, I's knows what a parlor is."

Rosenberg blew a cloud of cigar smoke into the front seat.

"Sorry, boss," Ziggy said. "The money's on the seat next to you. Didn't have time to count it, but it looks like it's more than that spic Jones had stashed up his chimney."

Gus looked at Ziggy. "Tell me again why you didn't shoot that asshole who found it in Jones's apartment? Just asking?"

"Would have been too loud. The hotel was as quiet as a church, and I heard somebody coming up on the elevator. I slugged the guy with the jack, and he went down quick. Besides, I knew he was a cop, and as far as I know, clean."

"No such thing," Gus said.

Rosenberg let another smoke cloud drift into the front of the car. He asked, "I take it from now on, you will be more thorough in your searches?"

Ziggy nodded. "Yes, sir. You can be sure I'll check every vent, flu, and chimney."

"Good boy. Ziggy? Ever hit a cop before?"

There was a long silence from the front seat as both gunzels looked at each other and shrugged.

"Nope," Ziggy said. "He never saw it coming. Cops drop as fast as any other man. He crumpled like yesterday's number sheet. Like I said, I put the bundle under my arm and took the stairs to the street. Then, likes I said, I watched from the street. Easy-peasy."

"You were lucky, fucking lucky."

"Yes, sir. I was lucky."

Gus continued east down Roosevelt Road toward the high-rises of the Loop. As they approached Douglas Park, he slowed and stopped at the park's entry on Albany Avenue. Across the intersection sat a massive black Packard.

"Jesus Christ," Gus said. "That sure as hell looks like Rudi Bandini's old Packard, the one the cops took after that raid last year. Goddamn, that's a sweet ride."

The stoplight changed. Gus slowly accelerated through the intersection; the Packard passed them. A man in a gray fedora was driving.

"Recognize him?" Rosenberg asked.

Gus and Ziggy looked closely. Gus said no.

Ziggy said, "There's something about the man that looks familiar, but the glare off the glass is bad. Shit, boss, it could be anyone. He looks Italian, but then again it figures; only Eye-Ties drive those fucking things. We Jews stick to our Cadillacs."

"You're an asshole, Ziggy."

"Yes, sir. I'm an asshole."

* * *

After a leisurely breakfast of pancakes and eggs at Lou Mitchell's, Alfano circled back around his old neighborhood of Little Italy and eventually to the station. He had to admit the previous afternoon had brightened his attitude, even though his head still throbbed when he snugged his hat. As he passed Douglas Park, he smiled—*it was a nice picnic.* He parked the Packard in front of the station, said good morning to McDunnah, and headed to his corner of the detective's room. The sergeant gave him one of his looks. Sitting, his desk phone rang.

He looked up, the sergeant pointed at him.

"Detective Alfano . . ."

He scribbled a few notes: snagged by a whitefish gillnetter . . . off the intake cribs in the lake . . . not yet identified.

"Man or woman?" he asked the caller. "How long in the water?"

For years, maybe for over a hundred, Lake Michigan had been a favorite location for dumping bodies. Tie an old iron wagon wheel rim or two to the legs and pitch the corpse over the side. Alfano had seen concrete blocks and even an anvil used, anything convenient to weigh down the body and take it to the sandy bottom of the lake. Sometimes the corpse would bloat with putrefactive gases and surface, at least for a while. Some washed up on one of the hundreds of beaches that ran from Milwaukee to the Indiana Dunes, making for a bad and unpleasant surprise for the beachgoers. Most, Alfano believed, were never discovered.

Abrahamson had said the body had been in the water for a day at the most. The early morning gillnetter who snagged it had pulled the body up with his catch of whitefish. He removed the fish before dealing with the body—money is money.

Alfano was upset with the doc; why call him? He had more than enough to deal with. Then again, the coroner had said that he knew the dead would get a fair break from Tony Alfano—thanks a whole lot, Doc.

"What's up?" McDunnah had come over to find out.

"A body pulled from the lake."

"Anyone we know?"

"Can't tell, but it's a big man, only a day or two in the lake. Should be able to get an ID—if he's on file."

"If he was dredged out of the lake, it's an even money bet that he's on file somewhere."

***

Duffy McGoin cooled his heels outside a conference room at the offices of the Illinois Boxing Commission. Crushed cigarettes filled the ashtray on a side table; most were McGoin's. Above the couch was a large black-and-white photograph of the recent June 23 fight between two of Chicago's lightweight favorites: Barney Ross and Tony Canzoneri. It had been a bruising ten rounder, and while McGoin, who had a third-row seat, felt that Canzoneri won the decision, the Jews stacked behind Ross's corner were rabid over the decision for Ross. Such was boxing these days, McGoin thought. It was as much a fight between men as it was a no-holds battle between Chicago's various races: the Irish, the Jews, the Negroes, and the Italians. He had a thousand Irish fathers wanting him to be their kid's manager. McGoin was looking for both talent and charm; with these qualities, your guy might just win a ticket to the big stage.

The door to the conference room opened.

"You may come in now, Mr. McGoin," a woman said.

The secretary led McGoin into the room and pointed to a small table with one chair. It faced a much longer table, around which sat a dozen men; some were politically appointed commissioners and some were lawyers. They all had a vested interest in the fight game. Sitting off to one side was a smartly dressed man in a three-piece suit, white shirt, dark tie. He addressed McGoin.

"Please sit, Mr. McGoin. This should not take long. I'm Dexter Dortman. I am the general counsel for the boxing commission, and I will be asking you a few questions. This is strictly an informal and preliminary hearing to try to understand what happened the night of Friday, August 11, at the Chicago Stadium. We will be taking your statement, but you will not be sworn in. Do you understand?"

The promoter looked at the stern and earnest faces of the men seated along the table. He'd met a few of them during the past few years, even had a drink or two with some of them after one of the fights. He knew that most were honest men who had the respect of the boxing community. He also knew they would, to save their collective asses, sell him down the river faster than a ten count.

"Mr. McGoin?"

"Yes, Mr. Dortman, I understand," McGoin said. "And I would like to thank the commission for taking the time to hear my comments regarding that tragedy."

He nodded to the men; no one nodded back.

Dortman lied. The questioning was not short. For three hours, the counselor and another attorney by the name of Schlagle grilled McGoin. Their questions were perfunctory at the start: How long had he managed boxers in Chicago? How many boxers did he manage? What was his connection to the Catholic Youth Organization? What was his relationship to the deceased boxer? They went on and on. McGoin was sure one of the next questions was going to be about his hat size.

Three hours into the interview, McGoin's stomach growled. He glanced at his watch, 1:30 PM. He was surprised that the commission had worked through lunch.

"Do you have somewhere to go, Mr. McGoin?" Dortman asked.

"As a matter of fact, I do, and you are making me late. You said this was to be a short conversation; however, I do realize that you bill by the hour so this must be one of the shorter interviews."

McGoin stared at Dortman, and then ran his eyes over to Schlagle. "So, what else can I help you with?" he asked them.

There were murmurs around the table. A commissioner seated toward the middle of the long table said, "I'm sorry for the inconvenience, Mr. McGoin, but this is necessary. Two men died."

"Yes, I know. I was there."

Dortman interjected, "Then can you tell me why the coroner believes that both men died as a result of injuries sustained by gloves that may have been loaded?"

McGoin glared outright at Dortman.

"Three hours, and you finally get to the real heart of the matter. I have no idea why he would come to that conclusion. You have seen his report; I have not."

Dortman said nothing.

"The gloves looked all right to me," McGoin said, still looking at Dortman. "I saw nothing about O'Shea's gloves that were any different than the standard mitts the guys wear."

"You have nothing to say about whether they were packed with lead shot or some other hard material?"

"What I am saying is that I have no idea about what you're taking about."

"Where are the gloves that Tommy O'Shea used that night?"

"I have no idea."

"Why not?"

"It's not my responsibility to take care of those things. The gloves were in the training room when we arrived. Neatly boxed, new, and clean. The trainer dealt with them. My job is the venue, the match, the rent, the promotion, and the—"

"Bribes and gamblers?" Dortman said.

McGoin let out a snort. "I beg your pardon?"

"The commission has tried for years to keep the sport clean and upstanding. It is you *gentlemen*, with your disreputable associates, who are causing this cancer on the sport."

McGoin looked again at Dortman, with even more fire in his expression. His voice grew loud.

"Mr. Attorney, without men like me, there would be no boxing, no Golden Gloves, no prize monies, and no boxing commission. You would not have a job."

Dortman pretended to ignore McGoin's outburst.

"Do you know where the gloves went?" he asked again.

"I was dealing with the after-fight press and getting Tommy out of the Stadium. I have no idea where his gloves did or did not go."

"I'm through with this witness. He can be excused," Dortman said, now speaking about McGoin rather than to him.

Without waiting for any further sign from the commissioners, McGoin stood, secured his fedora, and walked out of the hearing. He brushed off the secretary, who was telling him to remain available if the commissioners had further questions.

"You know where to find me," he snapped.

Sitting in the same hallway chair McGoin had waited in was Eggie Stingly. He looked at McGoin, and then stood.

"Tough?" Stingly asked.

"Enough so—they are fishing. Be very careful not to take the bait. If you do, they will gut you like a carp."

McGoin walked down the hall. He heard the door open and the secretary speaking to Stingly. "Yeah, I'm Egmund Stingly," came the reply just as McGoin started down the stairs.

16

THE DEAD MAN'S THICK, black, wet hair was pulled tightly back against his skull. The ghostly white color of the face was unnatural, almost transparent. The man's lips were the same color as his cheeks. The nose was large and twisted to the right, an old injury. The eyes, wide open, once had been dark brown but now were faded, vacant, washed out. A pair of neat and clean holes, a thumb's width apart, sat about two fingers above the right eye and extended deep into the skull.

Alfano traveled his eyes down the rest of the body; it was as pallid as the face. The dead man's body was hairy; a thick black mat on the chest, stomach, and groin was exposed in coarse contrast to the spectral pallor of the white skin. Scars, obviously from old bullet wounds, peppered the upper right side of the torso. A long scar ran down the left arm, another across the left thigh. Numerous puncture wounds that looked newer covered the trunk.

"Jesus," Alfano said. "This guy has been in a lot of fights. I'm amazed that he lived through them."

"From what I see, these were over maybe ten years. The man was in his early forties; the cause of death was, expertly speaking, two bullets to the forehead. I won't know until the autopsy if there might be something else. These contusions and bruises"—Abrahamson pointed to the dark splotches on the man's lower side and stomach—"were done before the coup de grâce."

"Nice phrasing. So, marinating in the lake didn't kill him?"

"No," Abrahamson said. "The lividity evident on the back says he was killed and then later dumped in the lake. I'll do a fluoroscope of the head to see if there are bullets still there. I found no exit wounds, so the chances are good."

"These wounds?" Alfano pointed to the roughly one-inch cuts that striped across the torso.

"I suspect those are from a substantial knife, also done post-mortem. See, no bruising. The punctures are to the lungs, stomach, and a few other organs."

Alfano nodded. The killer or killers had known to let the putrefactive gases out, which would help keep the body submerged.

"Pleasant thought," he murmured. "Anything else?"

"The clothes he was wearing"—the coroner jerked his head toward an adjacent table where the still-damp garments were carefully laid out—"nice labels, good stores. No shoes, just stockings. Also, when they pulled him up, he had a black hood over his head. There's two holes in the fabric."

"Like Jones?"

"Too similar. I'd even guess the caliber of the pistol to be the same. Maybe we can find markings on the bullets to match them to the same weapon."

"Yeah, but right now, I want to find the shooter, not the gun. Anything about the weights?"

"It's an old iron wagon wheel. I haven't seen one of those since I was a kid. Iron spokes, rim, and axle hub."

Abrahamson explained that most wagon wheels were wood with an iron rim; this one, which had been placed in the next room, was all metal, heavy, and durable—"like the kind used for farm machinery," he told Alfano. "Wide rim and all, it must weigh a hundred pounds. The body was secured to it with barbed wire twisted around the ankles. If it weren't for the fisherman and his net, this body never would have popped up."

"Professional?"

"Beyond that. These guys would have taught the school on lake body dumping."

"Doc, if these were the same guys who killed Iggy Jones, why the lake instead of another hole in the ground?"

"That's for you to figure out. In both cases, the bodies were disposed of hoping not to be found. Their professionalism is coming into question."

Alfano gave the coroner a wry smile. "Even the pros screw up, sometimes."

He lit a cigar as he walked from the morgue to the Packard. The smells in the place hung on him like the musty odor of mothballs clung to a winter coat. He found that only a Romeo y Julieta would mask the stench.

The body lying on Abrahamson's exam table had been pulled up along with five hundred pounds of whitefish, a hundred yards from the Carter H. Harrison intake crib, two and a half miles off the Gold Coast along Lake Michigan. To think that Chicago's drinking water was sucked in through the intake pipe a hundred yards from a rotting corpse was a lot more than Alfano wanted to think about. But then again, there were many things that Alfano did not care to think about.

However, yesterday's picnic lunch with Debbie Tillerman was not one of them. It had been a pleasant hour, even though a bit rancorous. That was okay; he appreciated it, even enjoyed a woman with strong convictions. His other recent dating experiences sadly had left him with a less-than-ideal impression of the fairer sex. He'd grown weary of the posturing and frivolity that many of his dates displayed. Maybe it was his being a cop, maybe it was the kind of women he met on the job, maybe it was because he was a cynical bastard at heart.

He glanced at his face in the rearview mirror. Gable? He smiled; in the midst of dealing with politicians, lowlifes, and dead bodies, the offhand comment by Debbie Tillerman had made his day.

The case—and he was pretty sure there was one case and not just random, disconnected crimes—was a jumble. He'd stopped to see the latest body more out of curiosity; the murder was all too professional. Someone had to have had a boat at the ready to move the body from where the man was murdered. The iron wheel suggested farm equipment, which was absolutely no help. Chicago was surrounded on three sides by a million acres, or more, of farmland. Alfano believed that the body was that of Igor Kozlov, the missing bookie. The face on the slab sure reminded him of the Russian. He would soon have the photos of the body from the coroner to match to the photos on the board. If it was Kozlov, he'd been killed less than twenty-four hours earlier. And he'd probably been snatched about the time they'd found Jones's body, two days ago. Someone laid down a series of big bets, all were losers, and it looked like the loser was taking out his revenge on the bookies.

The fight had been last Friday night, six nights ago. The fight, in which, increasingly, it looked like one of the boxers was intended to take a dive—which fighter he hadn't figured out yet. In the end they'd accidentally killed each other, but with weapons stealthily provided by someone else. Both fighters' gloves had to have been doctored, but now both pairs of gloves were gone—maybe they would show up, but Alfano doubted it.

The Catholic Church and important rabbis and politicians of the Jewish faith were tangled up in the events. Also involved in the crime, and he was positive it was a double murder, were gangsters, dead bookies, fight promoters, and more politicians. A grieving mother and a young pregnant widow were left with almost nothing and no answers to their questions of who and why. This case was like a puzzle with all the pieces strewn willy-nilly across a tabletop. It was time to start putting the picture together.

17

FRIDAY MORNING the coroner's photo of Igor Kozlov had joined that of fellow bookie Ignacio Jones and the other photos and carefully penned labels on the crime board. Sergeant McDunnah came up behind where Alfano stood with his hands in his pants pockets, staring intently at the board.

"Damn you, Detective, when were you gonna tell me what happened at the deli? You okay?"

"I'm fine. Harvey is fine. I'm pissed because I had to shoot that boy."

"He would have killed you."

"He was too nervous to hit anything."

"You don't know that; he could have gotten lucky, although I learned it was his first robbery. So, it's good you didn't kill him, or any of the others as well."

"Stupid kids—they weren't even eighteen, none of them. Shit, what's this world coming to?"

"For that, Detective, I have no answer. This summer has been seriously fucked up. The fair, guns, bombs, airplanes; now these boxers' death, and it's only August."

Alfano looked at his sergeant and then at the dozen or so detectives sitting around the room. "It's a war zone out there."

"That it is."

Alfano looked back at the board. "The story on the street is that four bookies took the big bets that night for Schwartz," he said.

"That's the word," McDunnah answered. "Your club owners said it, and I have a couple of frightened bookies saying the same thing. And O'Shea won with a knockout. Maybe he wasn't supposed to?"

"You think O'Shea was expected to lay down. Now we have two bookies dead, both under similar circumstances. But there is nothing that directly connects the bets to the fight. It could be a coincidence."

"A possibility. However, there are connections."

"Only if you look for them. Nothing is obvious. After going though both Kozlov and Jones's apartments, it is obvious they were thoroughly searched. I found in Jones's what was most probably a bundle of money. We can, for now, assume that something similar was found at Kozlov's. So, are our killers out for revenge, the money, or something else?"

"With these guys, I'd put money first and revenge second," McDunnah said. "The something else could be that these killings were object lessons. The mob's brutal way to tell the bookies to be very careful. Talk about trying to change a cat's stripes to spots."

"I'm also of the opinion that the killer or killers are old-school, maybe from Capone's days. The killings have that look about them. Do you have the names of the other two bookies?"

"First, Capone and the Outfit wasn't all *that* long ago. Second, yes, one is from Bridgeport: Oscar Xavier Macaulay. I've known Oscar since we were kids. He has an office down the street from the recently blown-up 11th Ward offices. It's in an office building on the same side of Halsted as Schaller's. I believe you are very familiar with that particular location."

"Too familiar. The other bookie?"

"The current rumor on the street is that Jimmy Applebaum is gone. Otherwise known as 'Two Fingers.' Two guys who know him say that he took a first-class cabin on the 20th Century Limited to New York. Left Tuesday—said something about an ailing aunt. My gut says that he's got no aunt, ailing or otherwise, in New York."

"Smart man—where was Applebaum's office?"

"It's not far from here, actually. A third story walk-up a block from Chicago Stadium. The guys say he wanted to be near the action to pick up any last-minute wagers."

"The city is not short of bookies. I'm sure that the two positions that have recently opened up have already been filled."

"Most likely," McDunnah said.

He stuck two handbills on the board. One was printed on bright yellow paper:

WORLD'S FAIR
BOXING IN THE LAGOON
A Stellar All-Star Program. Twelve-round Welterweight contest between Tim (Terrific) Callahan and Otto (The Fist) Werner. Preliminaries include two ten-round bouts and a special dance program, between bouts, of the "Fairy Dancers."

The fight was for Saturday night. The details at the bottom of the handbill were about prices and times.

"Tomorrow—that will be some kind of battle. Callahan and Werner do not like each other," Alfano said. "What's the other?"

"Next Saturday night at the Stadium. Heavyweights—one of your boys, Italian Primo Carnara, is taking on Jack Gross. This should be good. Carnara knocked out Ernie Schaaf in New York. I think it was in February."

Schaaf, as a matter of fact, had died a few days later. Carnara was the current world champion, McDunnah told Alfano.

"The undercard has Leo Rodak taking on Tommy Paul," he said. "There's lots of local talent in the other bouts. A couple of the fighters are from this year's Golden Gloves—they're debuts. I've heard that one of the fighters is Sammy Schwartz."

"Benny's brother?"

"Yeah, not good. I don't like it."

"You going tomorrow night?" Alfano asked.

"Can't. Saturday is that concert at Soldier Field. I told you, Moira already has our tickets. So, if you decide to go, you are on your own."

Still looking at the board, Alfano said, "Four important things are missing: the gloves from both the boxers. I looked for them, and they weren't in the Stadium. I think it's time to have Duffy McGoin and Eggie Stingly picked up and brought in for questioning. Send out a couple prowlers and see if they can find them?"

"I was wondering when we'd get around to those two. I also think we should find that trainer for Benny Schwartz. Strange-looking fellow; his name is Shem something. I've seen him in a lot of corners over the past ten years. He knows his business, but he never stays long with a fighter."

"Yes, get him, too. The attendants who cleaned up the room after the fight said that Stingly and the Shem guy got into it."

"Myerhoff, that's his name. Shem Myerhoff."

"He took off just after Benny was put in the ambulance," Alfano said thoughtfully. "This will make for some good conversation."

He looked again at the handbill for the Saturday fight at the Stadium. Here was another one that Debbie Tillerman and her father could use as a reason to stop the fights. Ernie Schaaf had been a New York fighter. He'd gone up against Max Baer as well as the colorful Tony Galento. Schaaf's death was a tragedy. Alfano reminded himself not to mention the Carnara fight during his movie date with Debbie that evening.

* × *

A loud ruckus interrupted Alfano's paperwork—he was filling out his report on the Tuesday night deli robbery. He looked up as McDunnah approached his desk.

"We have Egmund Stingly, ace fight promoter, waiting for you in Room Two. You interested in talking with him?"

McDunnah had a smile on his face.

"I also have Shem Myerhoff sitting on the front bench."

"Where did you find them?"

"They were both at the gym at the Hebrew Institute. Stingly, according to the patrolmen, was watching a kid box, and Myerhoff was the trainer. They were not happy about being interrupted. I also found out that the boxing commission interviewed both Stingly and McGoin. I'll see what I can find out. And, by the way, the kid they were handling was Benny Schwartz's brother, Samuel."

"I'll be there in a few minutes. Give them some of your coffee. That'll soften them up."

When Alfano walked into the interview room, Stingly was pacing the floor, mumbling to himself.

"Egmund Stingly?" Alfano asked as he looked at the top page of the folder McDunnah had given him.

"Yeah, who the fuck wants to know?"

"Watch your mouth, Stingly. I'm not partial to punks spouting off in my interview rooms. Changes my opinions of them before we start. So, tough guy, sit."

Alfano pointed to a chair behind the metal table that was bolted to the concrete floor. Hat in his hand, Stingly pulled the chair out and sat. He immediately began to rock back and forth. One of the chair's legs was a quarter-inch shorter, requiring the sitter to keep adjusting their seat. One more thing to keep them off-balance, along with the overly bright ceiling light. Alfano slid a chair to the opposite side of the table and sat down.

"Mr. Stingly, I have a problem, and maybe you can help me find a solution. Can you do that?"

"Problem? Who are you?"

"Detective Tony Alfano. That's all you need to know, other than I may be the only guy, right now, keeping you out of prison for either manslaughter or murder. Still trying to figure out which."

"Murder? What the hell do you mean by that? I did not kill no one."

"If you didn't do it, then who killed your boxer Benjamin Schwartz last Friday night? Somebody did it, and I'm just as happy to stick you with it as I am to put it on your associate, Shem Myerhoff."

"He ain't my associate. We goes our own ways."

"But those paths crossed all too often, so maybe you were in it together. Big payoff, split the winnings, help out a bookie or two."

"O'Shea killed the kid."

"And O'Shea is conveniently dead as well. I'll guess that you killed him, too. A double homicide."

"Jesus Christ, Detective. I had nothing to do with any of that. The fight game is tough. Sometimes these things happen. Benny was a good fighter, so why would I want him dead? The kid was making me money, not as much as a few others I have, but it was steady money. He had five KOs in the last year. My percentage was good, and he took some good money home to his mother."

"Did you know he was going to quit?"

"Who told you that?"

"His mother."

Stingly sat quiet for a few beats, and then said, "Yeah, I knew. He told me a few weeks ago. But we kept it quiet. If the other promoters knew, we'd never have gotten another fight. It's the rematches that make the big money. If they knew Benny was quitting, they'd never take the bout. So, after O'Shea, Benny had one more fight booked in late September. He was going to fight Barney Ross. It was going to be big in the Hebrew community."

"He'd have no chance against Ross."

"Maybe, maybe not. Nevertheless, the up-front prize money percentages were good. Schwartz was going to retire after the fight. So, why would I want the kid dead?"

Alfano merely stared at him.

"It was all an accident," Stingly said. "It happens in this sport. Boxers die, and jockeys fall off horses. Shit happens."

"You gave Mrs. Schwartz a thousand dollars. Why?"

"I made some good dough from the kid. We had a good ride—the money was a mitzvah. Something for the mother. What else could I do? Shit, Detective, I was torn apart by the kid's death. McGoin said he's gonna take care of O'Shea's family."

"Yeah, he gave the wife two hundred."

"Only two hundred? Jesus Christ, he is a cheap son of a bitch."

"Where's the gloves?"

"The gloves? Don't know nothing about the gloves," Stingly said. "When we left the Stadium—I was in the back of the ambulance with Benny—I left his mitts on the floor in the prep room. Maybe that rat Myerhoff knows where they are. He was still there when we left."

"The coroner says that both fighters wore gloves that were spiked. He's not sure with what, maybe shot or sand. He's leaning toward lead shot."

"Not a chance. The gloves were in their original packaging; they was brand new. McGoin and I agreed to that, and that was about all we agreed to. They were delivered to the rooms before the fight. They were there when we arrived."

"Do you know from where?"

"No, I assume that the Stadium took care of it. Talk to them. All I know, they were there when we arrived, on the training table—all fresh and new. Myerhoff wrapped Benny's hands and laced on the gloves. There was nothing different. It all looked good to me."

"Any ideas where they went?"

"Honest to God, Detective, I haven't a clue."

Alfano's interview with Shem Myerhoff went along the same lines as Stingly's. The major difference was when Myerhoff accused Stingly of cheating him out of fifty bucks he was owed for the fight.

"The son of a bitch still owes me for the night's work."

Myerhoff said that he remembered the gloves. Stingly had asked where they were, and Myerhoff had pointed to where they lay on the floor in a corner of the ready room. The trainer said he hadn't gone back for the gloves. He hadn't come to the Stadium with the gloves, so he wasn't sure who the gloves belonged to. And, he said he didn't know who delivered them to the room.

"How did it go?" McDunnah asked after Myerhoff walked out of the station.

"I'd like to arrest them both for complicity in stupidity and moral turpitude. Neither of them gives a thought to Benny Schwartz and what happened. They've both moved on. There's something bad going on here, but these two wouldn't know it if it punched them in the face. And they don't know what happened to Benny's gloves."

"They are still looking, and I talked to someone at the boxing commission who was there during the interviews," McDunnah replied when Alfano asked if there'd been word on McGoin.

"Good."

While Alfano was interviewing Stingly and Myerhoff, Mc-Dunnah had added a newspaper ad for Everlast boxing gloves to the crime board; he stuck two hand-drawn question marks over the clipping.

Alfano looked at the board, his mind still working the gloves question.

"What about Benny's brother?" he asked.

"Yes, one second," McDunnah said and began to look through the pile of fight promotion handouts he'd collected. "Here it is. Sammy Schwartz was listed on some Golden Glove preliminary bouts earlier this year. Can't say I've seen him fight. But it says here he's out of Davey Miller's gym on Kedzie and Roosevelt. It's called the Edmille Health Club. If I remember right, it's upstairs over a restaurant Miller owns. He's a power guy in the fights, especially the pros. Barney Ross may have trained there. Maybe Sammy is there."

"He's now next on my list," Alfano said and set his hat.

"This last bookie, the one I know, Oscar Macaulay, is a few blocks from my house. I'll drop by and see him on the way home."

"Be careful. I hope he's heard what's been going on," Alfano said as he walked out of the Racine Street station.

18

ALFANO ROLLED the Packard to a stop against the curb on Roosevelt Road, lit a cigarette, and watched the side door of the building on the corner. Over the entry hung a neatly printed sign: *EDMILLE HEALTH CLUB*. At the corner of Kedzie and Roosevelt, a wall of restaurant windows faced the streets. The name "Miller's" was painted on the glass in large gold letters.

Alfano couldn't remember having eaten there. A steady parade of men and women went in and out of the front door—lunch crowd. The side door opened and two men walked out, each carrying a gym bag. One had a pair of boxing gloves hung around his neck. They talked for a few minutes, and then each went his separate way up Kedzie. The big guy, Alfano recognized; it was Kingfish Levinsky, one of the toughest Jewish fighters from the neighborhood. In fact, Alfano had a third-row seat at the Stadium a year earlier and had watched Levinsky thrash Dempsey when the thirty-six-year-old world champion tried to make a comeback. Dempsey had retired after the short and brutal fight.

Alfano climbed out of the car, dropped his cigarette, and crushed it with his heel. He crossed Roosevelt and entered the gymnasium building by the side door. As soon as he stepped inside the entryway, he heard the muffled sounds of jump ropes and footfalls, the staccato banging of gloves against leather punching bags, and the gravelly voices of men yelling from the gym up the stairway. Alfano briefly closed his eyes; the sounds signaled that he could, at that moment, be in any gym in the world. He climbed to the second story; light streamed in from high windows across the floor of the sprawling gymnasium. Training equipment lined the walls. Men punched bags, skipped rope, lifted weights, and huddled in small groups. He was hit with the smells of sweat, liniment, and old socks. Everyone ignored him. In the center of the room, two boxing rings stood. Two men sparred in the nearest ring, gloves pounding practice pads. The thuds of body blows added a base beat to the din.

One man, in a suit and tie, spotted Alfano. He left the three men he was talking to and headed toward the detective. The man moved with grace and swagger. Alfano braced himself for the assault.

"If it isn't Detective Tony Alfano, the darling of the Chicago police force and chief ass kisser for the new mayor. What the hell are you doing here?"

"Didn't think I'd find an old buddy of Alphonse's in a legit place like this, Solly."

The big man wrapped his thick right arm entirely around Alfano and with his left hand gently slapped the detective's left cheek. Years earlier, that left could have killed Alfano.

Solly Goldberg had been a strong world heavyweight contender twenty-five years earlier. He'd won maybe thirty fights, all by knockouts. He'd lost all his prize money to gambling and other corporal pleasures. Capone had given him some odd jobs that eventually crossed tracks, the wrong tracks, with Alfano. Solly had been sent to Joliet prison for a deuce. He got out about the same time Capone's Outfit was disassembled through arrests, indictments, and murder. The Feds had done most of the heavy lifting, but the Chicago police did their fair share. It was Alfano who'd put the cuffs on Goldberg.

"I'm completely legit, Detective," Solly said now. "Seen my ways, got out, got married. In fact, I've got two kids."

He released his grip on Alfano and stepped back.

"Who'd have thought an asshole like me could find a way out of the shit I'd buried myself in? Davey gave me a break, been six or seven years now. How are you doing? I hear you're still pulling a city paycheck?"

"Doing okay, Solly. Same old shit: find the bad guys and throw them in jail. Cleaning up the streets as best I can."

"I'd start in city hall if I were you, just saying."

Alfano ignored the remark, not that he hadn't thought the same thing. Instead he said, "Good to hear all is jake with you and me, I hope."

"If it weren't for you I'd be dead or worse, as they say. I assume you are here on business? Never knew you to be a big fan of the ring."

"I like a good match now and then; I leave the technical stuff to my sergeant. I hear that the late Benny Schwartz's brother trains here."

The ex-fighter looked genuinely remorseful.

"That was terrible what happened," he said. "Yeah, Benny trained here, too. God, he was a good kid, had a real chance to move on. But he was stuck with that shit, Stingly. I tolerate a lot, but that man is as worthless as tits on a tick. I think he'd sell his mother for a sawbuck. Benny didn't deserve what happened."

"And Sammy Schwartz?" Alfano asked.

"He's in the ring over there, sparring with Davey Day. Now that's a kid that's up and coming. He took out Art Donovan a few months ago."

"Day's a pro. Why is he boxing Sammy?"

"And Sammy is five years younger, too—they's just sparring. Day's giving him some pointers."

According to Solly, Day and the Schwartz family went way back.

"Day is watching out for the kid," Solly said. "This last week has been rough on Sammy."

"And he's here working out?"

"Keeps his mind off all the crap. Plus, he's keeping in shape for next year's Golden Gloves. You want to talk to him?"

"Yeah, thanks."

Goldberg walked to the side of the ring.

"Sammy, there's a guy here who wants to talk with you. Davey, give him a rest."

"Yes, Mr. Goldberg," the skinny professional fighter said.

Alfano watched as both boxers climbed out of the ring. Day was a lightweight, maybe 135 pounds, and thin as a rail. His stature fooled every fighter he'd met. The "String Bean" had won his last fifteen fights, with only one loss somewhere in the middle of the string. He was known for his incredibly fast hands. Alfano guessed that Sammy Schwartz was the same weight class, but the younger fighter was fuller through his chest and arms. He was also a couple of inches shorter—and a good-looking kid.

"See you, Mr. Goldberg," Day said as he walked toward a door marked "Locker Room."

"Take it easy, Davey. You've got Engle at the Marigold in six weeks. Rest, keep in shape, and don't forget the road work."

Day waved and disappeared into the locker room. Sammy stood a few respectful feet away from Goldberg and Alfano.

"Sammy, this is Detective Alfano, an old friend. He has a few questions."

Sammy was holding his sparring gloves; he turned and pitched them in the corner near a pile of training pads. He stuck his right hand out. "Detective Alfano."

Alfano responded in kind, noting from habit that Sammy's

hand was strong and wiry, a workingman's hand.

"Sammy, it's a pleasure."

"You here about my brother?"

"Yes, I have a few questions."

"I got one first; why haven't you found the son of a bitch who killed him and broke my mother's heart all at the same time?"

"Now, Sammy," Goldberg started.

"That's okay, Solly. If anyone can ask that question, it's Sammy Schwartz. Can you give us a little room to talk?"

"No problem, I understand. Sammy, you be straight with Detective Alfano. In this fucked-up world, he's one of the good guys."

Goldberg left the two and headed over to where another fighter was punching a bag.

"I talked with your mother a couple of days ago. She's worried about you," Alfano began. "And she needs you. She doesn't want you ending up like your brother."

Sammy grabbed a towel from the nearby pile and began to dry away the sweat on his chest and shoulders.

"It shouldn't have happened," he said, his voice low enough that Alfano had to strain to hear. He hadn't seen the fight, Sammy said. He'd wanted to be there but he stayed at his mother's house to watch his little sister, Rebecca. Their mother went to the fight. Sammy told her to stay home, but she had to be there for Benny.

"Mom came home a wreck, and then the next morning we found out what happened. Something ain't right about it, too. The rumor around the gym is that there were a bunch of big wagers, maybe someone was supposed to take a dive. I don't know what to believe."

"I'm still sorting it. I've told your mother that as well. Did you see your brother the day of the fight?"

"Yes, he was here for a while, keeping loose. Worked the

light bag and the heavy a little. Just enough to get his heart going. Then he got a rub-down over there."

Schwartz pointed to a padded table on the other side of the gym.

"Eggie Stingly was here talking to him the whole time. That man wouldn't shut up! He acted more nervous than Benny, and Benny was the guy in the ring."

"What about Stingly?"

"I don't like him," Sammy said matter-of-factly. "He makes me jumpy. Talks too much, made promises that Benny said he never kept. Benny's first couple of fights made no money. Stingly said there were unavoidable expenses, but I bet his car never ran out of gas. Stingly gave Benny money, but he said it was a loan against Benny's future winnings. Then he kept the prize money—little that it was. Benny said he was going to leave Stingly, but Stingly said they had a contract. I told Mr. Goldberg, and he said he'd see what he could do. Nothing happened, and then Benny died. Stingly gave Mother some money; that's the least the chump could do."

"I heard," Alfano said. "Who's your manager?"

"Nate Orenstein. He works with a lot of us kids at the Hebrew Institute. I got no beef with him, but when I turn pro, maybe I can get with Sam Pian and Art Winch. They handle Barney Ross. I'm good; maybe I can be great."

"Sammy, do you remember anything about Benny's gloves from that night? They are missing, and I need to find them."

"As I said, I wasn't there. The rumor around here is that they were loaded," Sammy said. "That why you need them?"

"Don't know until I find out. But there's a chance. It was said they were delivered to the Stadium; they were new, in their box. Is that usual?"

"Not as far I know," Sammy replied, becoming the first person Alfano had talked with to innocently confirm that the way the gloves had arrived was, as he'd suspected all along, highly unusual.

"They check my gloves before a fight to see if they're okay," Sammy told him. "I can't afford new gloves. In fact, I borrow my sparring gloves. Mr. Orenstein helps the boys get leftovers. Detective, I don't know where Benny's gloves are, but I'll tell you one thing. If I find the asshole who loaded them, I will kill the son of a bitch with my own fists."

19

HALSTED STREET was the north-south corridor that connected the Irish Bridgeport neighborhood with the Loop about three miles north. Schaller's Pump, where Tommy O'Shea had collapsed a week earlier, sat on the corner of 37th Street. Halsted was fronted with stores, meat packers, and barbershops. Half of what you heard on the street was Gaelic or accented English. To the east, ten short blocks, stood Comiskey Park, the home of the White Sox.

The front window curtains of the second-story office in the gray brick structure half a block south of Schaller's were drawn tight; Oscar Macaulay wanted no one to know that he was in. He even parked his Buick a block away, over on 38th Street. He could hear the radio from the barbershop one floor under him. The phone call, from a not-so-close friend, had come two hours earlier: Igor Kozlov's body was on a slab at the morgue. He'd been found in the lake, two holes in his head. That call had followed the one from the same source with the news about Iggy Jones. Macaulay was petrified. Over the past week he'd set up a few hundred bets, mostly five or ten bucks on a baseball game or a horse race. For all his hard work, he was three hundred ahead, not a way to make a high-hat living.

He knew Kozlov and Jones were dead because of the

O'Shea fight. He knew he shouldn't have taken the bet, but his guy said that it was a cinch. The bet was for Schwartz to win in three—O'Shea was going down, guaranteed. That's what Kimble said, guaranteed. But Macaulay's guy said that Schwartz was going to take the dive. And his guy had never been wrong. Macaulay liked the Jew, but a bet's a bet. When O'Shea won, he was thrilled; it had been a long time since he'd made a decent return on one bet. Now, he was sure it wasn't worth it. Schwartz's loss put some good coin in his bag, but if Rosenberg was going to put two in his skull—shit, it wasn't worth that. Maybe he could square the bet with Rosie? He sneaked a peek between the curtains; nothing on the street said that they were coming for him. But then again, how would he know? If they could get to the paranoid Kozlov, they could get to anyone.

He glanced at the safe that sat against one wall. Trumbull Safe & Vault Co. was emblazoned in gold and red on the black face. Everything that Macaulay had was in that vault. He could have found a more lucrative and safer way to make a living during the last twenty years. But he was in now, and he could not—would not—turn back. He'd worked hard for the thirty thousand and change tucked away in his safe, and he would not let anyone take it from him.

He'd stocked up on food, beer, and a couple of extra pairs of underwear. Fortunately, he'd rented an office with its own bathroom. Having to walk down the hall to take a piss scared the hell out of him. He sat at his desk and waited.

Another friend, this one in the mayor's office, said that the investigation was moving along. They were close to finding whoever had killed the bookies. Macaulay did not believe it one bit; the police never found anyone. He knew this for a fact. Three friends of his—business associates, if you will—had been ruthlessly gunned down during the last ten years. Were their killers ever punished? No. The police just walked away from the case. Macaulay had known who the killers were, even told the police, and nothing happened. No, he'd get no protection or justice from the police or his so-called friends in city hall—fuck 'em, fuck 'em all.

He jumped a foot off the seat of his chair when someone banged on the door to his office. It felt like his heart nearly stopped, but he kept quiet.

"I know you are in there, Macaulay. Open up."

Macaulay raised the .45 caliber revolver from where it lay on the desktop and held it with two hands, the muzzle pointed at the door. He still remained silent.

"Come on, Oscar. Open the door. I don't want to break it down."

Macaulay slowly began to squeeze the trigger; three rapid-fire shots might just about clear the hallway of the killers. No one would convict him for self-defense. He took a breath.

"Oscar Macaulay, come on, open up. It's Sergeant Mc-Dunnah from the neighborhood. Put that .45 down and open up. Listen, you Irish shit, I'm here to help."

Stunned, Macaulay slowly lifted his finger off the trigger and slumped in his chair. Good God, he'd almost shot a man he'd known for forty years.

"Is that you, Sarge? Really, is that you?"

"Of course it is, you old sot. Who else would come banging on your door in the middle of the day, risking a bullet through the door? We need to talk."

Macaulay went to the door, revolver in his hand. He still wasn't convinced. He removed the two-by-four he'd used to brace the door, turned the lock, and took a step back.

"It's open."

He raised the Colt and pointed it.

The door handle rotated, and then the door slowly opened. The bright face of Sergeant McDunnah greeted the terrified face of Oscar Macaulay. The cop was in street clothes.

"Jesus, Oscar, put that cannon down before you hurt someone," McDunnah said as he walked into the room. "I'm going to guess from your reaction, you've heard."

"Yeah, Kozlov and Jones, I've heard. And you were about one second away from being blasted to St. Peter's heaven. Sorry, McDunnah, I'm scared, damn scared. Too scared to try and even leave town. What the hell's going on? Who are they?"

Macaulay went to his desk and pulled out a cigarette. The ashtray next to the package was overflowing.

McDunnah told Macaulay enough to make the bookie even more panicked than he was before.

"You said that Applebaum is gone?" Macaulay asked.

"Yeah, he got out a couple of days ago. We can put some guys out front to watch you."

"And tell the world that someone's after me. That would not be good for business, not good at all. Thanks, but no thanks. I can handle myself."

"Yeah, like shooting the cleaning lady when she comes down the hallway. I don't want to come back here just to arrest you for murder. Where's Lila?"

"She's in Waukegan, at her mother's. She's all right. Don't want her anywhere near this."

"Good." McDunnah replaced the plank across the back of the door. "Not very fancy or secure."

"All I need is five seconds. They try to bust in, I can clear that hall instantly. I was in the war; you know that. I know how to use this thing."

McDunnah was sure he did but reminded Macaulay that age could affect his reflexes. So could fear.

"I need to ask a few questions," he told the bookie. "You have the time?"

"Cute—I got all the time in the fucking world."

"Well, then, who placed the O'Shea-Schwartz bet with you?"

* * *

McDunnah took a cigar from the case he kept inside his jacket. He lit it and stood outside the closed door to his Model A Ford, mulling over what Macaulay had told him. Hymen Rosenberg had placed the bet. He hadn't heard that name in over a year. It figured, though—the man was a killer and a gambler. One more picture to add to the board.

The traffic was heavy on Halsted Street. Trucks lumbered up and down the road. Those with panel signs for meat-packers headed south; most others traveled north toward downtown. The stockyards were a few blocks away; some days you could smell them. Those were not good days, although as a Bridgeport kid, McDunnah had grown used to it. He watched a black Cadillac pass him, heading south. Then the driver made a U-turn and pulled up to the front of Macaulay's building.

Two men exited the front seats, one out each door. McDunnah instantly recognized Rosenberg's two gunzels, Ziggy Feldstein and Gus Teitlebaum.

"Jesus, Mary, and Joseph." He spat the cigar to the street. He was hidden behind the tall passenger box of the Ford as the two men walked to the door that led to the upstairs stairway. After looking up and down Halsted, they entered. McDunnah casually walked down the sidewalk away from the Cadillac. When he knew he was out of view from the street, he jogged quickly to the rear of the building and took the stairs, two at a time, up to the second floor. He tried the door that led to the inside hallway on Macaulay's floor; it was locked. He pulled his revolver and contemplated shooting out the lock and charging in.

"Now, that's a good way to get yourself killed," he said out loud.

The decision was made for him. Two explosions from a heavy pistol fired from inside the building shook the door. McDunnah shot away the lock and yanked the door open. The hallway was dark; the only light came seeping in through the rear door he'd just opened. He could make out the figure of a man sprawled on the floor just outside Macaulay's door; the dim silhouette of a second man was visible in the hallway. The shape spun and raised his weapon toward McDunnah. The sergeant fired. The hoodlum also fired, his aim going wildly upward into the ceiling as he was spun around from the impact of McDunnah's round. He collapsed on his partner. Two streams of light in the center of Macaulay's office door, like miniature spotlights, reflected off the walls and through the haze of smoke.

"You okay, Macaulay?" McDunnah yelled. There was a pause.

"Aces, Sarge. Did I get 'em?"

"You got one. They are both down," McDunnah yelled back.

A shadow appeared at the top of the front stairway, and another explosion ripped the air. McDunnah felt his leg give way before the pain reached his brain.

"There's another shooter. I'm hit," he called out. "Fuck."

The shooter came toward him; it had to be Rosenberg, the sergeant thought. The impact of the bullet had stunned his right side; the hand with the pistol wouldn't move. Hymen Rosenberg's features became visible as he stepped into the light coming through the rear doorway, where McDunnah was managing to stay partially upright, balancing on his left knee. The sergeant grimaced when he saw the hideous grin on Rosenberg's face.

"You're a dead man, Macaulay. No one fucks with me. I'll find your family and then—"

Rosenberg instantly staggered in the wake of the two explosions and flashes that came from the far end of the hall. In the dim light, McDunnah watched as Rosenberg dropped to his knees. For a split second, McDunnah was transfixed by the sight of the now mangled visage of the man who once ran one of the most heinous murder-for-hire gangs in Chicago. Then Rosenberg fully collapsed onto the mush that had once been his dapper face.

"God, I hope that wasn't you, McDunnah," Macaulay yelled from the open door of his office.

"You are one lucky fucken' Irishman, Oscar Macaulay," McDunnah answered.

"Told you I could shoot."

20

ALFANO SAT in the Packard down the block from the address that Debbie Tillerman had given him when he called to confirm their date. The day was surprisingly mild for a late-August evening. He hadn't wanted to appear anxious by parking in front of her house, and so he sat, gathering his wits, a block down the street. Her house was a block off Division Street on the east side of Oak Park, a pleasant neighborhood. Very nice, he'd thought, as he'd driven by her front door ten minutes earlier. Certainly, different from the two-room apartment he lived in.

He took another drag off his cigarette; he had no idea what she did for a living, even if she had a job. Maybe she worked for her father, which was not unheard of. Many aldermen employed members of their families, but then again, that's when a lot of the troubles started. When did you stop employing your family and putting them on the public payroll?

He slowly pulled back into traffic on Division and turned onto Forest Avenue and stopped. To his surprise, she was sitting outside on the brick steps. She waved as he parked and then walked to the car. Alfano opened the door and climbed out, coming around the front of the car so that he met her halfway.

"Without a doubt, this is one of the biggest cars I've ever seen. I didn't pay much attention the other day, but now, in this neighborhood setting, it just seems to fit. I didn't take you for a big car kind of guy."

"I told you, it's the department's," he said. "They let me drive it."

"What kind of engine does it have?"

"I have no clue, and do not ask me any more questions. It sucks gasoline like a drunk sailor. It is fast and scares the hell out of me. I drive it to impress the girls."

"Well, Detective, I'm impressed. But then, I love cars, their sleek lines, their power, what they project about the driver."

"Project?"

"When I see a man, I often can tell what he is by what he drives."

"Really, that's making a big jump—weird, if you ask me. And I don't own it."

"True, but you haven't given it back to the department, either," she said with a smile.

"Slight change in plans. The Gable movie is gone. Are you up for a little song and dance, something fun?"

"Like what?"

"*Gold Diggers of 1933* is playing at the Roosevelt. Interested?"

"I've seen it, and it was fun. What's your backup?"

"Your call."

"*The Masquerader* with Ronald Colman."

"Done."

She looked at him. "That was quick."

"I'm easy when someone else is making decisions."

"I find that hard to believe, but no arguments. Besides, I'm hungry, so where are we off to?"

"I'm Italian, so I'll give you one guess."

"Italian it is."

She looked at his profile as he drove toward downtown, the dusky light illuminating his face.

"I said Gable earlier, but I'll have to amend that to say Ronald Colman. Yes, definitely Colman. You've a harder and more experienced face."

"Not sure how to answer that," Alfano said.

"Then don't and accept it."

Alfano drove south on Cicero Avenue and then turned east onto Roosevelt Road. They passed Miller's Edmille Health Club. Alfano said nothing about his conversations earlier in the day. For a Friday, the traffic was slow but moving. Even during the hard economic times, people labored and had to get home from work. He stopped in front of a corner restaurant in Little Italy.

"I guessed you might be heading here. It's one of my favorites," Debbie told him.

"Good. It's one of mine as well."

A valet took the car, and the two walked into the comfortably dark and cool restaurant. A broad-shouldered man in a white suit and black tie walked up to them as they stood in the entry.

"Signore Alfano, it is so good to see you this evening."

"Thank you, Signore DeLucca. It is good to be back."

"I have your table ready. Please follow me. Signora, may I take your wrap?"

"Thank you, but I may just need it. Your restaurant is enjoyably cool."

"Like the movie houses, you need to step up with the times," their host answered, looking pleased. "It's the latest in refrigeration. Lord knows, I don't know how it works, but it was expensive. Please, this way."

They followed Mr. DeLucca to a small booth that overlooked the spacious room. On the far side, a violinist played a tune to a couple sitting at a small table; they held hands as they listened.

"Wonderful," Debbie said, "and thank you for getting me out of the house. I don't think I could spend another Friday listening to the radio and reading. The weather is just too pleasant. And, I meant to say this earlier, you look quite handsome this evening. It's hard to think you're a police detective."

"I'll take that as a compliment, and you look very lovely yourself. That is a beautiful dress."

"Thank you, sir. I bought it in New York this spring. I was visiting relatives in Yonkers. It was fun to shop somewhere other than a Chicago store."

"I wouldn't know. Shopping is not one of my favorite things."

"My husband was the same way. He was just out of Brandeis College, near Boston, and was going to Loyola for a law degree. He never had time to dress well. We met when I was visiting my relatives outside New York City. He was from the same Yonkers neighborhood. We fell for each other; I was in college here at Northwestern, studying something or another. We came back, got married, and he finished his degree. I went to Loyola for my law degree. Then he decided to join the Army; he was an attorney in their courts system. I wasn't afraid. He was far away from all the fight."—she paused. "I'm sorry I'm going on and on like this. Nervous chatter, I guess. And we haven't even ordered a cocktail."

"Please, I understand. Martini?"

She nodded. Alfano waved at the waiter and ordered.

"Now, you were saying?"

"Are you sure?" Debbie said.

Alfano smiled and nodded. He was interested.

"Well, they sent him to France to deal with some court-martial case. On his way there the train derailed, a hundred soldiers were killed—he was one of them. Wars can kill in so many ways. Were you in the war, Detective?"

He shook his head. "No, I've been on the force since 1912."

"So, you were fighting a war, just the ones here in Chicago. Through the Capone and the Outfit days, and now the country-wide depression."

He appreciated her assessment. Not everybody saw it that way.

"I made detective ten years ago," he told her. "I like it. It suits me."

Their cocktails arrived.

"What should we toast to?" Debbie asked, raising her glass.

"How about to us and an enjoyable evening. L'chaim."

She smiled. "L'chaim."

They clinked their glasses and sipped. Alfano again noticed how dark Debbie's eyes were, how they drew him in. He consciously let his mind wander.

"Detective," Signore DeLucca said, approaching their table. "I'm sorry for interrupting, but there is a phone call for you. You can take it at the front desk."

Debbie tilted her head in a questioning movement.

"I had to let my station know where I was, sorry. I'll be right back."

Alfano took a quick sip of his drink and smiled at his date. Damn, she was pretty. He followed DeLucca to the front desk.

"Detective Alfano," he said, when DeLucca handed him the receiver.

It wasn't good news. He finished his call and talked with Signore DeLucca, and then returned to Debbie.

"Is everything all right?" she asked.

"No, my sergeant's been shot. He was caught in a gunfight in Bridgeport. There's three dead. But right now, I need to get to the hospital. Sorry, but can you find your way home?"

"Not a chance. I'm going with you. Maybe I can help."

"It's not necessary . . ."

"Try and stop me. It's been years since I had a date with a

decent guy. You are not going to lose me that easily, Detective. I'm sticking to you all night, if I have to."

She then shot the rest of her drink and nodded to him. He did the same. Together they walked to the front of the restaurant; the Packard was waiting at the curb.

* * *

Sergeant McDunnah stretched out on the hospital bed, his bandaged right leg raised on a pillow. The woman standing next to the bed, holding his hand, was cute and on the demure side. Her red hair fell to her shoulders.

"It's good to see you again, Moira," Alfano said when he entered the room. Debbie Tillerman stood outside.

"And you, Tony." She looked out into the hallway. "And who's the lady with you?"

"My date, Miss Nosey," he said, before gesturing to Debbie to join them in the room. He made the introductions, and then said to Moira, "Seems that your husband has a way of upstaging my nights."

"I'm sorry, Detective," McDunnah said. "It seems the bad guys just don't know when you decide to finally have a date."

"Ha. What the hell happened?"

McDunnah told him a short version; he named names but did not include a lot of gory detail.

"Good thing you were there," Alfano said. "Macaulay might not have made it."

"We Irish stick together. But actually, I'm not sure they would have got him. He's a tough bird, and he can still shoot like a doughboy. Bottom line, there's three less problems to deal with now."

"Don't I know that."

"Bridgeport station is handling it," McDunnah said. "The boys are going over the Cadillac. Oak Park has been read in; they are going through Rosenberg's house to see what shows up." He told Alfano what Macaulay said.

"So Rosenberg was the one who put the money down on the O'Shea-Schwartz fight," Alfano said.

McDunnah nodded. "My guess, him and his thugs also were responsible for Iggy Jones and Igor Kozlov. Been trying to nail those sons of bitches—excuse me, miss—for years."

"Your sergeant is quite efficient, even from a hospital bed," Debbie said.

"I'd be lost without him."

"Without my sergeant, Tony would be more than lost," Moira added with a smile.

"Now, love, no need to say that," McDunnah said.

"Well, someone has to. You two are thicker than Irish cream. Some days, I'm not sure who you are married to, me or this thick-headed Italian."

"That's not how you talk to my boss," the sergeant protested.

"See what I mean, Mrs. Tillerman? He even defends the man in front of his own wife."

"He is a dear. I'm beginning to find that out," Debbie said. "Tell me more."

"All right, you two, stop it," Alfano said, a touch of red in his cheeks.

"And he blushes. I think I'm falling for the man," Debbie said.

"Out, you two. McDunnah and I have business to discuss," Alfano said. He pointed to the door just as a nurse walked in.

"And who are you, your high and mighty lordship, to be giving orders in my hospital?" the nurse wanted to know.

Alfano told her.

"And I'm supposed to be impressed." She looked at the sergeant. "I'll give you ten minutes, then everyone out. My patient needs his rest. After that, he can go save the world, for all I care."

McDunnah told Alfano the story again, but this time he

included the details and near misses that he hadn't wanted Moira to hear. They both knew he was one lucky Irish son of a bitch.

21

ALFANO STOOD outside the entry to his apartment in the morning light, wondering why he was standing here. He knew damn well where he should be. With a bag of groceries under his arm, he fumbled with the key in his other hand as he unlocked the mailbox.

He'd kissed Debbie Tillerman on the cheek after he'd dressed. She stretched, pulling the sheet tight over her lanky body, smiled, and put her hand against his cheek when he leaned in for another.

"I need to see how McDunnah is doing."

"Liar, he'll be just fine. He looks tough."

"He is that. However, there's things that need to be done."

"And things that need to be done here. Come back to bed, it's Saturday."

She slowly slid the sheet down her naked body. He slid it back up.

"You weren't that much of a prude last night," she said.

He couldn't tell if she was irritated or not. He kissed her again, this time on the lips.

"Being prudish has nothing to do with it," he promised. "I'll slip out. No need to announce to the neighbors."

"They are all older in this part of the neighborhood. None

are up yet."

"So much the better."

"You are a strange one, Detective. I'd think there was someone else if even my womanly ways can't keep you here."

"No one else, not even a cat."

"Then stay."

"I have to follow up McDunnah's shooting. Sorry."

Now she did look irritated. "I can't believe you'd choose an Irish cop over me."

"Not fair. It's just that . . ."

"What?"

"Last night was wonderful, and unexpected. But McDunnah's shooting, three dead gangsters, and the ongoing investigation into the fight."

"Really, really bad excuses, Tony. That's not what you tell a woman after—"

He kissed her again.

"I've got to go."

"Am I going to see you again?"

"Of course."

"Tonight?"

"Can't. There's a fight at the fair, some people I need to see. The bouts are on the Floating Stage in the North Lagoon." He paused. "Do you want to go?"

"You want me to go to a fight? You know I can't do that. Besides, my father is attending the music show at Soldier Field. We have excellent seats. Maybe I can entice you to join us? Some bribery?"

She began again to slowly slide the sheet down. He grabbed the hem of the sheet and stopped her.

"It would be wasted on me and my tin ear."

She slid up in the bed, sat back, and wrapped her arms over the sheet around her knees. "Call me tomorrow?"

"Of course. After last night, I'd be a cad not to call. With my sergeant in the hospital, it may take a few days. But I will call."

"So, this isn't goodbye?"

"No. Be a good girl and pull up that sheet before I arrest you for solicitation. Have a good time at the concert."

He leaned in to kiss her again, and this time she pushed him away.

After he retrieved his mail, he climbed the stairs and elbowed his way into his apartment. Still holding the groceries, he opened a window and let in fresh air—the day promised to be mild. He clicked on the radio over the sink; the soft, bluesy strains of "Sophisticated Lady" filled the small kitchen and living room. He took off his jacket and removed his tie; he needed a bath. As he started to fill the tub, someone tapped on the door. He knew that tapping, and he did not want to talk to Alice Kowalski.

"Tony, I know you're in there. Just a moment, please."

Alfano sighed, turned off the water, put his shirt back on, walked to the door, and looked through the small peephole. At least she was alone. He pulled the door open.

"Out all night? Big case?" Alice asked. She was holding a plate covered with another plate.

"Yes, big case. What can I do for you, Mrs. Kowalski?"

"I brought you breakfast. The old man left for work late this morning and didn't have time to eat it. He's on the weekend day shift, and the money, well, we need it. So?"

"So, what?"

"Do you want this breakfast? It's still warm. There's eggs, some sausage, and toast. I sure as heaven can't eat it. I'm trying to lose weight."

Alfano did not want to get in that conversation.

"Alice, you always look wonderful. So, thanks. I will take it. It's been a long night—police business—and you are too kind to think of me."

"Anytime, Detective, anytime. I'm just across the hall. And Mr. Kowalski won't be home until after eight. There's a baseball game on later. You want to come over and listen?"

"Thanks, but after this, a bath, and a little sleep, I have to get back to the station. Sorry."

"That's what neighbors are for, Detective. So, remember, the Cubs start at one o'clock."

"Sorry, but I'll be at the station."

"Anytime, Detective, anytime . . ."

He slowly pushed the door closed, and then carried the plate to the kitchen. He had to admit it smelled wonderful, and his empty stomach growled with each step.

* * *

He was a cad, he knew it. This was the first day he'd had off in so long he couldn't remember the last Saturday he'd spent off. Why couldn't he ask Debbie to spend it with him? Had he gotten that bad with women? Yes, she was right, he was a liar, and not a good one. That's probably why he'd asked her to go to the fights—he knew she'd say no. He called the hospital and talked with his sergeant; McDunnah was good. They said he could go home Sunday. Alfano said he'd call him.

After his breakfast, he scanned the *Tribune*. As Alice had said, the White Sox were in town to play against the Yankees at Comiskey Park. It was a short drive from the park to the fair for the boxing matches at the North Lagoon. Not that it would have changed his plans otherwise, but the weather was perfect. All he wanted to do was see who showed up at the fights. Now that Hymen Rosenberg was out of the picture, there was a big hole in the fight game. He needed to know who was trying to fill the gap.

He picked up Alice's dishes and knocked on her door; she answered before the sound finished echoing in the stairwell.

"Hope you enjoyed it," Alice said as she gathered up her

housecoat across her bosom.

"It was delicious. I haven't had as good a breakfast in ages," he said.

"More coffee?"

"I'm good. I have to go to work. You and the hubby okay?"

"We're good, Detective. And thanks for asking. The arm's still a bit tender, but it won't slow me down. I can make that coffee to go?"

"Thanks, but no. You take care of yourself. Maybe see you tomorrow."

As he turned and started down the stairs, he heard Alice's door close behind him. Six weeks earlier, a bomber who was plaguing the city had tried to assassinate him in this same stairwell. The man laid in wait, and as Alfano turned on the landing, the killer took a shot through the glass window. Alice, who had come out of her apartment to greet him, was hit in the shoulder with the bullet intended for him. Alice mended well and so did her relationship with her husband. The economic times took their toll on everyone, and her husband worked seven days a week. She felt neglected. Surviving the bullet brought them back together. Alfano felt sorry for the woman; she was young, pretty, lonely, and bored. She wanted Alfano's company, but he had declined more than once to go into her apartment to find out how much.

He drove to the Racine Station and spent an hour going over the reports of the Macaulay shooting. The paperwork had been delivered from the Bridgeport station and was a mess; he missed McDunnah's usual deft organizing.

His sergeant was lucky, damn lucky. If the slug had been two inches to the left, it would have broken the bone and possibly sheared his femoral artery. He never would have made it to the hospital. As for the three dead men—Gus Teitlebaum, Ziggy Feldstein, and their boss, Hymen Rosenberg—Alfano could have wallpapered the back of the station house with their rap sheets and arrest records. Six pistols and revolvers were found on or near the bodies. The weapons had been sent to the crime lab for testing and ballistic checks against the bullets found in the heads of Jones and Kozlov. Police also found shovels and tarps in the trunk of Rosenberg's Cadillac.

Macaulay had been detained after Sergeant McDunnah had been taken to the hospital; the last note in the file said that Macaulay had been released after a detective from Bridgeport station had interviewed McDunnah. The sergeant was clear enough in his statement that it was Macaulay who had fired his weapon, killing Rosenberg, and saving the life of the sergeant. Ballistics would sort out which of them shot which of the thugs. Search warrants had been issued to go through the various residences of the dead men.

Still mulling over what he'd read, he said goodbye to the two detectives manning the room, and the replacement sergeant at the desk, and drove the four and a half miles to Comiskey Park, where he parked in the police lot. After waving his badge at the service entry, he strolled into the ballpark that had hosted the All-Star Game just six weeks earlier. When the New York Yankees came to town, no matter where the Sox were in the standings, you could be sure of a crowd, a loud, boisterous, and somewhat inebriated crowd. The Bronx Bombers with their Murderers' Row had never been a favorite in Chicago, and were in second place behind Philadelphia, but the chance to see Babe Ruth and Lou Gehrig still drew the crowds.

After wandering around the stadium for most of the game, Alfano found a seat in the late innings and watched as the Sox pulled out a win in the twelfth inning after Berry doubled and Rhyne drove him in with a single. Ruth and Gehrig went one for six. The crowd went home happy.

Three miles to the north from the ballpark and built along the Lake Michigan waterfront was The Century of Progress

World's Fair. Since its opening in May, the fair had drawn almost ten million visitors from all around the world. It had pumped millions of dollars into the depression-racked city of Chicago and had piled more than headaches onto the Chicago police force. Gambling and prostitution had grown, catering to the desires of the visiting guests, and even though it now was assured that Prohibition would end at the end of the year, illegal liquor easily was found everywhere. A special dispensation for wine and beer at the fair assured a steady return flow of visitors.

Alfano hated the place.

On the opening day of the fair, three months earlier, he'd helplessly watched as his girlfriend—heartbroken over the loss of her only child—killed herself on the steps overlooking the North Lagoon. She had financially orchestrated a psychopath who had killed dozens of people in Chicago in a methodical vendetta against the city and the mayor who she held responsible for the child's death. Her suicide had left Alfano in a tailspin. He still wasn't sure he'd recovered and Deborah Tillerman was only confusing him. He thought he sensed her ghost as he walked along the crowded midway of the packed fair. The music from the concert at Soldier Field drifted over the din of the midway, adding to the cacophony of over two hundred thousand visitors filling the fair.

He'd parked in the police lot and, after leaving his name at security, wandered the extensive fairgrounds. A soft and refreshing breeze blew in off the lake. The overhead Sky Ride, with its spaceship-like cars, lazily drifted over the crowd. The last and only time Alfano had taken that ride, he had watched the psychopath jump to his death. He shook his head to try and toss off the memories.

He ate dinner in the restaurant of the Italian pavilion and relived the few days, a month earlier, when Italo Balbo, the second in command to Mussolini, had flown in twenty-four seaplanes and was the toast of Chicago. Alfano had chased down and foiled an assassin who was sent to kill radicals who wanted to embarrass the Italian dictator; after that, the assassin was supposed to kill Balbo. Stopping these crazies had added another notch to Alfano's reputation; he didn't see it that way. All it did was add to his cynical attitude toward both people and politics.

He left the pavilion and strolled out to the point behind the planetarium that overlooked Lake Michigan. There, for an hour, he enjoyed a cigar, and for the moment left the troubles of the past week behind him.

22

THE FIRST BOUT STARTED at precisely eight o'clock. The sun was a glow to the west behind Soldier Field, and the sounds from the music festival climbed over the upper parapet of the stadium and filled the air.

He took one of the temporary seats set up on the broad landing that faced the floating stage where the fights would take place. A wiry kid with a scrunched cap walked up to him. It was Sammy Schwartz.

"Detective Alfano?" the young man asked, removing his hat and twisting it in his hands.

Alfano put out his hand. Sammy released the hat with one hand, took Alfano's, and smiled.

"There's some good fights tonight," the young fighter said. "These guys are all amateurs. Some of them are in training, like me, for the Golden Gloves next February."

"Are you boxing tonight?" Alfano asked.

"No, not tonight. I tried, but the card was full. Six fights, four-rounders, some good kids, no heavyweights, all bantam-, light-, and middleweights. They's set up a temporary dressing room in the administration building over there."

Sammy pointed to a building a hundred feet away.

"Most of the guys are grumbling that the rooms are too

small with no place to warm up. And, for the love of Mike, they's boxing on a floating stage. I wonder about that. And what's that music? I feel like I'm in some creepy circus side-show."

"Sammy, this is a circus sideshow. How's your mother?"

"She's good. Family's been over, and she's not been alone. I saw her this morning at temple."

"You're not living at home?"

"No, I share a place with two guys near the gym. I got a job at a grocer near there. But I see her a few times a week."

"Good boy. Where did Benny live?"

"At home with Mom. He took care of her. Linda, my older sister, is staying for a few days to help with Rebecca."

"I met Linda. She seems like a good person."

"Yeah, I guess. She's up in Skokie, all high and mighty. Her schlemiel of a husband is in banking or something. When he comes along with Linda to see Mom, I go to the gym."

Alfano smiled to himself, thinking about his own family, one that was long gone.

The fight bell sounded. The first two boxers, lightweights, were in the center of the ring, bobbing up and down on the balls of their feet, heads and shoulders weaving as they pawed the air with their gloves. Alfano was sure that none of the fighters had ever fought to the sounds of a band and chorus.

"The guy in the red trunks is Danny Zuko," Sammy said. "He's from the South Side. The other is Arnie Feller. It used to be Fellman, but he changed it. Arnie trains at Edmille's, like me. He's good, fast. His left is where his power is."

The detective and the young fighter watched with the crowd as Feller moved in and threw a flurry of midriff jabs at Zuko. Zuko pulled in his elbows and used his forearms to ward off the blows. It was a fight strategy Alfano had seen play out time after time: try to reduce the impacts of the opponent's blows and not get hurt. Then, at the right moment, find that opening where you could hurt the man.

Zuko dropped back.

"He's a smart fighter," Sammy said. "He's testing Feller."

He leaned forward in his seat.

"Watch it, Arnie. Watch it," he said under his breath.

Zuko ducked and moved laterally. Feller dropped his right. Zuko stunned him with a left to the face that Feller only partially blocked with his elbows. Zuko dropped back, bouncing lightly on his toes as he moved left.

Alfano was amazed by the speed of both fighters. He put it to their weight, guessing that they both were about 130 pounds. The first round scoring leaned toward Zuko and the left he'd slipped in between Feller's arms.

"Good round for both of 'em," Sammy said. "I've sparred with Feller. Took everything to keep up—then again, he's four years older. I need a few pounds to take him on. Maybe after next year's Gloves. That's my ticket."

"Sammy, you're a smart kid. Why do you fight? Honestly, it seems a bit crazy to me."

"Mr. Alfano, I love it. I like the people and the exercise. Being in the ring, well, it gives me something to do. I'm not a brainiac like my sister and some of my friends. So's, I'm not sure where I'll be in ten or twenty years. Benny had his whole life in front of him, then he died. Make do with what you got now, that's what I say."

"Carpe diem."

"Huh? What's that, French or something?"

"No, Latin. It means to seize the day, although I like your version better."

Zuko took the bout with a unanimous decision by the three sportswriters, who doubled as judges, sitting at the edge of the ring. Sammy said it was closer than the decision.

"Feller had him in the third when he put Zuko against the ropes. The ref stopped him too soon. Then again, this crowd ain't a boxing crowd. You said we was a sideshow. I think you were right."

Sammy stood and stretched his arms and back. He scanned the crowd that was gathering for the next bout.

"What the hell is that son of a bitch doing here?"

Alfano turned toward where Schwartz was looking. Eggie Stingly—Benny Schwartz's former manager—stood next to a small boxer who had a towel draped over his head.

"That kid's from Coulon's Gym. He *thinks* he's a tough featherweight—the guy he's fighting will kill him," Sammy said. "Stingly knows that. I don't get it."

Stingly and the boxer pushed their way through the crowd and crossed over a bridge onto the elevated stage. Alfano had been to dozens of fights, but this was the first time he'd seen such a theatrically staged production. He'd known something was different about the first fight, and now he understood: the crowd was all to one side. There was nothing but open lagoon behind the ring.

Sammy was right. Stingly's guy instantly was set upon by the other fighter, the thin yet lanky kid from the North Side gym Sammy had mentioned.

"The guy's been a pro for about two years. He fights in clubs all over the city. An Italian, if I remember," Sammy told Alfano. "He can take a beating, but his manager has never tried to get him a title fight. Rumor is he gets a cut of the gambling, but you didn't hear that from me. That's why he fights all the time."

Stingly's kid now was trying to stay away from the Italian. He'd take steps back, bounce off the ropes, trying every tactic to avoid getting hit. The Italian pursued and punished the kid. When the bell rang, Alfano heard the crowd exhale.

"Not good," Sammy said. "The kid's already cut above his eye."

The Italian was off his stool before the sound of the next

bell reached the seats. The kid, looking woozy, stumbled back into the war zone. The Italian clocked him with a left that did more than stun him. He essentially was out cold; his body just didn't know to fall yet. The kid was obviously defenseless, but the ref did nothing. The Italian hesitated, and then looked back at the ref, who ignored his look. The Northsider then threw another left that flattened the kid. He backed away to his corner as the referee counted out the kid. Stingly's trainer and cut man rushed into the ring. Smelling salts were held under the kid's nose; he jolted awake, and then collapsed back on the canvas. Even from fifty feet away, Alfano could see that this wasn't good. Three men helped the kid to his feet and bodily carried him out of the ring.

"That should not have happened," Sammy said.

"No shit. I'm following them. You want to come?"

"Absolutely."

The two made their way through the crowd and followed Stingly and the men carrying the kid. They were headed toward the administration building. Alfano and Sammy caught up just as Stingly's crew disappeared into a room off the hallway. A man in a white jacket—it was the coroner, Dr. Abrahamson—sprinted down the hall and pushed his way past where Alfano and Sammy stood. To Alfano's surprise, another man, wearing a suit, stood at the end of the hallway watching. The man's face was hidden in the shadows, but Alfano clearly could see the pair of boxing gloves that dangled from the man's right hand. When the suit saw the detective, or so it seemed, he quickly turned and walked away. There was something familiar about the man, but Alfano couldn't place him before he was lost in the crowd that started to fill the hallway.

Alfano debated following the man in the suit. Reaching a quick decision, he remained at the doorway, observing the action in the room. Dr. Abrahamson hadn't wasted time going to work on the kid. He flashed a penlight in the fighter's eyes, and then checked him thoroughly. Only then did he turn to the door and acknowledge Alfano.

"I saw you in the crowd. Did you see the fight?"

"Yes. Is he going to be all right?" Alfano answered.

"Too soon to tell. I'm getting him to the hospital. They are bringing in an ambulance."

"To where?"

"Cook County General."

Alfano nodded. It was the closest hospital.

"I'll meet you there," he told the doctor. To Sammy he said, "You coming?"

"If you don't mind?"

They watched the attendants lift the kid onto a gurney and roll him out to the waiting ambulance. The doctor climbed in after the kid. The vehicle left, its siren barely audible over the music from the massive stadium that rose high above them.

23

ALFANO, SAMMY SCHWARTZ, and Eggie Stingly stood in the hospital waiting room. Stingly didn't need to introduce Myerhoff. The rat-faced cut man left abruptly as soon as Alfano walked in.

"What's his problem, Stingly?" Alfano asked.

"He's allergic to cops, especially after your talk with him the other day," Stingly answered. "And I'm getting the sniffles myself—why are you here?"

"The doc and I go back a long time. He wanted me to follow. Anything you want to add?"

"About what? The kid got knocked out. He's good; he can take a punch."

"He shouldn't have been fighting that guy. You know that, Mr. Stingly," Sammy said.

"And you shouldn't be here either, Schwartz," Stingly said.

"Leave him out of this. I asked you a question," Alfano said.

"This official? You busting my balls for the boxing commission?"

"This is not official, yet," Alfano said. "So, what happened?"

"The kid got knocked out. It was a cheap shot. You saw it.

The referee was going to stop the fight, and that dago took a cheap shot."

"That's not what happened," Sammy said.

"Detective, he talking for you, now?"

"Sammy, take a minute. I need to talk to Mr. Stingly."

Sammy glared at them both and started to say something but then spun on his heels and walked out of the waiting room.

"The kid's a hothead, and still upset over his brother," Stingly said.

"I understand what he's going through. Now, what happened?"

Stingly sighed. "Here's the thing, the kid in there made a few bucks. He needs the money—knock out or win. So, he made fifty bucks."

"Your cut?"

"My usual percentage."

"Win, lose, or draw?"

"That's how it's done."

"God, you're a shit."

"It's a living."

Dr. Abrahamson walked into the waiting room. He was wiping his hands on a towel. He crooked his head to Alfano and then moved several paces away from Stingly. Alfano followed.

"The kid going to be all right?" Alfano asked.

"He should be. If he'd gone another round, I'm not sure. I'm seeing some of the same bruises I saw on the O'Shea boy. Did you collect the gloves from the other fighter?"

"No, never thought of it."

Damn, Alfano thought. He'd been too distracted worrying about the kid. Considering the last twenty-four hours, he wasn't entirely sure where his head was at the moment.

"I did see a man back there in the hallway—he was carrying gloves," he told Abrahamson. "The other fighter, the Italian, was his room next door?"

"Yes, I think so. You'd have to ask the kid's manager."

"Yes, that'd be one Eggie Stingly. Now, he's a piece of work."

"Yes, I've heard the name," the doctor said, looking over at the promoter. "That him?"

"Yes."

"Find the gloves."

"I will."

"I've got your three stiffs on ice," the coroner said. "I'll deal with them Monday. I understand they were not nice fellas."

"They were at the top of the menu of not nice guys. The evidence points to them as the killers of Iggy Jones and Igor Kozlov. It's when they went after Oscar Macaulay that things didn't work out as they planned. Sergeant McDunnah may have nailed one of them."

"Sometimes justice comes in surprising ways."

"Ain't that the truth!" Alfano said.

He left the doctor and found Sammy standing outside. The young man was pacing back and forth on the sidewalk and smoking a cigarette.

"I'm not sure your trainer would be happy to see you smoking. I've been told it affects your wind," Alfano said as he lit one of his own.

"Do as I say, not as I—"

"And don't be a smart ass. The kid will be okay. The doc says that if he'd gone another round or two it could have been a lot worse."

"Damn . . . You know, with O'Shea's gloves maybe being loaded?"

"Don't believe all the rumors, but that's why I'm here and why I'm talking with you. Doctor Abrahamson believes that the gloves Benny wore also were spiked. Did you hear that, too?"

Sammy took one last drag and crushed the half-smoked cigarette on the sidewalk.

"Yeah, there's that rumor. But I don't believe it. Benny would never do that."

"The rumor, as you call it, says that neither fighter knew, and that O'Shea was supposed to take a dive. But he didn't," Alfano said.

"That's news to me, rumor or not. Anyway, why would he take a dive? Benny was good. He'd have taken the Irishman, no problem."

"Someone wanted insurance."

"Or someone wanted them both dead or badly hurt."

Sammy seemed to come to some sort of decision. He squared his shoulders and looked directly at Alfano.

"Detective, there's been some fights over the last few months where one of the fellows took a beating worse than they should have. Nothing serious enough to get them killed, but the talk is that the mitts had been fooled with."

"Who knows about this?"

"Officially, no one's said anything. Even the boxing commission doesn't know, but mothers have been pulling their sons out of the Gloves."

"So, the word is getting around."

"Yeah," said Sammy. "Most of the gyms probably know by now, and I think Father Dominic and Rabbi Harris also know. But I'm not sure."

"Go home and get some sleep, and go see your mother in the morning. Take her to breakfast. She loves you."

"I know, I will. And, Detective, if the rumors are true, find the son of a bitch and put him away. Someone else is going to die if you don't."

*** ***

Monday morning Alfano stood in front of the crime board. His head hurt from his day off. He knew he needed to make some changes; he thought about calling Debbie, but put it off. He'd asked for and received photos of Feldstein, Teitlebaum, and Rosenberg from the records files and now added them to the cork panel. He wrote, with some degree of satisfaction, "Deceased" on small slips of paper and pinned them over the tops of the photos. His gut told him they all were a dead end, at least as far as the O'Shea-Schwartz fight. According to Macaulay, Rosenberg had put the hundred thousand on Schwartz. Sure, he put down a bet, but he thought it was the bookies that screwed him. Alfano was certain that Rosenberg and his two goons were the ones who'd killed Jones and Kozlov. He'd have to wait and see what turned up at Rosenberg and his associates' houses and what would show up in ballistics on the slugs. Hopefully, more evidence to prove what Alfano already knew to be true. Justice done was justice served.

"There's a woman here to see you," McDunnah's temporary replacement said and dropped a piece of paper on Alfano's desk. "Daisy O'Shea" was scrawled on the paper.

"Show her to Interview One. Tell her I'll be right there. And would you get us a cup of coffee, Doud?"

"Yes, sir. In the interview room?"

Alfano nodded.

When he walked into the small interrogation room, Daisy O'Shea sat in the chair opposite the door. She held one hand over her swollen belly and rubbed it lightly. Mary sat in the chair next to her, fidgeting with a baby doll. A large bag sat on the floor to Daisy's right.

Alfano took the seat opposite the woman. "I'm Detective Alfano. Mrs. O'Shea, I'm sorry for your loss. I understand that Tommy was a good man and a good father."

"Thank you, Detective, this is my Mary."

There was a knock on the door.

"Coffee, sir," a voice said from outside.

Alfano opened the door, and the young patrolman placed two cups on the table.

"Mrs. O'Shea, would Mary like something?" Alfano asked.

"Do you have some milk?"

Alfano looked at Doud. The patrolman shook his head no.

"Some water?" Alfano asked.

"That's okay, Detective. I'll only be a moment."

"Thank you, Patrolman Doud."

Doud nodded and silently departed, closing the door behind him. Alfano slid the coffee to Daisy.

"Thank you."

Her voice was soft, and Alfano had to lean in to hear her.

"Yes, my Tommy was a good man and"—she looked up at the detective—"I saw you at the church. You were waiting for Father Dominic."

"Yes, I was. I assume you were there to arrange for Tommy's funeral?"

"Tommy won that night—did you know that? But, the money is almost gone. I had to use a lot of it for Mary . . . and then there was the funeral. That was Saturday."

"I wish I could help," Alfano said gently. "All I can do is find out who was involved in his death."

Daisy O'Shea stared at the cup of coffee without taking a drink. Her hand moved to the handles on the bag. Alfano had noticed it upon entering but hadn't been curious. Most women in her condition carried a bag, or perhaps it was for Mary's things. Now he wondered.

"Why are you here, Daisy? This is no place for a lady in your condition and with Mary. I would have come to see you, or met you at the church."

"It took two buses for us to get here, Detective Alfano. I needed to talk to you where no one else could see me. I brought you something."

She placed the large paper bag onto the table, turned it on its side, and withdrew its contents: the balloon-like shapes wrapped in newspaper were unmistakable. Whether they were Tommy's, well, that was another question altogether.

"Yes, these are Tommy's gloves," she said, answering his unasked question. "When he didn't get home that night, I had my neighbor drive me to the Stadium. I went to the dressing room that a Negro gentleman working there had said was where Tommy dressed for the fight. There were piles of bloody towels everywhere. And his gloves."

"How do you know they were Tommy's? They could belong to any of the boxers who fought that night."

"I thought so, too, until I looked at 'em."

She picked up the left-hand glove and held it palm-side up.

"Look here"—she pointed at the palm area—"there be three crosses drawn on 'em. See, here."

Alfano looked at the three crudely drawn crucifixes; two small Ts flanked one large one in the middle. It looked like someone had used a sharp pencil to dig into the smooth leather. The lines were smudged but legible.

"Before every fight, Tommy would draw these on his gloves. The first few times it was one cross—that was for me. Then another one for our Mary. The last time was three, for us and this one."

She patted her belly.

Alfano looked at the gloves like they were religious objects dropped from heaven. He couldn't dispute the explanation she gave for how she'd identified them as her husband's.

"Someone told me there's a rumor that the gloves were loaded," she said. "Tommy would never fight with loaded gloves, never. I brought 'em here to you, so you can tell me truly whether my Tommy did something wrong."

She pushed the gloves away from her as if they were diseased.

"Please place them back in the bag," Alfano said. "I don't want to touch them. We may be able to get some fingerprints."

He watched as she did what he asked. She left the sack on the table.

"Is there anything else I can do for you?" he asked her. "Do you want these gloves back?"

"No, I don't, and yes, Detective, there is something you can do. Find who killed my Tommy and make him pay."

24

ALDERMAN SOLOMON said to Rabbi Harris, "I understand there was another incident Saturday night at the fair."

The alderman smoked a cigarette as he paced about his office.

"And I also heard that that thug Hymen Rosenberg met his just fate along with two of his gang."

"Yes, on both counts, Isaac," Rabbi Harris said. "Would you just slow down, sit? You're going to throw an embolism."

"Our children keep being injured by this barbaric sport, if you can call it that. And yet we continue to receive little support from the politicians, the boxing commission, city hall."

"You actually believed that you would? Isaac, they all have interests in keeping this going. It's good for the kids and for those involved in it, politically and financially."

"You are right. It is good for the bribe-taking politicians, the gamblers, the racketeers, not to mention the people who sit in the seats and watch our children beat each other to death."

"They aren't children."

"Really? They start at age fourteen and by the time they are twenty-four, they are deformed, injured, scarred, and possibly touched in the head. You can see men in their forties who look twenty years older. This is not a sport; it's a gladiatorial exhibit for the masses."

"You know that you are fighting a losing battle. Even the newspapers don't want to hear from you. What did that reporter say to you when you asked to be interviewed after the Dempsey-Tunney fight?"

"He asked me what I thought of the fight."

"Yes, and you said you believed it was fixed, that all fights were fixed. Fighting is a criminal sport enjoyed by criminals. That didn't help you with the politicians in this town."

"But my constituents liked it. That's why they reelected me. You see, Rabbi, this city is more than gangsters and politicians. There's the people, and the people want this cleaned up or shut down. With the death of Rosenberg, maybe it's beginning."

"You condone this police shooting, this street justice?"

"I understand it was in self-defense."

"Maybe so. I don't know the facts. But it seems convenient."

The alderman lit another cigarette.

"God does work in mysterious ways. You should know that more than most, Rabbi. We are just His tools."

At the sound of a knock, the alderman turned to the door. "Yes?"

The door swung open. His daughter walked in, a stack of papers in her hands.

"Sorry I wasn't here to greet you, Rabbi. It has been busy this morning."

"Quite all right, Mrs. Tillerman. Your father and I are almost finished."

"It's a long-running discussion," the alderman added.

"And one that most probably will not end soon," Debbie said. She turned to her father. "It's ten o'clock. Your medication—you know what Dr. Bernstein says."

"You see, Jacob. Deborah has become so much like my

Susan. She watches over me."

"I miss her, too, Isaac. Mrs. Solomon, Susan, was a force in this community."

The widowed alderman touched the left side of his chest.

"There still is an empty spot here after five years," he said.

"Stop it, you two, or you will get me crying," Debbie told them.

"That boxer from Saturday night, the one from the fair—is he going to be all right?"

"I asked my friend Detective Alfano. He was there. And he says, yes, the damage was minor, a concussion. He didn't say much else."

"That's good. And to think we were just a few hundred yards away having a good time at the concert when this mayhem was going on."

"Father, please. The schedule for the fair is posted weeks in advance for all the events. That exhibition was just one more event."

Rabbi Harris stood and said his goodbyes. Deborah walked him to the door and then returned.

"Yes, just one more event that shows man's brutality." He crushed his cigarette. "What else do we have today?"

Debbie looked at the ashtray.

"Dr. Bernstein told you to quit smoking. Weren't you listening?"

"It's a minor vice, not a big deal."

"Yes, and it puts a strain on your heart."

"The schedule today, please?"

Exasperated, Debbie said, "This afternoon there is a tea with the synagogue's women's group, then a few short meetings with businesspeople from the Ward back here. And don't forget the Thursday noon lunch at Hull House. They are celebrating Miss Addams's birthday next month, so she will be there."

Solomon picked up another cigarette, saw his daughter's look, and put it back in the tray.

"Tell me about this Detective Alfano?"

"Father! Are you prying into my personal life, as little as I have, now?"

"I always am concerned when it comes to you and your, as you say, personal life. I am worried about your happiness. So, this man, this detective?"

"He's a good man, a simple man. No pretense, and he is dedicated to this city. He has the mayor's ear, such as that is, and is loyal to his fellow officers. Yes, I like him." She was surprised by her assessment, which was all true, but there lingered a huge however . . . where would it lead? Would she be able to expose herself to a man with such simple tastes, narrow ambitions, a strong moral compass, and obviously a guarded heart? Did she need more challenges in her life?

"Good."

* * *

Alfano stood on the porch of Sergeant McDunnah's house and watched the kids playing stickball in the street. Thirty years earlier, he'd played the same game on a similar street twenty blocks north. Easier days and simpler times. Then again, for most eleven-year-olds, all of life was simpler. These dozen kids would say the same thing someday, on some street, in some neighborhood, watching their kids play the same game. Baseball, in any form, was a unifying sport. Simpler days and simpler times—a mantra spoken by people from time immemorial.

Moira McDunnah came to the door.

"How's the sergeant?" Alfano asked.

She held the screen door open for him.

"He's good, Tony. Been bellyaching all weekend to get back to work. He's in the front room, drinking his coffee."

The small clapboard house was like hundreds of others in Bridgeport. Comfortable, as modern as the owner wanted, and warm in winter. Alfano remembered McDunnah complaining about the coal furnace. Alfano walked through the house to the parlor that overlooked the wide tree-lined street.

"Can't stand to be away from me, can you, Detective?" McDunnah said, setting down his cup on the doily draped over the small table next to his chair. The room smelled of jasmine.

"Patrolman Doud is doing a good job," Alfano said with a smile.

"Still wet behind the ears, but he's a good lad."

Alfano told McDunnah about the gloves Daisy O'Shea had dropped off.

"I left them at the coroner's office to have the doc take a look at them."

"Why not the crime lab?"

"I wanted his take on them first, to see if they match the marks on the Schwartz kid. If they do, I'll have forensics look for prints."

"Wouldn't you do that first?"

"I didn't want them to cover the gloves with all their goop before the doc could look at them," Alfano said. "He'll be careful. He wants answers as much as we do."

Alfano told him about the fight on the lagoon platform and the beating the young boxer had received. Then he told him what the coroner said and what Sammy had heard about other fights.

"This is getting stranger and stranger," McDunnah agreed. "You actually think someone is out there trying to sabotage boxing in this city?"

"Yes, and whoever it is has been at it for a while. With all the chaos that occurs just before and after a fight, it's possible they could be switching the gloves."

"Gambling rackets?"

"Maybe. A lot of money changes hands after one of these fights. I'm waiting for more evidence. What Abrahamson is doing will help. Maybe a fingerprint or two would also help. I'll keep you informed."

"You can tell me directly. I'm back in the station tomorrow."

"No way. I want you here recuperating."

Alfano turned to the doorway where Moira stood.

"Keep this Irish mug here, will you? Tie him to a chair or something. If that leg becomes infected, there will be hell to pay. I hate breaking in sergeants."

"Yes, Tony. And you be safe, too. He tells me he hates breaking in detectives. You staying for dinner?"

"Love to, but I'll take a rain check. There's a match tonight at the Marigold, and the owner doesn't know it, but he's buying me dinner."

25

A MISTY RAIN FELL as Alfano tossed his keys to the valet in front of the Marigold Gardens. He quickly walked to the main entrance, where a small crowd was gathered. People stood talking under the broad awning as they waited their turn to be allowed inside. After flashing his badge at the bouncer, the door was opened for Alfano. Inside he knocked the rain off his fedora and looked down the entry hallway to the bar at the far end. Off to the right, Eddie Dietrich stood against the railing that overlooked the large main hall. Dietrich had a cigar in one hand and an alluring, well-endowed platinum blonde on his other arm. She smoked a cigarette and looked bored. Alfano aimed himself at Dietrich. The blonde, no longer bored, slipped out from under Dietrich's arm and slid into an intercepting position.

"Nadine, cool your high heels. The guy's a cop," Dietrich said.

Nadine noticeably slumped and leaned her well-shaped bottom against the railing. She blew a smoke ring in the air.

"He looks so harmless," she said. "You sure? I've seen cops, even dated a few, and he don't look like one."

"Nadine, he is. So be careful, he bites."

"Interesting," she mused.

"Here for the fights, Detective?" Dietrich asked.

"Yes, and to watch the menagerie that's attracted to them. Full house?" Alfano said as he looked around.

"Yeah, the house looks good. So, Hymie Rosenberg is dead. Not sure whether to be thankful or upset—but I also knew never to get into that Cadillac of his. I forgot where to send flowers."

"It's been impounded. The flowers? Haven't a clue."

"If it comes up for auction, would you let me know?"

"Sure, I'll even put in a word."

"I adore a man in a Cadillac," Nadine said with a sigh.

"Don't we all," Alfano answered as he lit another cigarette for her. "I'm partial to Packards myself," he told her.

"Ooh, a man with a big Packard. What else you got, Detective?"

Alfano smiled, then ignored the question. "How many matches tonight, Eddie?"

"Six. Four three-rounders, one a five, and the main event is eight rounds. Most are club fighters, no big names. Just locals from the North Side clubs and gyms. The rest are regional, except for the last bout. It's a surprise. I'm calling it Italian Night; all the fighters are dagos."

"How creative—anyone I would know?"

"Depends. Who do you know?"

Alfano could see this conversation was going nowhere.

"I take it no one's disappointed about Rosenberg and his two sidekicks?" he asked Dietrich.

"Sometimes the trash man becomes trash himself. No, I can't think of one tear I've seen. A few lifted a drink, I can tell you that. And not a few are breathing a little easier. They tell me he'd have put his own mother in the ground for the right price."

Alfano looked at Dietrich and shook his head. "Who knows? But for the rest of you bums, I'm sure he had a standard price. He was a businessman, after all. Some days maybe he offered a special discount."

"I understand it was your man who put the dog down."

"True, and it was self-defense. My sergeant was protecting a citizen."

"Ah, the Chicago police to the rescue. Nadine, why don't you show Detective Alfano to table fifteen, and his night is on me." Dietrich looked at Alfano. "You off the clock?"

"I'm never off the clock, but I'll take that offer. Lead on, Nadine, my sweet."

Alfano followed the blonde down the five steps to the main floor and was more than entertained watching her as she glided through the crowd. At a table with a front-row view of the boxing ring, she removed the "Reserved" sign and pulled a chair out for the detective.

"May I get something for you, Detective?"

Joan Blondell could not have asked in sexier fashion.

"You wouldn't have Canadian Club back there, would you?"

"For you, Detective, I have the whole state of Canada."

"A double, and it's a country."

He watched her scrunch her forehead thinking about what he'd said. As she walked away, he forgave her for the small error in geography. Other men in the room furtively watched Nadine walk up to the bar; one gent had the side of his face slapped by his date. Alfano guessed it was worth it.

He looked up at Dietrich who was directing Duffy McGoin with his hand to a table, his table. Two very young women flanked either side of the manager. Two rough-looking Irish kids stood behind each of the girls. One lad was a heavyweight, the other lightweight to maybe middleweight. Alfano looked back to the railing, where Dietrich still stood. The club owner smiled and shrugged. Nadine leaned in so that one of her full breasts rested on Alfano's shoulder and then placed his drink directly in front of him. Her perfume nearly choked him; he held his breath. The pressure on his shoulder eased, and he looked up at the smiling Nadine.

"Thank you," he told her, letting out his breath.

"My pleasure. If there's anything else you need, just wave. I'll be up there keeping Mr. Dietrich company."

Another young woman had come to stand next to the table.

"Detective, this is Missy. If you need dinner or a refresh, she will take care of you. Anything you want, just ask."

Nadine leaned in, and Alfano again felt something full and soft on his shoulder.

"Mr. Dietrich said *anything* you want is on the house," she whispered and brushed his cheek with hers.

After she left, Alfano discreetly checked his suit coat pockets to see if anything was missing.

"So, Detective," McGoin said. "Was it you who shot the Jew? If not, I'd like to shake that mug's hand. The world's a safer place."

Alfano nodded and then looked at McGoin's guests.

"Where's me fucking manners?" McGoin responded. "Detective Tony Alfano, I'd like to introduce you to the O'Donnell sisters. They be the cutest twins in all of Bridgeport. These others are my clients. The big redhead is Shamus O'Toole, two hundred and sixty-five pounds of pure Irish guts and brawn; twenty-seven and two he is. This past year, he has won fifteen straight. This other Mick is Lucius Dorneky, middleweight, eighteen wins and one draw. We're doing a little sightseeing, checking out the competition, if you know what I mean."

"Glad to meet you," Alfano said.

If the twins were eighteen years old, he'd be surprised, and neither of the fighters looked much beyond twenty-two themselves. What a screwed-up world, he thought. He took a sip of the Canadian. It was his turn to be shocked; it tasted like the real McCoy.

Beyond the façade of arched and open windows that flanked the main room, Alfano had a view of the old beer garden area, full of tables and chairs. The light rain had pushed a few brave souls under the awnings that stretched out and over the tables near the windows. The tables inside the hall filled the entire floor, except where the ring had been set up and, next to it, a rectangular dance floor. The ring was small, sixteen feet on a side. Most of the bouts in the Chicago Stadium were fought in a twenty-foot sided ring. Somehow the smaller version felt just right in this nightclub venue.

At the far end of the large hall was a stage, the curtain pulled shut for tonight. Just beyond the edge of the canvas, to the right, he saw Debbie Tillerman. Sitting next to her was an older gentleman, and to his right an alderman Alfano knew well. The two men were talking. Debbie was looking around at the crowd. As she glanced toward Alfano, McGoin stood, blocking his view. Another man came to her table and leaned down to talk with the alderman.

"Your card, sir," Missy said, interrupting his attempt to see Debbie.

The waitress handed him a four-by-eight-inch lineup card. Printed on the handout were the bouts scheduled that night. Tony knew only one of the names, an Italian kid he'd seen fight before here at the Marigold. The kid fought out of the North Street gym. The others not from Chicago came from Kansas City, Gary, and Milwaukee. The main event was an eight-round, 160-pounds-each battle between an Italian fighter from Chicago and a true Italian from Rome. Dietrich loved his theme nights. Alfano looked back toward where Debbie had been seated. She was gone and so was the man who'd been sitting next to her. Only the alderman remained.

The fight bell clattered and directed everyone's attention to the center of the hall. A short parade of fighters, trainers, and cut men bounced their way down an aisle that cut through the tables. The men split into two groups, each taking a corner of the ring. Not wasting time, an announcer dressed in a tuxedo climbed into the ring and tapped on a microphone that had been lowered from the ceiling.

He began: "Ladies and gentlemen, thank you for braving the weather and coming out to the Marigold Gardens' fabulous Italian night. We have six bouts for you tonight. Please check your card for the particulars and for your favorites. Let me remind you not to forget that the spaghetti is the special, only a buck, and you get a glass of illegal red wine with it."

There was a general chuckle from the crowd.

"The first bout is at one hundred twenty-nine pounds. Two lightning-fast Italians with hands of steel. In the red shorts is Tony 'Il Duce' LaRocca out of Jimmy's Gym, and in the opposite corner in black is Bobby 'The Fist' Campania out of the Coulon Gym. Gentlemen?"

The two fighters approached the announcer as the microphone was reeled back to the ceiling. They bounced on their toes as they listened to the referee; then they touched their gloves and went back to their corners. At the bell, they both ran at each other and collided like two bucks in rutting season. Il Duce fell and lay momentarily sprawled across the canvas as the crowd roared with laughter. He found his feet and began bobbing and weaving. The Fist mimicked him, and the two began a dance that was seldom interrupted with punches. The crowd began to boo even before the bell.

Alfano looked at his fight card; this was a three-round bout. He looked for Missy and waved. He pointed at his glass, and she nodded. He also looked at the food menu on the table, and then shrugged. He'd take the spaghetti and pass on the wine.

The fight, halfway into the final round, changed. The men began to pummel each other—fists found their mark, clenches drove each fighter against the ropes more than once. Il Duce was bleeding from a cut over his right eye. Half blind, he was swinging wildly. The Fist, seeing an opportunity, came in for the kill and walked into a right haymaker that put him to the mat—out cold.

Il Duce danced in place; blood from his cut face dropped on the canvas. The Fist rolled onto his side at the end of the count. His trainer stuffed some smelling salts under his nose; the kid got to his feet, and with the help of his cut man stood next to the referee as Il Duce was declared the winner. The crowd mildly applauded and then went back to their spaghetti.

Alfano looked past his tablemates and perused the crowd. He spotted a couple low-level gangsters he knew from the old days; they wore shabby tuxedos. Both had put some time in at Joliet prison. The girls they were with weren't bad-looking. Nothing ever changed, he thought. Some women followed money like moths to a flame. And the results often were the same.

The band had restarted just after the decision was announced. They were good; they played swing, and the fellow on the clarinet drove the band. The dance floor was full. Some of the dancers were excellent, in a carefree, athletic, and extremely bawdy way. If someone had asked Alfano to dance, he would have feigned a broken leg.

He looked up at the railing. Three men were talking to Dietrich. One of them, in a nice tuxedo, pushed his finger into the club owner's chest. Dietrich put his hands up and then stepped back. The other two pushed their way past the one bouncer standing next to Eddie. They both then scanned the crowd. Alfano recognized all three.

"McGoin, get your fighters and the twins out of here, now. Go through the doors to the beer garden, and then get the hell out."

"What? Why?" O'Toole, the redheaded heavyweight, said.

"In about a minute, there will be bullets flying everywhere," Alfano answered. "Get them out."

"Come on, kids. You heard the detective," McGoin said, gathering up his flock. He shepherded them through the crowd to the glass doors.

Alfano heard one of the twins say as they passed him, "But, Mr. McGoin, it's raining."

"Yeah, soon to be raining bullets, doll face," came the answer.

Slowly weaving in and out between the patrons, all unaware of what was about to start, Alfano worked his way around the room to the end of the railing near the steps up to the bar. In the ring, the announcer walked up to the lowering microphone and prepared for the next event. Spotlights were aimed at the entry for the fighters. The band started playing "It Don't Mean a Thing." Alfano climbed the steps and positioned himself behind the man standing with Dietrich. Now close enough, he saw sweat rolling down the cheeks of the club owner. Alfano leaned into Dietrich's antagonist.

"I suggest that you keep your hands right there, Fredo. And call your men back."

Before Fredo could answer, a single gunshot sounded. Instantly, people were screaming and running. Men and women alike overturned chairs as they tried to move away from the sound. Another gunshot answered the first. More screams. Alfano took a quick look down to the floor and saw one man reaching inside his coat. A third blast spun that same man to the wooden floor.

Fredo no longer waited. He made his move and pushed Dietrich over the railing. Dietrich fell the short distance, to the main floor, knocking over a brunette in the process. She collapsed to her knees, the two-hundred-pound owner on top of her. Fredo used his momentum and fell forcefully back into Alfano. The detective had anticipated the move. He threw the thug to the floor and then withdrew his revolver from his shoulder holster.

More gunshots, with a different sound, echoed in the hall. Alfano pistol-whipped Fredo, purposefully knocking the gangster out cold. Then he turned back to the chaos on the dance floor. Dozens of patrons were rushing to the already jammed exits. Four men stood their ground, or rather, had squared off in the center of the ballroom. Two in shabby tuxedos, and Fredo's men in ill-fitting suits; each man held a revolver.

Alfano took a second to decide his next action. In the cacophony of the screaming, frightened patrons, no one would hear him calling to drop their weapons. He raised his own revolver and fired once into the ceiling. Then he swung his aim down and at the larger of the two in bad suits. The noise startled everyone. All four turned to look; the big man saw Alfano's gun and immediately figured that it was pointed at his head.

"Drop them, now!" Alfano yelled.

The room instantly quieted.

"On the floor, or, Gordo, swear to God, I will blow your fucking head off." He caught the eyes of the other men; they all froze. "The floor, now!"

The two men in tuxedos lowered their weapons, and then Gordo and his associate did the same.

"On the fucking floor, all of you," Alfano yelled.

The four slowly took a knee, then laid themselves out on the parquet dance floor. Alfano heard chairs shifting behind him, and then three men rushed past him and down to the floor. He recognized Dietrich's bouncers; they gathered around Fredo's men and the two in tuxedos. One of the bouncers began collecting weapons.

"Stay right there on the floor!" Alfano yelled.

Behind the two men in monkey suits, another man lay sprawled on one of the banquet tables. Blood stained his white formal shirt. A woman in a sequined dress was pushing a handful of cloth napkins against the man's chest. They were not sufficient to stop the bleeding. Alfano had seen too many shootings to know this was not going well for the man, who weakly reached up to the woman, clawing at her, grabbing the strap on her dress. Blood from his hand covered her bare shoulder. Then the arm fell. In a final effort, the man tried to rise from the table but instead he rolled off onto the floor. His body went rigid. The woman took a step back, glanced at Alfano, and then turned and ran out the now clear exit door behind her.

Police appeared at the main entry, and more poured in from the exits. Eddie Dietrich had gotten to his feet and was helping the woman who broke his fall. She seemed more frightened than injured. One of the cops moved toward Alfano.

"Drop it, or I'll drop you," the patrolman yelled, as he held his service weapon up and pointed it directly at Alfano.

Alfano slowly placed his pistol on a small table next to the railing and raised his hands.

"I'm Detective Anthony Alfano, Racine station, Corporal. May I?"

The patrolman, a kid not twenty-five, studied the detective. "Badge?"

Alfano slowly moved his hands to his coat pocket and removed his credentials and badge; he held them up in either hand.

"Sorry, sir. The call said multiple gunmen."

"It's those guys on the floor. There's one shot; he's over there. Probably dead. We need an ambulance." He pointed to the man at his feet. "And put cuffs on this one."

The patrolman moved to do as told. Alfano looked down at Dietrich.

"You were lucky, Eddie. Fredo Tucci swore he'd kill Donnie Conti years ago. Even Joliet prison didn't take that vendetta out of him. You okay?"

"My shoulder hurts to high heaven, and it looks like I'm out a few thousand."

"Who else should we arrest?" a sergeant asked Alfano.

"Those four for sure and anyone with a gun."

"Detective?" a soft voice said from behind. It was Nadine. "Your hat."

26

MCDUNNAH SAID, "You look like shit," when Alfano walked into the station. "Then again, after the excitement last night at the Marigold, I'm not surprised. Coffee's fresh."

"Why are you here?" Alfano asked. "You are supposed to stay off that leg."

McDunnah ignored the question and they both headed for Alfano's desk, where the detective set his cup down and gingerly lowered himself into his chair. He took a sip of coffee and shook his head. He was positive he heard rattling. Upon leaving the chaos of the Marigold the night before, Dietrich handed him the almost full bottle of Canadian Club as a personal thank-you. His reward was a thick head this morning. He swung his chair around to face the crime board. Someone, it had to have been the sergeant, had put neat black ribbons over the pictures of Rosenberg and his two gunzels.

"Nice touch. How's Macaulay?"

"After he was questioned, he disappeared. My guess is that he's up north with his wife. I don't think anyone will go after him. However, there are a few that would like to give him a party. The word in the neighborhood is that he's a hero. Just what that fool needs, an adoring public."

"Really, how's the leg?" Alfano asked him.

McDunnah grabbed the back of a chair from the next desk and pulled it over. He gingerly sat down next to Alfano, and put his leg up on another chair.

"I'm fine. Sore, but I'm okay. No way I was staying in the house, bored stiff after three days. Moira dropped me off; she took the car to work today. What happened last night?"

"Fredo Tucci decided to collect on his promise to kill Donnie Conti. Looks like he made good on that threat."

Tucci was one of the, as Alfano generally phrased it, "not dead or still in prison" surviving members of Capone's Outfit.

McDunnah let out a low whistle.

"In the Marigold, with all those people. Jesus, Mary, and Joseph."

"That's not all," Alfano continued. "It seems that one of Conti's nephews was on the card last night, in the second event. Tucci was going to kill the kid in front of Conti, and then shoot the old man. I saw Tucci come in with his men. He took Dietrich by surprise; the German damn near peed in his pants. Then, all hell broke loose. Lucky only Conti got whacked."

McDunnah nodded. It went without saying that dozens more could have been hurt in the crossfire had Alfano not intervened.

"These Italian vendettas, how long will they go on?" the sergeant wondered.

"You Irish certainly hold onto yours," Alfano said. "This coffee could be considered a weapon in some places."

"Stop with the criticizing of my coffee, or you can make your own."

McDunnah pointed at the three message slips he'd placed on Alfano's desk.

"The first is from Doc Abrahamson. He has news about the gloves Daisy O'Shea gave you; you need to tell me about those. The second is from the mayor; he wants to see his hero.

The last was from a woman, and she didn't leave her name, just a number. She said you knew it."

Alfano looked at the messages; the last was from Debbie. "My Tuesday is full, and it's not even ten o'clock."

* * *

After parking in front of the morgue, Alfano waited ten minutes in the small lobby of the coroner's office. His head still throbbed from too little sleep and too much alcohol. He crushed his cigarette in the ashtray when he heard the familiar click of the coroner's shoes.

"You need to quit those things," Abrahamson said. "They will kill you."

"In my job, it's maybe fifth or sixth on the list. What do you have?"

"This way."

They walked through the maze of halls; a dozen or so occupied gurneys filled the corridors.

"Been a busy weekend," Alfano noted.

"Working in this city seems to come with job security. By the way, Donnie Conti is under that one."

They passed the sheet and gurney. Alfano could only shake his head over the strange justice from the night before. The doctor directed Alfano to a small, dark room. The boxing gloves lay on a large boxlike table in the center of the room. A lamp hung low over the contraption.

"Nice setup. What did you find?" Alfano said looking at the fluoroscope machine.

"Quite a lot. The fluoroscope allows me to see into bodies without having to cut them up; same goes for these mitts."

The doctor, who wore a heavy thick apron that covered most of his front, picked up a glass plate in a metal frame with handles on all sides.

"When I hold this over the gloves, you can see what I saw. But stand back. I don't want to get you exposed to the radiation."

When the doctor passed the plate over the left-hand glove, the vague outline of the mitt could be seen. In the center mass of the largest part of the glove was a neatly defined four-inch pad encircling a cluster of small, unmistakably shaped objects. The pellets looked like white BBs under the medical X-ray.

"Lead shot?" Alfano immediately guessed.

"Looks like it, Detective. Twelve-gauge or similar. They are in a pouch of some kind that then was sewn into the gloves. It is a very good job; the gloves weigh almost ten ounces, just a little over the standard weight."

"Practically no one would notice the difference," Alfano mused. "Even the fighters wearing them."

"Yes, and the mass is more than enough to help increase the effectiveness of a punch. One blow wouldn't necessarily make a difference, but repeated shots to the head"—he clicked off the buzzing machine.

"The fighter is dead before he leaves the ring or not long after," Alfano finished. "Okay, so there's no doubt the gloves are loaded. The bigger questions are who did it and why."

"My quick analysis found four sets of fingerprints. I suspect one set is Mrs. O'Shea's. The crime lab needs to match the others. They are layered under some of Mrs. O'Shea's prints, assuming they are hers. Other than the crosses scratched into the leather, there's nothing else about the gloves that is peculiar or even helpful."

The coroner picked up the gloves by their laces, and placed them in the same paper bag Daisy O'Shea had brought them in.

Alfano forgot his headache. The familiar and not entirely unwelcome excitement of being a step closer to the answers he sought took over.

"The three crosses on the hide in the lower palms by a pencil," Abrahamson said as they exited the lab. "You said that

O'Shea did that to remember his wife and children?"

"That's what she said."

"Are you sure he's the one who scratched in the symbols?"

"No, I'm not. I believe her, but there's no way to prove it."

When they reached the office, the coroner handed Alfano a folder and the paper bag with the gloves.

"There's fluoroscope images in there as well as exterior photographs of the gloves," he said. The coroner's expression was sober. "Find out who did this. Someone in this town is killing our young men by proxy. You need to stop them, Tony."

* * *

After delivering the gloves to the crime lab, Alfano drove crosstown to city hall. Not for the first time, he mulled over the impact that boxing had on the city—it was huge. Over ten thousand young men were registered in Chicago to box and compete in the Golden Gloves and the professional matches. There had to be more than a hundred gyms and clubs that catered to the needs of those inclined to punch the lights out of their fellow men. The pugilistic arts went back thousands of years; he knew that. To put a stop to boxing would be like trying to stop drinking by imposing Prohibition. True, the CYO, the Catholic Church, and the Jewish organizations were there to protect their young men from getting their heads bashed in during no-holds-barred backroom fights. But in Alfano's mind, it was all about money, plain and simple. The kids could earn a few bucks while getting their bells rung; the gyms made a few more dollars in monthly memberships; the promoters even more *dinaro* by getting a piece of the gate; and the city's big halls and stadiums were full of patrons paying five and ten bucks a ticket. And that didn't include all the gambling, backroom venues, and fixes that seemed as natural to the game as suds to soap. Except nobody was clean—no one.

Alfano waited in the lobby of the mayor's office. It was a

two-cigarette wait. At least the mayor had good magazines. The latest *National Geographic* featured articles about spiders. He looked at the door to the mayor's office: *spiders and webs— how apt.*

The secretary's intercom buzzed.

"The mayor will see you now, Detective."

Alfano crushed his cigarette, crossed the room, and, as he waited for the door to be buzzed open, he noticed a thin strand of spiderweb in the upper-right corner of the doorframe. The web caught the late-morning light; its owner was hiding or gone. *How appropriate.*

"Good morning, Detective," Mayor Kelly said from behind his desk. He stood and stuck out his hand as Alfano walked into the room.

"You know Pat Nash and Police Commissioner Hayden? Of course you do. What was I thinking? You and the commissioner go way back. Take a seat."

The mayor pointed to a large leather and oak chair on the far side of the desk.

Alfano shook hands around the room and then settled into the chair. Not much had changed in the mayor's office; in fact, his predecessor's photos still hung on the walls. The only differences now were family pictures on the desk and a large portrait of the new president, Franklin Delano Roosevelt, adorning the opposite wall. Nash was Chicago's most important political fixer. Hayden was working his way up the political food chain.

"The funeral was Saturday," the mayor said.

"What?"

"The funeral for my godson, Thomas O'Shea. You okay, Detective?"

"I'm sorry, Mayor. It's already been a rough morning. I've been following up on the shooting of Donnie Conti by Fredo Tucci . . ."

"I understand you were there?" Commissioner Hayden asked.

Alfano and Hayden had a long relationship, some days good, some days bad. Alfano wasn't sure which it would be today.

"No, Commissioner, I wasn't at Tommy's funeral."

"No, Detective, I meant the Marigold."

Alfano looked at Hayden, then said, "Yes, Commissioner. I dropped in to watch a couple of bouts and spotted Tucci, but I was too late to stop the hit. Tucci just got out of Joliet a week ago. He always swore he'd kill Conti. My guess, his next date is with the chair."

"Stupid dagos think they can do anything in my city," the mayor said as he lit a cigar. He then looked at Alfano. "Present company excepted."

"Sure. I was in the right place at the wrong time. Duffy McGoin was there with a couple of his fighters. I got him out just before the shooting started."

"That son of a bitch is partially responsible for my god-son's death. You could have left him there."

"I was more concerned about his associates and the girls he had with him. I can find him when I want him."

The mayor shrugged but said nothing. Apparently, the floor was Alfano's.

"I found out that the gloves Tommy used were loaded with lead shot," he continued. "I can guess that Benny Schwartz's also were fixed. Sadly, it looks like they both beat each other to death."

"Someone had to doctor those gloves," Nash said.

"Absolutely, Mr. Nash," Alfano answered. "And, according to people in the business, this isn't the first time. I saw the effects last Saturday night at the fair. One of the fighters was severely beaten; the marks and bruises were the same as those on Tommy and Benny. I'm hearing that there have been others. The boxers are skittish."

"This was another incident?" Nash asked.

"Yes, looks like it. The kid will be alright."

"That's good," Kelly said. "Keep on it, Detective."

"I was told that your sergeant took down a few associates of the latest version of Murder Incorporated: Misters Teitlebaum, Feldstein, and Rosenberg," Nash said.

"Sounds like a law firm, not a bunch of killers," Mayor Kelly jibed.

"They were killers, contract killers, Mayor," Alfano said. "Our numbers say that they may have been responsible for more than three dozen murders over the last five years. Good enough that Rosenberg had a nice home in Oak Park."

"Killing pays well," Hayden chimed.

"I understand there were a few politicians on his list that he hadn't yet gotten to," Alfano said, looking at the commissioner.

"Screw you, Alfano."

"Boys, stop that," Mayor Kelly said. "Detective, are you any closer in chasing this guy, this fixer, down?"

"To be honest, not sure. I may have seen him on Saturday night at the fair. Someone, in a suit, was leaving with boxing gloves, but I didn't see his face clearly. The crowds from the music festival made it impossible to follow."

"I was there. It was something," the mayor added. "The gloves?"

"Like I said, the suit was carrying a pair as he left. Later, I couldn't find the gloves the boxer was beaten with that night. My guess, they were taken by him or someone else—either way, no evidence."

"What do you need from me? I owe it to the O'Sheas," the mayor said.

"Time. Whoever is doing this is trying to stop boxing in this town. If the gyms and the boxers begin to believe the fix can come from anywhere, maybe they will stop. Wrongheaded I know, but that's my take."

The mayor turned to Nash and Hayden. "Any ideas?"

"There's a couple of groups that want fighting stopped," Nash said. "Some are from the old temperance leagues. They've lost the fight to the liquor lobby and are shifting their focus. Most are old biddies, hardly people you'd find at the fights. The most organized is a group pushed by Isaac Solomon, the alderman from the 24th Ward. He's been adamant about how boxing is injuring his people. He wants it stopped, outlawed in fact. He's been hounding the boxing commission to have better referees and shorter fights."

"I'll look into it; it's something," Alfano said, his thoughts turning to the daughter of the alderman. He said nothing to the politicians about Debbie Tillerman.

27

MCGOIN OWED HIM. Alfano sat in the Packard in front of the Dublin Health Club and Gym in Bridgeport. For the last thirty minutes, he'd watched a dozen men and boys enter and leave the club. All carried gym bags; some had boxing gloves tied to the grips. The last pair to enter were Duffy McGoin and the red-haired heavyweight boxer Alfano had met the previous night. Alfano left the car and followed the promoter into the club. The faded sign painted on the brick above the gym's sign read that this building once was a meatpacker's warehouse. That seemed appropriate to Alfano.

The cavernous room held three boxing rings, exercise equipment arranged along the walls, and the usual stench. A couple dozen men jumped rope, pushed weights, and pounded both the heavy man-sized bags suspended from the rafters and the speed bags mounted to the walls. The staccato of leather on the smaller speed bags filled the room with a constant background drone of popping and thumping.

Shamus O'Toole was stripping out of his sweat suit and talking with another fighter. McGoin was engaged with another man; the roll of papers in McGoin's hand was being used to punctuate the air.

"You do get around, don't you, McGoin?" Alfano said.

"I'd been looking a couple of days for you, and then, there you are at the Marigold. We need to talk."

McGoin feigned a look of surprise and for a moment studied Alfano.

"Alfano, I want to thank you for getting us out of Dietrich's last night. I understand it got ugly."

"A couple of old-school gangsters shooting it out? Yeah, it was bad. Could have been worse."

"Donnie Conti is dead. It was pretty damn worse for him. Why are you here, Detective?"

When the man McGoin had been talking to heard the word "detective," he got the clue and walked away.

"Did you know Hymen Rosenberg?" Alfano asked McGoin.

"No, not really. Sure, I knew about him, but I never met him."

"The street says otherwise."

"The street's known to lie."

"True, so I need some help. Someone is targeting fighters. I've been told about fights that had loaded gloves."

"Always a possibility. Recently, there's been some strange things happening in some of the bouts around town. They don't include my guys—I'm legit."

"Nothing about you is legit, McGoin. What things?"

"Guys with more head trauma. Damage I've not seen since we started using the bigger gloves. Maybe the boxers are getting stronger. Better training. That might be part of it."

"What's your take?"

"Someone is fucking with us. None of my boxers goes into the ring with gloves I've not checked personally, certainly not since the O'Shea fight. I've told all the other managers and promoters here; they are doing the same thing. Nothing's been found."

"And the other gyms?"

"Can't say. I can tell you that the boxing commission is taking this seriously. They grilled me for hours about it."

"When was that?"

"Last week, just after the fight. They're on a witch hunt. This scares them, too. Right now, it's not hit the papers—who knows what would happen if it was broadcast over the sports pages: loaded gloves, fixed fights, busted-up boxers. It would be the end of us."

O'Toole walked up to where the two men stood.

"What'cha want me to do, Mr. McGoin?"

"Warm up, jump ropes, and then the speed bag. I've got a sparring partner coming in. We need to work on your back-pedaling and footwork. Last fight you were clumsy, almost tripped over your own feet."

"Yeah, but he was down in the third."

"You should have had him in the second. Work on those. I'll be there in a minute."

Alfano watched the big man walk away and pick up a jump rope. He was surprisingly quick for a heavyweight.

"He looks good," Alfano said.

"He is, instinctive. Fast hands, fast but clumsy feet, but a little slow on the upbeat. I need to tell him anything three times to get it to sink in."

"He reminds me of an Irish Kingfish Levinsky."

"Yes, but without the scary sister who's his promoter and manager. Now that's a pair. Shamus can be a contender in a year, if I can get him the right fights."

The big man right now was Barney Ross, McGoin told Alfano. "After the Canzoneri fight last June, that Jew can take that win and do just about anything. I want O'Toole to take him next year."

"Good luck with that. What do you hear about Alderman Isaac Solomon?"

"That meddler? Shit, he's been sticking his big nose into

almost everything for the last two years, all since he won that Ward. He thinks he's some kind of crusader or something, that's what I hear, at least. Never met him."

McGoin then echoed Sammy Schwartz's statement that mothers were pulling their sons out of the gyms, although McGoin also was concerned that the Jewish gyms were losing fighters.

"A lot of good fighters are Jews. I'm hearing that Solomon is having an impact in the neighborhood around Maxwell Street," the promoter said. "That will make it harder to get fights for my boys. I always need a little of the racial thing to help sell tickets."

"That's a cynical thing to say."

"It sells tickets, tickets mean money, money means bigger purses, and that's why we're here, Detective. Money does make the world go round and round."

"I was wrong. You're a cynical Irish asshole, too."

"Screw you, Detective."

"You're the second one to say that to me today."

"Doesn't mean we aren't right."

"Are you Detective Anthony Alfano?" a thin man asked. The sleeves of his white shirt were rolled up, exposing Navy tattoos. He wore a straw boater, even in the gym.

"Yes?"

"Phone call for you. Says he's Sergeant McDunnah."

McGoin raised his eyebrows.

"I always leave a number where I might be found," Alfano said. "Where?" he asked the thin man.

"It's on the table in the office, there." The man pointed.

"Alfano here . . . Did she leave a name? . . . A number?"

Alfano didn't need to write it down; it was on a note in his pocket.

"Yeah, I know who it is. If she calls back, tell her I'll call her . . . That, Sergeant, is none of your business."

Alfano held the receiver in his fingers, but held down its cradle on the side of the phone. He looked at McGoin through the glass window of the small office. McGoin's back was to him. O'Toole was climbing into the ring, and another boxer was pushing through the ropes from the other side. Both wore sparring gloves and leather headgear. Alfano thought for another few moments, then lifted his finger and dialed.

"Hi, Debbie . . ."

He apologized for only just now getting her message. She wanted to meet him tonight. "The Berghoff . . . what, not Italian?" he asked her. Then, "Just kidding . . . seven. See you then."

He walked back into the gym, and stood ringside for the next twenty minutes, watching the heavyweight go through the motions. He turned to McGoin.

"That kid's heart is not in it today. He okay?"

"Last night scared him. He's never been that close to being killed—it shook him up. The twins thought it was a lot of fun, though."

"The naiveté of children. Youth is wasted on the young."

"Ah, the detective philosopher. You should leave that to the Irish, Alfano. The only ones who have that much blackness in their souls are the Irish. Look at our writers and poets."

"I'll take Dante over Joyce any day."

"Aren't you an illiterate toad? But then again, it's to be expected. You Italians may be great painters and lovers, but it takes an Irishman to rip your fucking heart out."

"Your boy still keeps his arms too low."

"Yeah, his weakness. Think you can take him?"

"I wouldn't even try. If you think of anything, McGoin, let me know. And it was a good thing you did, giving the fight winnings to the wife; she needs it. I just wish your heart was as big as Stingly's. He gave Benny's mother a grand."

"Stingly's a sucker and has a bigger heart."

"At least his beats."

28

ALFANO HAD A LATE LUNCH and then returned to the station, where he found a note and a cardboard box on his desk. The note was from McDunnah. He was going home; the pain in his leg was killing him. He would try to get in the next day but offered no promises. *Tried to do too much, not as young as I used to be,* was the last line. *Who is?* the detective thought.

He cut the tape on the box. Inside was a sheet of paper with "Chicago Crime Laboratory" neatly printed on top and information about the gloves Alfano had dropped off earlier that morning. Telling the lab that the analysis was important to the mayor must have sped things along.

He scanned the report. As Abrahamson's examination had predicted, the lab had found five sets of distinct finger-prints and a few unidentifiable smudges on the gloves. One set matched a man named Clive Kimble, another a referee who worked pro fights; the other three were unknown. Alfano knew about the cut man Kimble, Kibbie to his friends; the included rap sheet for minor stuff was added to the crime board. The referee's prints were understandable; he probably had his hands on the gloves during the fight. Presumably, one set of prints belonged to Daisy O'Shea; he'd have McDunnah clear those when the sergeant came back to the station. That left two. One might be McGoin's, but most likely the promoter wouldn't get his hands anywhere near the gloves. Two unknowns; Alfano felt a small step closer.

He removed the gloves from the carton. Both were covered with the black carbon used to raise the fingerprints. The gloves had been neatly and sharply cut along their padded tops. Also inside the box were two manila envelopes, labeled "Right Hand," "Left Hand." He opened the right-hand envelope; inside was a flat, round, rough leather bag about three inches across. It, too, had been slit open and was empty. He slid out the small paper envelope tucked inside the larger envelope. He found a clean, empty coffee cup, and emptied the contents of the small envelope into the white cup. Hundreds of small lead beads filled the bottom. The report from the lab verified Abrahamson's earlier guess that they were twelve-gauge buckshot, lead, most probably from a shotgun shell. Three ounces of lead in each pouch; the equivalent of what would fill three or four shotgun shells. He looked closely at the stitching on the pouches. It was neat, even, done by someone who knew how to sew. If he'd done it, Alfano thought, it would have turned out messy. No fingerprints had been captured on the pouches.

When he retrieved a magnifying glass from his drawer, he could tell that the extra stitching on the gloves was similar to the work on the pouch. He also saw where the gloves had been opened along the line of the manufacturer's stitches and where the new stitches began. There were subtle differences, but without a magnifying glass, almost impossible to tell. And when you were lacing on gloves over a fighter's wrapped hands, who would think to look that closely at the stitching?

He put the gloves back in the box and lit a cigarette. So, he had two sets of prints for unknown persons on the gloves, two three-ounce-plus pouches full of lead shot, stitches that showed skill with a needle, and the confirmation that the gloves were loaded. He had no way of confirming that the gloves were the ones used in the fight. He looked again at the report and saw that blood had been found in the seams. Tests were being done on the blood scrapings to determine the blood type. If it matched that of Benny Schwartz's, Alfano would have confirmation that the gloves had been used in the fight.

He spun to face the crime board. All this information was helpful; it affirmed his suspicions and those of the coroner. However, it didn't move the needle a notch. There were thousands of people in the Chicago area who might have come in contact with the gloves since their manufacture, and thousands with the same blood type as Schwartz. Trying to discover the identities of the two other people was more than daunting; it would be almost impossible.

Alfano wished that his wounded sergeant hadn't gone home; he needed his perceptive sounding board. He wrote a note and stuck it to the board under the picture of the gloves that McDunnah had mounted the previous week: *Two unknown sets of prints. Confirm D. O'Shea.* He added two parallel horizontal lines with a question mark at the end of each. He wrote another note and stuck it below the photos of Tommy O'Shea and Benny Schwartz. This one read: *Confirm reports of other boxers injured by loaded gloves!*

What drove someone to intentionally doctor the gloves? Fixing a fight, illegal wagers, gambling, all to predetermine an outcome to the bout for a couple of dollars. Rosenberg's wager had been huge, so he may have known the fix was in, but that option was now a dead end, literally. There were other ways to game a fight, tried and true ways; the easiest was to pay off one of the fighters to take a dive. Put up a good battle and then drop, in the right round. He'd heard of a few fighters who were very good at that bit of theatrics. They didn't last long and tended to be older boxers in their last days anyway. Sentimentality in the world of boxing would only get you a free lunch at Schaller's in Bridgeport.

Something else was going on. The scenario reeked of revenge, intimidation, and politics, but there was no pattern, or at least none that Alfano could see—yet. All he'd heard was that the damage to other boxers appeared in professional bouts at the larger venues, the Chicago Stadium, the World's Fair, and some of the bigger clubs. Those spots all were public, with easy access to the training rooms since most had minimal security. Whoever it was knew they could come and go as they pleased without being questioned.

Patrolman Doud came over to say that Alfano had a visitor. "He says his name is Sammy Schwartz."

"Thank you, Patrolman. Ask him to wait in Interview One. I'll be right there."

"Would you like some coffee or something?"

"No, I'm fine."

Alfano picked up a notebook and walked to the interview room. He wondered why the kid would come here to the station and, more importantly, what did he want?

The wiry, muscular teenager stood looking out the window, his back to the door. When Alfano entered the room, Sammy turned and faced the detective. A shiner haloed his left eye.

"Strong left, I'd say. You okay?" Alfano asked.

"You should see the other guy."

Alfano smiled. "How's your mother, Sammy?"

"She's good, all things considered. The last week's been tough. I've moved back temporarily to help."

"That's good. She can use it. So, what can I do for you?"

"I'm fighting on Friday night; it's an exposition bout against Ray Weiner. He's this other kid from the neighborhood. Rabbi Harris put it together. Weiner is tough and experienced, so it will be good for me."

"Where?"

"At the fair, on the lagoon stage. May not be as fancy as

Soldier Field and the bouts against the Irish team three weeks ago, but it's still a chance to be seen."

"I thought you said you didn't like the floating stage."

"I can get used to it. It's a fight, Detective. There's fifty in it."

"Your mother, she knows?"

"Yeah, but not happy. My sister says I'm a fool. It's too early since Benny died, she says—not good for Ma. But, Detective, I got to do something. There's nothing better, I tell ya, nothing better than being in the ring."

"Someday you'll find out differently, but I get it. What are you, one hundred thirty pounds?"

"I'm fighting at one twenty-six. Just made the number."

"Want a Coca-Cola?"

"Sure," Sammy answered.

Alfano went to the door and called to Doud, "Bring me a cup of coffee and a Coke."

"So, why are you here, Sammy?"

"I got this idea. Maybe I can help find out who loaded the gloves. Friday, I keep my eyes open and look for anything that don't look jake. Mitts where they ain't supposed to be, strangers, people wandering in and out, that kind of stuff. If I see something not right, I find you and tell you. Maybe it will point you to the guy who killed my brother."

"Interesting."

"I told you there's already some guys whose folks made them drop out of the gyms and competing for the Gloves. My sis tells me that Ma is thinking it, too. I need her permission to be in the gym and keep my registration, at least until I'm eighteen. I don't want to go behind her back, so if we can find the guy doing this, everything will be okay—again."

"Let me think about it," Alfano said. "It might work."

Doud came in with coffee for Alfano and handed a cold soda bottle to the kid.

"It's not too dangerous—certainly not like being a look-out for one of Capone's hideouts," Alfano continued, more to himself than to Sammy, but the young man answered him.

"I knew a kid that did that. He was ten back then, my age. Died in the crossfire of a shootout. Nice kid, but he didn't know when to duck."

29

ALFANO LIKED the Berghoff Restaurant, especially the snug bar off the main dining room; it was for men only. He slid in between two men in suits and pointed to one of the three bartenders standing behind the long mahogany dressed in white shirts, ties, and long white aprons. They were the only ones not wearing fedoras.

"Robert, a stein, please," Alfano said.

"Right away, Detective."

When the two men to either side of Alfano heard the bartender address him as "Detective," they gave him a little more room.

The bartender slipped a clear glass beer stein under the tap and began to draw out one of Chicago's better, and now legal, beers.

"Haven't seen you in a while. Where you been keeping yourself?" he asked Alfano.

"Unfortunately, I don't get downtown for pleasure as much as I like. It's been more than a month since I had lunch here. How's the wife and kids?"

"Doing well."

Robert's German accent was thick—his Ws sounded more like Vs. Alfano remembered the man's first day behind the bar. That was more than ten years ago. The war was still on everyone's mind, the Armistice was only five years old, and Germans still were somewhat unpopular. Robert was a cousin of Herman Berghoff, the restaurant's owner. Robert had survived the Hun trenches and, with a little help politically, Herman was able to get him and his young wife into Chicago. As far as Alfano knew, the man had never missed a day of work behind the bar.

"The oldest is going to middle school next year—good kid. The little one is now seven. She brightens my every day," Robert said.

"Prost!" Alfano responded and lifted his glass.

Robert smiled and sharply nodded his head.

Alfano was early by almost a half hour for his date with Debbie Tillerman, allowing him a rare few minutes to himself. He studied the crowd pushed up against the bar; it was a typical workday evening. The men told stories, drank, and prepared for the crowded trains and the commute home.

Twenty minutes later and halfway into his second beer, he felt a tug on his coat. A young boy stood next to him, holding a small piece of paper.

"Detective Alfano, this is for you," the boy said.

I am running late. Have a beer for me, the note read.

Alfano gave the boy a quarter and pointed to his stein. "Top it off, would you?" he said to Robert.

"A detective? Is that what I heard? You work for the city, or are you a P.I.?" the man to Alfano's right asked. He'd been looking at Alfano in the mirror behind the bar for most of the time the detective had stood there. His words were loud and aggressive. He was alone.

"The city, out of the Racine station," Alfano said.

"So, you drinking on the city's tab, or is your buddy just handing out free beers?"

"Hey, fella, quiet down," Robert said. "Keep it up, and I'll have to ask you to leave."

"That's okay. I'm off duty," Alfano told the bartender. He turned his back on the drunk.

"I'm talking to you," the man said, not lowering his voice. "You cops think you own the city. What a load of horseshit. You should be out stopping criminals and not drinking free beer."

"You, out!" Robert demanded and looked across the packed barroom to a large man near the door. He pointed at the man standing next to Alfano. The bouncer expertly pushed his way through the crowd.

"I'm not done with my beer."

"You are done now. That one's free, so go."

"And let this cop drink for free while decent people have to put up with all the crap from city hall and the police?"

Alfano put a dollar bill on the bar. "Make you feel better?"

The bouncer had come to stand behind the detective; he easily was a foot taller than the loudmouth. Alfano recognized the bouncer; he was a retired heavyweight boxer.

"That's okay, Lionel. He's all right," Alfano said. He put another bill on the bar. "Robert, this is for my friend."

The man brushed the bill off the bar; it fluttered to the black-and-white checkerboard floor.

"I don't need charity, especially from a cop. I can pay my own way."

He stepped too close to Alfano and put his face right in front of the detective's.

Lionel grabbed the man by his collar and yanked him backward, in the process propelling him around and away from the bar and toward the crowded floor.

"I'm getting you a taxi, sir. It's time to go home to the wife and kiddies," Lionel said, his tone pleasant.

"I haven't got one anymore, a wife that is," the drunk said. "She left me three days ago. Called me a drunk and an asshole and went home to dear old Momma, the bitch. I don't need her anyway."

Lionel slowly and methodically shoved the man through the crowd and to the door. A second later, they were gone.

"Sorry about that, Detective. I haven't seen him around here before," Robert said. He pointed at Alfano's half-full stein. "That one is on the house."

"And confirm what that drunk said? Not a chance."

Alfano picked up the dollar off the floor and placed it next to the first bill.

"Will this cover it?"

"More than enough."

Robert took the bills and turned to the cash register. In the mirror, he saw a woman standing in the front doorway. She was waving in Alfano's direction. He turned back to the detective.

"Detective, I think your date has arrived."

Alfano took a last swallow and then placed his stein on the bar. "Later, Robert."

"Detective," Robert said as he slipped the bills into the till.

Alfano navigated his way through the jostling patrons and, when he reached the doorway, removed his hat. Debbie leaned in and kissed him on the cheek.

"Sorry for being late, Tony. Father is keeping me busy."

Alfano returned the affectionate kiss with one of his own. Her cheek was soft and warm, and the fragrance of something exotic filled his nose. He inwardly relaxed, realizing he hadn't been sure how warm a welcome to expect from her. His fault for leaving so abruptly the last time. Now he might have a chance to correct that.

He reluctantly pulled away and waved to the maître d'. The man nodded and pointed across the room. Debbie and Alfano crossed the room and caught up with the host at a booth against the wall.

"It is good to see you again, Mrs. Tillerman, and you, too, Detective Alfano," the host said.

"Thank you, Howard. It is good to be back," Debbie said as she slid into the booth. Alfano followed.

Howard handed menus to each of them and announced the night's special: "A thirty-two-ounce porterhouse steak with an incredible pepper sauce, which is more than enough for two. We also have a recent delivery of excellent Rieslings from Alsace. And, of course, some excellent red wines; and a few other things, if you are interested."

A man, dressed much like a bartender, stood behind the maître d'.

"Frank will be your waiter," the maître d' said, his tone formal as ever. "Please have an excellent evening."

They watched as Howard walked away and Frank took his place.

"Cocktails?"

"Frank, this is Detective Anthony Alfano."

"Then what wine would you prefer?" Frank asked with a smile.

Alfano answered, "Canadian Club. That is, if you have any hidden away somewhere. Deborah?"

"Oh, it's Deborah now, is it?" She smiled at Alfano before looking at the waiter. "Champagne cocktail, Frank."

They ordered oysters and then the porterhouse with creamed spinach. A bottle of French Burgundy appeared. Debbie Tillerman snuggled close to Alfano. The soft silk of her dress lay tight against the linen slacks of his suit.

"How is Mrs. Schwartz?" he asked her.

"Doing better. She's resilient. She had a tough childhood in East Prussia, so she's known death her whole life. Two of her siblings died from the famines."

Alfano nodded, unsurprised at the revelation. The famines that raged through that part of Europe had been more politically inspired than natural. Sadly, Mrs. Schwartz's story was not uncommon.

"How someone could use starvation as a weapon is beyond me," Debbie was saying. "She misses Benny. And Linda has her own family to deal with, but they will be all right."

"I met Samuel—seems like a good kid."

"He is, but he wants to follow in his brother's footsteps. It's breaking her heart. Maybe you can redirect his energies. With Benny gone, he's got no one now to guide him. If it's left to those men in the gyms and clubs, who knows what he'll become."

Debbie picked up her wineglass; Alfano noticed for the first time that she had a Band-Aid wrapped around her left index finger. He gently took her hand in his.

"Did you cut yourself?"

"No, silly me. I stuck a pin in my finger. I've been sewing for most of my life and I can only remember a time or two when I drew blood."

Alfano wanted to believe her—did believe her—but a thought occurred nonetheless. He kept his face expressionless.

She took another sip of her wine and then added, "It's really just a hobby. Momma taught me to sew. I'm making a new dress. Something to do."

"Can I see it when you are done?" he answered and then kissed her finger.

"Absolutely. However, it's for winter. The fabric is thicker; the result is a needle in the finger."

The evening was mild. After dining, the two friends walked down State Street, past the Marshall Field's building, and north toward the Chicago River. Even at this time of the evening, the street traffic was heavy.

"Why are you a policeman, Tony Alfano? Why do you do what you do?" Debbie asked as she accepted a cigarette.

"It's a job, and today that's worth a lot," he answered as

he lit it.

"An evasive answer. You could work just about anywhere. You're confident, smart, and good-looking."

"And in this economy, that and a dime, if you had one, would get you a bad cup of coffee."

"I forgot to mention, modest."

"Stop that. I'm a cop because of another cop. His beat was my old neighborhood, a few blocks from Taylor Street. I used to get into a little trouble, nothing serious, the stuff idle and bored teens get into. One day, this man took me aside and told me what my future would be if I kept on the road I was on. Three of my friends ended up dead, shot down working for some of the gangs that were popping up after the war. This cop, his name was Shaun Dugan. He got me through high school and then helped me get a spot at the police academy. And now"—Alfano turned toward her and spread his arms wide—"one of Chicago's finest, at your service. I got my detective's star ten years ago and can call some politicians and bartenders by their first names."

"And that's a good thing?"

"Sometimes."

"What happened to Officer Dugan?"

They were standing on the State Street Bridge. Alfano gazed down at the river drifting slowly below them; a dozen small boats crisscrossed the water.

"Second year I was on the force, some punks robbed a bank on Halsted. There were three of them; two were kids I grew up with. Officer Dugan recognized them, and that delayed his reaction. The third kid had a revolver. He shot Dugan in the chest and killed him."

"I'm sorry."

"It broke my heart. Those two ex-friends of mine are still in prison. The killer was executed. That was eighteen years ago, but it seems like yesterday. I miss that big Irishman."

Alfano pitched the butt of his cigarette into the river. He thought of the Band-Aid on Debbie's finger. He'd never wanted so badly to be wrong about a hunch. He chose his words carefully.

"Generally speaking, I might not disagree with him. But exactly why is your father so adamantly against boxing?"

Debbie leaned against the railing as the cars behind them rumbled across the iron grating of the bridge; the whole structure shivered.

"My father was born in 1872. My grandparents had just emigrated from Odessa. Like a lot of Jews then, as now, they found a way to escape the pogroms. Father was born a month after they arrived in Chicago. They lived in a hovel off Maxwell Street. Three years later, my uncle was born—his name was David. Both boys grew up wild and free, certainly not what it would have been like in Russia. They both got into boxing, for the money, as Father says. Every dollar helped."

"Wow," Alfano said, truly surprised. "I find it hard to believe your father boxed."

"Yes, it's hard for me to believe as well. My grandmother told me he was very good; he fought with a chip on his shoulder. He quit at the same time as—so, to go back, in 1893, he and his brother were boxing in fights that were part of the activities for the last World's Fair. This was all before my time, of course."

"Of course," Alfano echoed with a smile.

"Father doesn't talk about it. According to grandmother, Uncle David was a middleweight. He fought this Russian who had just immigrated to Chicago. My grandmother said it was an awful fight. The referee wouldn't stop the bout even when it was obvious that my uncle could not go on; a day later, he died from damage to his brain."

"I'm sorry."

"That was forty years ago, but Father has carried it with

him since. My grandmother never recovered from the pain, either. It's been my family's sad legacy. That's when Father quit—when David died—and he swore he'd never stop trying to outlaw the sport . . . if you can call two men beating each other up a sport. After the Gans and McGovern fight, Father helped to ban it in the city for a while. Sadly, it wasn't outlawed for the boxing; it was for the illegal gambling and fixing—and only in Chicago. When it was allowed again, Father was furious. So, I support him where I can."

"It's tough to change people's attitudes."

"It's tougher to change their greed."

30

THE NEXT MORNING, Sergeant McDunnah phoned in to say he would be home for at least two more days. He was under doctor's orders to keep his leg elevated and change the dressing twice a day. He'd be in Friday.

"Damn leg still is killing me," the sergeant admitted when Alfano pressed him. "At least yesterday I could listen to both ends of the double header of the Sox winning two against Boston. And there's another double header today—glorious. I guess I could get used to this."

"Enjoy it while it lasts. I need you here. Listen to the doctor; no messing around with that leg, okay? If not, I'll talk with Moira."

"Got it. What's happening with O'Shea and Schwartz?"

Alfano told McDunnah everything he knew, including Sammy Schwartz's offer to act as lookout during the Saturday match at the lagoon stage.

"You be careful there, Detective. He's just a kid. He doesn't know the trouble out there waiting for him. And if you drag him in and something happens, you will never forgive yourself."

"I know. Although Sammy might be our best lead at the moment. He says there's been a few more instances of possible fixed fights and loaded gloves. He tells me there are even more that aren't reported."

"Just leave them alone and keep him out of it."

"Saturday, it's a series of exhibition fights at the fair. High profile and visibility. I'll be there."

"Just be careful. There's something else going on here."

"Yes, I know."

Alfano studied the crime board; half of it was taken up with items about Rosenberg and his gang—who now were the proverbial dead end. He stood and re-pinned the Rosenberg photos, with their black ribbons, off to one side. He then moved the various rap sheets and other crime-scene photos that the sergeant had posted. He couldn't accept that the Rosenberg crew was responsible for the injuries to the fighters at the fair; they now were lying in the morgue. What remained on the board were images and notes about the victims, including the two fighters, O'Shea and Schwartz; the picture of the gloves; his notes on the fights; and mug shots of McGoin, Kimble, Stingly, and Myerhoff. The promoters, yes, he thought, they could be loading the gloves, tilting the odds on the fights—but it would be chump change. Rosenberg had lost the most and, Alfano assumed, recovered much of it from the dead bookies. He smiled at the irony of the bookies getting even in the end—even if his sergeant had been one of the avenging angels. McGoin and Stingly might be the perpetrators, but Alfano believed that this operation required a lot more finesse than either of those two inherently had.

The perpetrator had to be someone who had easy access to the venues; someone no one would question: a security guard, a boxer, a manager, a known fixer.

Debbie Tillerman had mentioned greed the night before. One of the seven so-called deadly sins. Greed, that had been Rosenberg's angle: turn money into more money, no matter how he did it or who got in his way. Alfano discounted the other six sins, even though he'd put away a lot of bad guys for most of them. He'd always, since his days on the beat, believed that one was missing; that sin was revenge. He also knew why it was missing from the Bible's list; half of the Good Book was written with revenge as its theme. But the need for revenge, to resolve a vendetta, take an eye for an eye, was even older than those ancient religious words. The court system was established precisely to remove vengeance as a private and primal tool. Revenge became the state's jurisdiction, as if that could stop someone from privately exacting their pound of flesh. He, a cop, was the state's tool in seeking vengeance or, as some called it, justice. There were times when he resented being placed in that role, becoming a paid sword of vengeance.

He looked at the box sitting on the floor under the board, the box with the O'Shea gloves. He made a note to find out if the crime lab had typed the blood yet. Maybe it would help.

"Detective Alfano," a voice said behind him. He turned around, masking his irritation both at being interrupted and that it wasn't McDunnah.

"Yes, Doud?" he said.

"There's a woman here to see you, name of Linda Gottschalk. She says that she is Benjamin Schwartz's sister."

"Interview One, and two coffees. Is it fresh?"

"No, Detective. I'll make a new pot."

Again, not McDunnah. Alfano sighed inwardly and headed to the interview room.

Linda Gottschalk was dressed in an expensive-looking beige linen suit, white blouse, and a strange hat that sat to one side of the tight curls of her dark hair. She was smoking a cigarette. Prosperous floated around the room and mixed with the cigarette smoke and her high-priced perfume.

"You don't mind, do you, Detective?" she asked, dropping an ash into the ashtray.

"No." He lit one of his own. "What can I do for you?"

"Samuel told me that he'd talked to you. Told you about his boxing match this Saturday."

"He did. The kid seems excited about the fight, even confident."

"He's a child. He knows nothing. Even what happened to Benjamin hasn't changed his mind about the sport. Our mother is beside herself."

Alfano nodded politely and said nothing. He anticipated the speech that was coming when Gottschalk leaned closer to him and squared her jaw.

"For the last fifteen years, since our father died from the Spanish flu, she has done everything to keep the boys out of the ring. Benny was headstrong, too much like Papa. Sammy is just like his brother."

Again, Alfano nodded and chose silence. It occurred to him that Debbie Tillerman wasn't the only woman who could sew.

"I was nine when Papa died, leaving the four of us to be raised by Mama. She couldn't give the boys a father, a man to follow. When they were old enough, they went to the gym. I think it was then that she lost them. Thank God for that, I guess. It kept them from being recruited for the gangs. But now Samuel won't give it up; he has dreams in his head."

"What boy doesn't? Mrs. Gottschalk, what do you want me to do? This is really a family issue."

"I want you to convince Samuel to quit, get out of the fights, stop all this foolishness."

"You said the boys were like their father?"

"Yes, when Papa was young and new to America, he also was a boxer. He saved enough from fighting to open the newsstand. That's where they met, at the newsstand. They were older than most when they married. Mama was thirty-three, if I remember correctly."

"I admire her spirit. She is quite a force."

"But she can't make Samuel stop. It's his life, she says. He has to make his own decisions, she says. But I know she wants him to quit."

"You said she's upset."

"I know she's upset, even though she won't say anything to him. But I know it. He admires you, he said so. Can you make him stop?"

"I'll talk to him. I've been to the gym where he works out. It's a good place; good people run it. Frankly, it's better than a lot of places today for a teenager. I'll see what I can do, but no promises."

He watched her gather up her handbag and slip the package of cigarettes back into the pocket. She extended her hand.

"Thank you, Detective. Please do what you can. It would make my mother very happy."

"I'll walk you out."

Alfano opened the door to Racine Street. A massive black Cadillac sat at the curb. A tall man in chauffeur livery stood next to the rear passenger door. When he saw Mrs. Gottschalk, he opened the door and waited. She turned back to Alfano and looked at him.

"You need to talk with Rabbi Harris, ask him about the Ukraine. Thank you."

She then disappeared into the dark cavern of the Cadillac's back seat.

Alfano, back at his desk, mulled over what Linda Gottschalk had asked of him. He would say something to Sammy. The kid was sharp and smart; despite his passion for the sport, the road he was on was dangerous. It was like walking down a dark street at night. At anytime, something might hit you, even if you were careful.

He decided that the crime board was better for all his reorganizing. He looked at the picture of a pair of boxing gloves McDunnah had posted, and then flashed on the man in the suit he'd seen at the fair—the man who had been holding a pair of boxing gloves. Was he connected? Alfano made a note about the man in the suit and then scribbled a second note and stuck them both to the cork. The second note read: *WHY?*

He took out his notebook, checked a page, then called.

"Rabbi Harris, Detective Anthony Alfano here. Do you have a few minutes to talk?"

After scheduling the meeting, he watched Doud cross the room.

"Phone call, Detective," Doud said.

"Who is it?"

"Didn't say."

Alfano picked up the earpiece and grabbed the phone. It was Father Dominic calling about a matter he deemed urgent.

"I may know someone. I'll call you back in five minutes," Alfano said after the priest explained.

He clicked the cradle for the earpiece and then dialed Sergeant McDunnah's house number.

"It's Daisy O'Shea," he told McDunnah after Moira had picked up and then passed her husband the phone. "Father Dominic just called. She's with him, and she's starting to fall apart. All of this and the baby are getting to be too much . . . Do you think Moira can help? Would you ask her?"

He waited while McDunnah talked to his wife. Moira came back on the line, asking what she could do.

"The sergeant will fill you in, but this woman—still a girl, practically speaking—needs some help. If you could sit with her for a while?"

Moira agreed, and it was arranged that Father Dominic would drive Daisy to the McDunnahs' house.

When Daisy had dropped the gloves off, Alfano could see she was under a lot of strain. He was upset with himself for not understanding how much.

"Thank you," he told Moira, hearing the relief in his own

voice. "That would be great. Thanks. I'll stop by in a while."

* * *

Alfano sat in the Packard in front of the McDunnah residence thinking about what Rabbi Harris had told him. It was all circumstantial at best, but still there was a lot to consider. He rang the McDunnah doorbell; Moira opened the door.

"She's resting," she said as she led the detective to the small back room off the kitchen. "I have her in the upstairs bedroom, and the child is taking a nap, too. The poor woman is about to collapse."

"Thanks for taking her in."

"That's not a problem—the problem is, what to do tomorrow?"

"Tomorrow?"

"Yes, tomorrow; what to do with the family after today? She talked and cried about the funeral last Saturday, but is still at her wit's end. Father Dominic is helping, but Daisy is totally frazzled. The money the priest gave her, that blood money from McGoin, is all gone. I'll do what I can to help, but it's going to be a tough road for her."

"Thanks for your help."

"Stop saying that. It's what I do. But long term? We need to work something out for her. Her friends have their own troubles, and as much as they want to help, they have very little money and their own priorities. She's a lost soul—actually, they are two lost souls, with a third due in two months."

Sergeant McDunnah was stretched out on the couch, his leg braced up on the sofa arm. Daisy's little girl, Mary, was tucked in the crook of his arm, asleep.

"Detective," McDunnah whispered; the sound of a baseball game drifted in the background of the small room.

"Sergeant, good to see you are putting yourself to work. How's the game?"

"Sox are winning. Moira told you?"

"Yes, any ideas?"

"We are working on a few. The Hull House people said they might have room," Moira said.

"You have been busy."

"He's been a help." She pointed to her husband.

"You've trained him well," Alfano said.

"Cute. I am lying right here."

"And doing an excellent job of it." Alfano looked at Moira. "Hull House? If they have room, yes, they would be a big help."

"There's a luncheon there tomorrow for Miss Jane Addams. It's for her birthday in a few weeks. I'm meeting one of the social workers afterward at two o'clock. We will see what we can arrange then, but for today and even the next few days, they'll be just fine here. It's a pleasant diversion from the demands of his lordship."

They both looked at the sergeant. He had nodded off, the child quiet and nestled in his big arm.

31

IT WAS LATE in the afternoon when Alfano parked the Packard in front of the Hide Away. He told the valet to leave it where it was; he'd be back in a few minutes.

"Want me to rub it down, Detective? It could use a little TLC, if you know what I mean?" the kid asked. "Won't take but a minute."

"Sure, kid, do your best—have it ready in fifteen, got it? There's five bucks in it if you can."

"Yes, sir!"

Alfano pushed his way into the gambling joint. The noise was penetrating. What was going on, even at this time of the day, wasn't his concern. Standing just inside the entry was the same flat-nosed bouncer who managed the front door.

"He ain't here, Detective," the man said.

"You don't know who I'm looking for. Maybe it's you."

Fear flashed for a split second on his face, and the bouncer took a step back.

"Got ya! I saw his car in the lot. Tell Mr. Johnson that Detective Alfano wants to talk."

"I's know who's you are."

"Then be a good little boy and go find him. I'll be at the bar."

Alfano crossed through the room, weaving between the craps and roulette tables. The mingled sounds of the dice games and spinning black balls bounced off the low ceiling. He took a position at the end of the bar, every inch of which was jammed with some swell or a good-looking babe. One woman caught his eye and followed his wanderings through the casino. She left the nearest craps table and headed directly toward him. She stopped a foot away and smiled.

"You work long hours, Nadine. Does Eddie know?" Alfano said.

"What I do on my own time is my business, Detective."

He watched her slowly remove the long gloves she wore. She was one hip throw short of being a show stripper.

"And what do you do on your own time?" Alfano said, pleased with the impromptu and playful striptease. He signaled to the bartender.

"I like to have fun. Is that a crime in this city?"

"Sometimes. It depends on how much fun you're having."

He turned to the bartender and started to say that he'd have—"A Canadian Club on the rocks. Same for me, Tanya," Nadine interjected.

"Good memory," Alfano told her. He was enjoying this.

He watched as the cute bartender removed a bottle from a low shelf and began to pour.

"It pays to have a good memory," Nadine said, turning his cheek to look at her. "You never know when you need to forget something." She then lightly slapped his cheek.

"Funny girl."

"So, after all the excitement of the other night, Eddie was disappointed that you didn't stay around. To be honest, I was disappointed, too."

"Life is full of them."

"What?"

"Disappointments."

"Now you're just being rude."

"He's always been a rude guy, Nadine."

They both turned to look at Tim Johnson, who had come up to stand behind Nadine. Alfano felt almost disappointed to see him. He wouldn't have minded a few more minutes of Nadine's tease.

"Good evening, Mr. Johnson," Nadine said.

"Nadine, why don't you run along and stop bothering the detective. Powder your nose or something. We have things to discuss."

Nadine gave Johnson a smile that simultaneously said, "Yes, sir," and "Go to hell." She turned back to Alfano. She took the gloves she held in her hand and softly slapped him on the cheek. "Later."

"You know her?" Johnson asked.

"In what sense, Johnson?" Alfano said as he sipped his drink. "As in biblical?"

"Never mind. What do you want?"

"You've heard about Rosenberg and his boys?"

"Who hasn't? The rumors about who's filling his shoes are running up and down State Street like an Italian Day parade. Personally, whoever killed him did the city a favor. It's a little safer out here now."

Alfano glanced around the casino.

"Safer for who? Some of your patrons can barely buy breakfast, yet here they are dumping their quarters into your slots and stacking their chips on your numbers."

"I give them a meal, and drinks are on the house. They get home safe."

"You are a regular social worker and hero of the people."

"Alfano, what do you want?"

"Some information," the detective said and slipped a five on the bar.

"Your money's no good here."

"Tanya, this is a tip. Okay, boss?"

The bartender looked at Johnson, who nodded. She slipped the five inside her well-endowed blouse.

"I'm looking for someone who wants to shut down boxing in this city, maybe the whole state. Rosenberg was a dead end. He wasn't involved with the fix—it was someone else."

The gloves had been loaded with lead shot, he told Johnson. "In fact, a lot of the fights in recent weeks have been fought with tampered gloves. If the word got out that no fight could be considered honest, what would that do to your sports book?"

"It would collapse, or at least the boxing side would. Why would you do that?"

"Tim, we go back a long time. So, some help here—what have you heard?"

Johnson nodded. Over the years, the two men had shared a few good stories and run-ins that ended up a little off-book. I scratch yours, you scratch mine definitely applied.

Johnson looked at Tanya and pointed to Alfano's almost-empty glass. She nodded when he held up two fingers.

"The current rumor is that there's an avenging angel who's trying to kill boxing," Johnson said. "Some of the clubs and gyms think this person wants to make it so dangerous to fight that the commission or the politicians will shut it down. You're right about the loaded gloves. A few pairs turned up last month, same deal. Lead shot. But most of the mitts from the fights, especially when one guy is seriously hurt, have just disappeared. But most of the fights were good."

Alfano swirled his replenished glass.

"Is there any one venue that's had more of these fixed fights?" he asked Johnson.

"The Chicago Stadium, the World's Fair, and the Marigold," Johnson said without hesitation.

"The Marigold?"

"Yeah, Dietrich's joint. I can't tell you exactly why, but the nights there's big fights in his ring, I watch the book real careful-like."

"Like the night of Rosenberg's big bets?" Alfano said.

"They weren't placed here. I told you that. And those two bookies that got themselves killed, well, this ain't a racket for the fainthearted."

"You should all be swept out into the river and flushed to St. Louis. Why didn't you tell me this last week?"

"It wasn't my business."

"Of course it is, and you know it. This place stays in business because there's politicians with one eye closed and the other looking the other way. I saw three cops playing dice over there and a judge who can't stay away from the Blackjack table. You watch your business like a cock with his hens and chicks. I want a name. Can you get me that?"

Alfano watched as the wheels seemed to spin in Johnson's head: the pros and cons, the plusses and minuses, the ups and downs.

"I'll see what I can find," Johnson eventually said. "This isn't coming from the street, I can tell you that. There'd be hair on it; someone would say something. I'll let you know."

"Thanks. You know where to find me."

Alfano finished his drink, winked at Tanya, and headed toward the door. Halfway there, someone grabbed his arm. He spun around and almost knocked Nadine to the floor.

"Need company?" Nadine asked, nonplussed.

"Working, and a long night ahead."

"I could say the same thing."

"Goodnight, Nadine. Be careful."

Alfano tipped his hat to the bouncer as he passed and found his car, shinier than a new penny, right in front. He slipped the kid the promised fiver and drove off down Devon. He had one more stop.

* * *

It was dark both outside and inside. The sign on the front door read, *Closed*. Alfano peered through one of the small side windows into the dark entry hallway of the Marigold Gardens. At the far end, a panel of light from a single open door washed across the dark floor. He banged hard on the front door; it boomed like thunder. He waited ten seconds and did it again. A shadow appeared in the white door panel, and then a silhouette was visible in the hallway.

Alfano smiled to himself and pounded on the door again. A shaft of light from a flashlight pierced through the glass, someone muttered "son of a bitch," and then came the heavy click of a door latch. The owner of the flashlight shifted the beam from the glass to the opening in the front door.

"Put that fucking thing down, Dietrich. We need to talk."

The flashlight went out.

As Alfano followed Dietrich down the hallway, he saw the revolver in Dietrich's hand reflect the light from the floor. Further inside, in the dim light of a single light bulb high over the boxing ring, he saw that the great hall was a chaos of overturned tables and chairs. The mess continued inside the boxing ring, where two stools had been overturned and towels flung about. The smell of stagnant beer and liquor lay in the air.

"Why the fuck did you close me down, Detective?" Dietrich said when they reached his office.

"I didn't."

"Like hell. When I asked the lieutenant—who showed up after all the shit that happened—he said the order came from downtown. You, Alfano, are downtown as far as I'm concerned. So, it had to be you."

"Sorry, Dietrich. Wasn't me. My guess, it was one of the aldermen I saw sitting ringside with their wives or girlfriends. Not sure which, but probably girlfriends. They would not have been as pissed if it were their wives."

Dietrich pulled two glasses from the glass shelves of his bar, and put two fingers' worth of bourbon in each. He handed one of the glasses to Alfano.

"You're still a downtown flunky."

"Believe what you will, Dietrich. You always do."

"*Prost!*" They clicked glasses, and Dietrich shot the drink down.

"Which alderman?" Alfano wanted to know. "I didn't see any."

"From the 11th. He's a close friend of the mayor's."

"As I said, a flunky."

"Cut the crap—you saw the alderman and recognized him. He was talking with two other people, a man and a woman. The man was older. Do you remember who they were?"

Dietrich poured more bourbon in his glass and then held the bottle up to Alfano. The detective shook his head.

"He's another alderman, a Jew from the 24th, and it wasn't his girlfriend with him—it was his daughter. Name's Solomon, Isaac Solomon. Why he was here, I haven't a fucking clue. He's been trying to kill boxing in this town since it was legalized."

Dietrich took a swig of bourbon. "Yeah, and she's a knock-out. I don't know her name."

Alfano didn't volunteer a name or even recognition.

"Did they say when you could reopen?" he asked.

"No, and I got forty people with no income until I do."

"I'll make a call. Sometimes, Eddie, it's good to know someone who's a flunky for downtown."

32

FIVE DAYS EARLIER, Tommy O'Shea had been laid to rest at Mount Olivet cemetery, in the far South Side of the city. Father Dominic had presided and the mayor had attended. This morning, before Daisy and Mary were to visit Jane Addams's Hull House, she asked the McDunnahs if they could visit Tommy. Alfano drove and then stayed off to one side as Sergeant McDunnah and Moira stood at Tommy's fresh grave with his pregnant wife and their little girl. When they returned to Alfano's Packard, the detective helped Mary settle onto her mother's lap in the back seat.

"Thank you, Detective Alfano," Daisy said as she fiddled with Mary's collar. "I wish you could have known my Tommy. He was a good man."

"I'm sure he was. Are you ready for this afternoon?"

"Yes, Detective, ready as I can ever be."

Moira and McDunnah stood outside the car and waited.

"I've a few things to do back at the station," Alfano said to Moira. "I'll drop you at the house and then I will pick you up at one thirty; and, Sergeant, there's no reason for you to go. I want you off your feet."

"I'm fine," McDunnah protested.

"I'm selfish. I don't want fine. I want healthy and no limp."

"See what I have to put up with, Moira? He's like that at the station," the sergeant said.

"You wish," Alfano said. "Do I have to ask for a note from your doctor before you come back?"

An hour later, Alfano sat at his desk, tapping his notebook with a pencil. He'd written Deborah Tillerman's name and, in parentheses, the name "Solomon." The man with her at the Marigold fights had seemed somewhat familiar, but it wasn't until Dietrich put the two of them together that it finally began to crystallize in his mind. Why had Debbie gone to the fight at the Marigold? Why was her father there with her?

He wrote the alderman's full name next to Debbie's and then ripped the page out of the notebook. He stuck the sheet of paper next to the note on the board that read *WHY?*

"There was a call for you, Detective," Doud said, handing him a note.

"Did he leave his name?" Alfano looked at the note. "Oh, never mind."

"Eddie, what's up?" Alfano said when Dietrich picked up the receiver. "What do you mean, you found them?"

Dietrich was sure, he insisted, when Alfano pummeled him with questions: "Gloves? What gloves? You sure? Lead shot sewn in? Do you know which fighter? You have both pairs?"

He would send a patrolman over to collect the gloves, Alfano told Dietrich. "No, we are not square," he added. "But you're closer. And thanks."

As he hung up, Alfano flashed on the man he'd glimpsed at the Lagoon Theater the previous Saturday night, the man in the suit holding the gloves. Even though he hadn't seen the man's face, right now he was sure the elusive figure he'd seen at the Marigold with Debbie and the man at the fair were one and the same.

Debbie, what reckless secrets are you keeping?

× * *

A little while later, Moira sat in the back of the Packard with Daisy and Mary as Alfano drove north on Halsted Street from the McDunnah residence in Bridgeport. Hull House and its collection of buildings sat on Halsted just north of the Jewish neighborhood on Maxwell Street and east of the neighborhood called Little Italy. If there was a confluence of ethnicities in Chicago, it was here at South Halsted and Polk Street.

Alfano had been inside the three-story red brick settlement complex only once, and that was more than ten years earlier. He remembered it had to do with a woman. She'd been reported missing by her husband, who said she'd left with their two children, abandoning him. What Alfano found in the building was a woman with black eyes, a broken arm, and two frightened children being cared for by the residents in the settlement house. Alfano made it a point, after having a serious and personal conversation with the drunk husband, to see that the man never found his estranged wife and children.

He parked at the curb and offered his arm to Moira and Daisy in turn as they stepped out of the Packard.

"I'll be right here when you are finished," he said to Moira.

"Thank you, Tony. They will take care of us. I can call you at the station when we are done," Moira said.

"That's okay, I'll wait."

Alfano lit a cigarette and watched Moira and her two charges enter the building through one of the three arches that faced the street. The street was full of parked cars, more than he'd seen in this part of town in years. What was more surprising was that many were new and expensive. His shiny Packard seemed to fit in. He recognized the chauffer of one of the cars; the man was a policeman.

"Hi, Herb. What's the mayor doing here?"

"Detective Alfano," the officer said. "It's the old lady's seventy-third birthday, so they are having a party for her. His

Honor would never miss something like this. He's a big fan of Jane Addams."

"Smart man. There's lots of votes in this part of town, too. He come alone?"

"No, Mr. Nash and Commissioner Hayden are with him."

Now Alfano wished he'd said yes to Moira's suggestion and gone back to the Racine station. From the triple-arch entry that the women had just entered, a crowd of people began to emerge. At the head was Mayor Kelly, directly behind him were Nash and Hayden, and following them a collection of the city's aldermen, department heads, and even the police commissioner. Alfano tried to hide behind the massive Packard, but the mayor spied him and waved him over.

"What are you doing here, Detective?" the mayor asked, shaking Alfano's hand.

Before he could answer, the mayor pulled over the police commissioner.

"Commissioner Allman," the mayor said, "this is one of your top people, Detective Tony Alfano from Racine."

"I know the detective," Allman said, returning Alfano's crisp salute. "He's been a busy boy since the fair opened."

"And done a lot for the city in the meantime. Detective, when you get a minute, stop by and bring me up to speed on what's happening in my city."

The last was said with a laugh. Alfano watched Allman look at the mayor and then at him; the police commissioner wasn't smiling. The mayor then moved on toward the street as dozens of questions were barked from the reporters that followed his entourage. Alfano slid back and out of the way.

"I didn't expect to see you here, Detective."

Alfano turned toward the familiar voice.

"Deb—Mrs. Tillerman, I didn't expect to see you here, either."

"It's an important birthday in this city. I greatly admire

Jane Addams. I am here with my father."

She gestured to the stout man who stood just behind her. His thick hair was white and neatly groomed. His suit was expensive.

"Father, this is Detective Anthony Alfano. Tony, my father, Isaac Solomon."

"Mr. Solomon, a pleasure."

They shook hands, and the alderman said, "Deborah has told me a lot about you, and it seems you have the ear of the mayor."

"I work at the pleasure of the mayor and for the city. Whether I have his ear is another matter."

"Well, my daughter likes you, so what more can I say. When you have some time, stop by the Ward office. We can talk."

With that, Solomon turned and walked away, hurrying to catch up with the mayor as he proceeded down the street.

"Busy man," Alfano said to Debbie.

"Yes, overly busy. He works too hard, and I can't get him to relax. He smokes too much and doesn't eat well."

She looked at him, clearly expecting some comforting words. He didn't have a smooth segue to what he needed to know from her, so he plunged in.

"I saw the two of you the other night. You were at the Marigold when Donnie Conti was killed. I thought you didn't like boxing."

Her reaction surprised him.

"You were there? Why didn't you say something, come and see us?"

"I was going to, but then all hell broke out. When it was over, you were gone."

"Are you just curious, or do you have your detective hat on?"

"Both."

She didn't seem taken aback by his bluntness.

"My father had a brief meeting with Alderman Scorsi; we were there only a few minutes. One of the evening's boxers was a friend of his. We were there for support."

"And you left early. Some support," Alfano said.

"What do you mean by that?"

"Just that you disappeared just before the match began that had Conti's nephew boxing. Strange."

She stared at him and then repeated, "What do you mean by that?"

Just as he was about to respond, Daisy's little girl came running up and hugged his waist. Moira and Daisy were a few paces behind. Alfano looked down and patted Mary on the head. When he looked up, Debbie was walking quickly away after her father.

"They can take Daisy and the child in next week," Moira reported. "It will work out exceptionally well for them. They have a room available, and they can help with the baby as well."

"I did very little," Alfano said.

"You did wonders," Moira said. "And the added comments from the mayor and Alderman Solomon helped to seal it."

"What comments?" Alfano said.

"Some very nice things about you and your relationship with the O'Shea family."

"I didn't know," he protested.

"Thank you, Detective," Daisy said as she picked up her child. "Mary, tell the detective thank you."

"Thank you, Detective. They have lots of toys."

33

PATROLMAN DOUD SAID, "Detective, that kid's here again. Do you want to talk to him?"

"What kid, Doud?"

"That Jew kid from the other day—Sam something."

"Samuel Schwartz, that's his name. You must do better, Doud. The sergeant would have you cleaning the Monday morning holding cells if you can't remember names. Do a better job of remembering and be more respectful."

"Yes, Detective. Samuel Schwartz would like a few minutes of your time."

"Thank you, Doud. Tell him I'll be right there. Same room as before. And be careful, your Irish is showing."

"What, sir?"

"You heard me! Tell Sammy five minutes—and get him a Coke."

When Alfano walked in, Sammy was dancing around the room, shadow boxing. The can of Coke sat on the table. Alfano had to admit that the kid was fast with his hands. His footwork wasn't too bad, either.

"Detective Alfano," Sammy said as he pulled off his cloth cap. "Thanks for seeing me. I got some information."

Alfano pointed to the chairs.

"What do you have?" he asked Sammy.

"There's a lot of press about the fights this Friday at the fair. You know, on the floating stage. I don't know who's ginning it up, but suddenly there's posters and handbills everywhere. And my name is on it—that's cool."

Sammy laid a handbill on the tabletop. The headliners were pros from two of the biggest training clubs in the city; the undercard listed four fights. Slammer Sammy Schwartz was listed in the first bout; both he and his opponent were posted as amateurs.

"Are you sure you want this? So soon after your brother?"

"I can make a few bucks. We can use the money."

"That's a bad reason," Alfano said. "And it says amateur."

"A little something to excite the crowd, us before the big boys—I'll show 'em. Besides, Mom can live on fifty bucks for the whole month."

"And if you lose?"

"I get experience. Every round is experience."

"It's all stupid."

Sammy looked at him patiently. Despite his promise to Sammy's older sister, Alfano realized he wasn't going to get anywhere trying to persuade the kid to give up fighting.

"Here's the idea," Sammy said. "While I'm in the ready room, I'll look through the gloves and see if any look off. Check their weight and see if the nose of the glove feels wrong. If I find out anything, I'll signal you. The way I see it, if anyone sees you walking around near the fighters, they will get cold feet. We'll have to wait for the next time."

"Not a bad idea, but I still don't like you boxing. Your last fight was just a few days ago."

"Too late for that. I can take care of Sammy Schwartz," Sammy said with a laugh.

"It's still too dangerous," Alfano answered. "Besides, I need to find out who's doing this, catch them red-handed, if

I can."

"What do you suggest?"

Alfano looked at the kid; he was still bobbing and weaving. "Sit, Sammy. Here's what I want you to do . . ."

Ten minutes later, Alfano asked Schwartz if he could pull it off.

"Aces, no problem. I'll be all right. I'm fighting a kid who couldn't punch his way out of a paper bag. Just watch, and wait."

* * *

"I'm sorry about the questions at Hull House," Alfano said into the receiver. "Seeing you there was so unexpected . . . I apologize. I've been wrapped up in this case."

Debbie murmured her concern when he told her that another young boxer had been injured, but she didn't ask for any details.

"Yes, it was a pleasure to meet your father," Alfano told her. "To make amends, can I buy you dinner? Someplace nice . . . Palmer House it is, seven o'clock. See you then."

Alfano thought about what Debbie Tillerman had told him that night on the State Street Bridge. Her father once boxed. The brother, a family tragedy, and Alderman Solomon now was a reformer. Could the stout, graying man he'd met on the street be the one doing this? Replacing the gloves, endangering the boxers, essentially fixing fights. Was his daughter actually helping him? It was too hard to believe. In fact, he didn't want to even consider it. There had to be something else driving these actions, someone else with access to the fights, someone else with a motive. Either way, he needed to know.

Alfano left the station and went home to change. As he climbed the stairs to his apartment, Alice Kowalski waited for him at the landing. This was the last thing he wanted, the very last thing.

"Good evening, Alice. How are you tonight?"

"I'm good, Tony. Mr. Kowalski is taking me to dinner tonight. It was a surprise, so I have this stew I made. Now, I don't know what to do with it. Do you want it?"

"Thank you, Alice, but I can't. I have an appointment, so it would be wasted."

"You could put it in your icebox for later," Alice suggested.

"Great idea, but the next few nights, I'm out—on an important case."

"That's too bad. You have always liked my stews."

"I do, and that's the unfortunate part for me. Maybe next week you can make me one. Is that okay?"

"I guess so. Maybe Mrs. Janko will take it."

"That's a good idea. Why don't you ask her," Alfano said as he maneuvered himself around Mrs. Kowalski. "I thought I heard her radio as I started up the stairs."

"Thanks, Tony. I'll ask her."

"Alice, either come back in or close the door—the bugs are getting in," Alfano heard through the Kowalskis' open door.

"Teddy is home?" Alfano asked.

"Of course, why wouldn't you think that? We are going out to dinner; didn't I say that?"

"Of course. Sorry about the stew. Ask Mrs. Janko. She would probably be happy not having to cook."

Alfano made it to his door, and as he closed it behind him, he heard Teddy Kowalski tell Alice once again: "Shut the door, Alice, the flies."

* * *

After a feeble shower under his wretched showerhead, Alfano dressed, lit a cigarette, and finished the half-inch of Canadian Club still left in the bottle. An hour later, he parked in front of the Palmer House Hotel. He slipped the valet a couple of bucks.

"Keep it available. If anyone asks, tell them it's Detective Anthony Alfano's automobile."

He flashed his badge.

"Yes, sir," the valet responded. "In fact, I'll park there." He pointed to an open spot against the curb. "Nice saloon, sir. Powerful, I'll bet."

"I wouldn't know, but thanks."

Alfano walked into the lobby and looked around. Debbie was sitting on one of the velvet-covered chaise lounges in the richly decorated lobby of the city's premier hotel. In the few hours since their chance meeting at the Hull House, she, too, had gone home and changed attire. Now she smiled, slowly stood, and in a slightly seductive manner walked toward him. She kissed him on the cheek.

"Thank you for the offer. I wasn't sure if you would ever call," she said. "Father had an evening planned that included a dinner with some veterans group and then a political session at the temple. I could not do that again. Today was long enough. You, thankfully, rescued me."

"At your service, or should I say, rescue."

"The evening is young. Let's find out."

Oysters followed cocktails, and then dinner was a rich fish soufflé. Dessert, when it came, was a slice of lemon meringue pie. The wine was a Chablis.

"It's amazing how much better the wine has become the closer we are to Prohibition ending," Debbie said.

"And how much more expensive it is as well," Alfano countered.

"Tony, this is my treat tonight. It's the least I can do."

"Why have I earned this honor? It was I who was out of line earlier."

"You, sir, when doing your job, are never out of line. I was tired and needed to catch up with Father. So, Detective Alfano, do you have to work this weekend?"

"Right now, I'm off Saturday and Sunday," he lied. "Just a little work tomorrow night, and then maybe a few days for myself. The weather is supposed to be good. Maybe I'll go up to the lake. There's a place I go near the Wisconsin border. Two days for myself."

"What, no company?"

"These few days help me keep my wits about me. Sorry, not this weekend. However, other weekends are negotiable."

"That is a deal. I've a new swimsuit and would love for you to see it."

"You are making it harder."

"I know. What's this work tomorrow night?"

Alfano signaled to the waiter.

"Coffee. Would you like some?" he asked her.

"No, I'll finish the wine. Tomorrow?"

"There's an event tomorrow night at the fair on the North Lagoon. I thought I'd catch it. Sammy Schwartz is boxing. I want to give him some support."

"His mother is trying to get him to stop."

"He's headstrong, and he loves the sport."

"Sport? Phooey, it's an excuse for gamblers to make money on our children," she said. "Nothing good comes from it. After what I told you the other night, I know."

Alfano noticed that her mood subtly had changed. She'd seem relaxed, and now she looked uncomfortable. She finished her glass of wine a little too quickly and then looked at her watch. He wasn't too surprised when she said it was late and that she needed to get home.

"I'm sorry. I didn't mean to bring up the match. Let me buy you a nightcap," he offered.

She looked at her watch again. "No, I am late to see Father. He's supposed to be back from his meetings at nine. Sorry."

"Let me drive you."

"Detective, Tony, I'm fine. They will put the dinner on my

account. I really must be going—don't worry. I'll take a taxi."

Alfano stood and watched as she hurriedly left the restaurant. He could only shake his head in wonder. The last thing he did, before following the woman out, was to carefully remove Tillerman's wineglass from the table, wrap it in a cloth napkin, and slip it into his pocket.

34

THE NEXT MORNING, two manila envelopes, a large paper bag, and Sergeant McDunnah were sitting on Alfano's desk.

"What the hell are you doing here?" Alfano asked knowing full well why.

"I had to get out, don't send me back. Please." McDunnah pleaded while he placed a large paper bag on the desk. "This came in for you."

"How's the leg?" Alfano asked and pointed to the chair next to the opposite desk. He then placed a small white bundle on the desk.

"Bored, both the leg and me. After last night, I knew I needed to come in. I love her, but . . ." Stopping himself, he pointed to the envelopes. "The envelopes are from the crime lab."

The sergeant changed his location from the desk's edge to the chair. He pointed at the box on the floor. "Those the gloves from Daisy O'Shea?"

"Yes, this is the preliminary report." Alfano searched his desk and handed the envelope to the sergeant. "The blood test results should be in the new report"—he nodded at the unopened manila envelopes—"as well as the fingerprints that they pulled from the O'Shea gloves in the box. They were transferred to glass slides."

He opened the larger bag on the desk. Inside were two pairs of dark brown boxing gloves and a note: *These are the ones found at the club. Sorry, I messed them up checking them out. You were right. The lead shot is in the envelope. Good luck. Eddie D.*

"How's your detecting skills this morning?" Alfano asked McDunnah.

"Good. I'll do anything so you don't send me home."

Alfano unfolded the white napkin and carefully removed the wineglass. Avoiding touching the outside of the glass, he set it on the table.

"I want you to compare the fingerprints on this glass to what's in the lab's envelope."

"Whose are they?"

"That would confuse your investigation, so please just check them. Someone left their prints on the glove, and I'm trying to find a match. After that, check these other pairs of gloves in the bag." He pointed at the bag from Dietrich. "You will have to dust them. See if there are any matches. The second pair may have a lot of different prints. Have Doud stay at the front desk. This is the highest priority—use Detective Emerson's desk."

McDunnah relocated the bags, the box, and the wineglass to the adjacent desk, and then he walked across the detective's room to the small storage room. A minute later, he returned with a simple wooden box and began to spread out his fingerprinting equipment on the desk.

Alfano read the short report on the blood test. The small sample from the seam tested O+. He wished there were some other way of determining blood properties or ownership. The report also noted that the blood tested by the coroner from Benjamin Schwartz was A+, and Tommy O'Shea's had tested as B+. Alfano wasn't surprised that neither fighter's blood type matched the seam sample. Now all he had to do was find someone with O+ blood who had been involved with the gloves. And if he remembered correctly, it was estimated that more than 35 percent of the United States was O+, so he'd already eliminated 65 percent of the population of Chicago. That left just one million Chicagoans to check.

He retrieved the paper bag with the Marigold gloves from Emerson's desk, and carefully removed the two pairs of gloves that Dietrich had found. One mitt, a left, had absolutely been tampered with—that was the one Dietrich mentioned. Now that he knew what to look for, squeezing hard he could feel the pouch of shot secured to the broad head of one right-hand glove. He took his pocketknife and gently cut the glove open. Secured inside was a leather pouch identical to the ones found in the O'Shea gloves.

It has to be the same perpetrator.

He looked over at McDunnah, who was meticulously using a fine-haired brush to dust the wineglass.

"How are you doing?"

"Not bad. There are at least three different fingers here. Makes sense; the busboy, the waiter, and the one who drank from the glass. Of course, I can't tell which is which."

"Pull them all, and then compare them to the ones from the gloves."

Alfano reread the report for the O'Shea gloves: five different sets of distinct fingerprints—Kimble's, the referee's, two sets of unknowns, and possibly ones for Daisy O'Shea; her prints still needed to be confirmed. The two unknowns were found on the smooth inside leather surface of the cuff of one of the gloves. Whoever doctored the gloves had wiped the exterior clean but forgotten about the inside.

"Make a note. We still need to get Daisy O'Shea's fingerprints," he told McDunnah. "I want to clear her on the gloves."

"No prints on the lead pouches?" McDunnah asked as he

continued to work on the wineglass.

"The leather is too rough. The only good source is the smooth finish of the mitts, inside and outside."

"Too bad. Those prints would have nailed the fixer."

"I'm going back to the fair tonight. There's a five-bout event at the Lagoon Theater."

He showed McDunnah the handbill that Sammy had given him.

"Your leg up to carrying you for a few hours?"

"Good God, yes. A couple of hours would be therapeutic. I have a cane," McDunnah added. "Moira is enjoying being a grandmother to Daisy and the baby. It was a pleasant surprise that the mayor threw his weight in for the girl."

"Tommy was his godson, and you Irish stick together. But I can't figure why Alderman Solomon would get involved."

"You said there's a connection to the Schwartz family. Could that be it?" McDunnah asked.

"Maybe. That's where I met Solomon's daughter."

"Yes, the lovely Deborah Tillerman." McDunnah paused. "It all just seems awkward."

A short time later, McDunnah put down his brush and carefully placed the wineglass back in a small paper sack he retrieved from his fingerprint kit.

"There, you little devils—I got the prints from the glass, Detective. This new clear Scotch tape does wonders. I'm placing it on a glass slide."

They spent the next hour confirming what they found and rechecking all the prints. Alfano was not as shocked as he thought he'd be. Sadly disappointed, but not surprised.

* * *

Alfano and McDunnah used their badges to get seats below the ring built on the floating stage. Across the narrow strip of lagoon, a stepped concrete amphitheater faced the stage.

Behind the stage, colossal geysers, illuminated from below, provided a surreal backdrop. The noise of the falling water obscured the din from the fair. Alfano noticed that there were fewer people sitting in the amphitheater tonight than last Saturday. Sitting next to Alfano and McDunnah were the timekeeper, judges, and a man holding a stopwatch.

The first two boxers, wrapped in striped robes—one blue and white, the other red and white—danced down a lane that cut through the meager crowd. Their entourage of trainers, managers, promoters, and cut men followed. Alfano watched as Sammy bounced through the fairgoers, his left arm obviously raised. As the group crossed over the bridge that connected the stage to the land, Sammy's eyes scanned the crowd until they found Alfano. He smiled when Alfano acknowledged him and then crooked his head toward the administration building and the ready rooms. When Alfano nodded in reply, Sammy climbed up into the ring.

After the fighters took their respective corners, the announcer began.

"All right, all right, everyone calm down and be quiet," he said as he tilted his face up to the microphone a foot above his head. He paused and waited, holding his crumpled fedora in his right hand, a card in the other. He began to wave the hat around.

"I said calm down . . . that's better. Now then, ladies and gentlemen, thank you for coming out on this beautiful night. I's hope you're having a fun time at the fair. Nothing better than a little boxing to get the juices flowing . . . I promise you a great night, five bouts of unequaled skill and ferocity. Our first match is a four-round, 126-pound exhibition bout between two homegrown Chicago amateurs. In the west corner and in the white shorts and fighting out of the Edmille Health Club with a record of eight wins and one draw is . . . Sammy 'The Slammer' Schwartz. In the east corner and in the blue trunks and representing Kid Howard's Gym with a record of six wins, two draws, and one loss, is Billy 'The Club' Jones."

The thin crowd applauded; the noise from the fountains behind the stage made it difficult for them to hear the announcer. Most were there because of the fireworks that would explode at precisely ten o'clock as they had for the last three months. The lagoon seats were excellent locations for the pyrotechnic extravaganza. Some of the fair visitors licked ice cream cones or munched on snacks from the vendors that lined the Avenue of Flags directly behind the seats. Many had never seen a live boxing event. A few had never even seen a match on film or in a newsreel.

"Schwartz just gave me the signal," Alfano said as he rose. "I'm going to check out the ready rooms. He said if he'd found something, he'd make sure the gloves would be there."

The sergeant began to stand, then frowned, and sat. "This leg is killing me. I'm staying put. You be careful," McDunnah said.

"I'll be right back."

35

AS ALFANO toward the administration building, he heard the bell for round one. The sound echoed across the open theater and was swallowed by the cascading fountains. He turned and watched the two boxers charge each other like young bulls, and then pull up, stop, and take preliminary and ineffective jabs. Both fighters bounced lightly on the balls of their feet and began circling left, their left arms and gloves batting each other, trying to find an opening. Right-side arms and elbows provided mutual defense.

The walk to the administration building took Alfano less than a minute. An attendant in a fair security uniform stood outside the short hallway with its four doors. Each, Alfano assumed, led to a prep room.

He flashed his badge.

"Any of the boxers in the rooms?" he asked.

"All are filled," the guard said. "The pros are in the last two rooms; the amateur pair are in the first two. Is everything okay?"

"Just a little bit more security. Were there any other people hanging around this evening?"

"There's always someone hanging around, Detective. I had to tell some girls to take a hike; they wanted autographs from the pros. Jesus H. Christ, they're just boxers, for heaven's sake." He pointed. "They are over there; it's the three girls smoking. Then, let's see, there were a couple of fair officials. They went through the rooms to make sure they were ready, but that was an hour or more ago."

"Any chance an older, heavy man and a younger woman came through here?"

"Yeah, they got here just after the officials. You mean the pair from the boxing commission, right? I let them pass, 'cause they were bringing in the gloves for the matches, or so they said. Then the first of the boxers and their managers started showing up, of course. So, I guess it's been normal."

"Which rooms did the people from the commission go into?"

The attendant thought for a moment.

"Those first two, and then I think they went into the room on the right. And then crossed over to the left one there. Pretty sure they left by the rear door."

"They weren't carrying anything when they left?"

The guard paused again.

"Come to think of it, they still had those bags they came in with. Now, that's strange, isn't it? They told me that they were leaving the gloves in the rooms for the boxers. Didn't even think about it until just now."

Alfano walked down the hall to the first door. A paper label had been inserted into a small metal frame mounted on the door. It gave the fighter's name and event number. He opened the door. Four people were inside; one wore a suit, two were in white T-shirts, one of them was lacing up the boxer's gloves. The boxer, in black silk shorts, sat on a padded table.

"Were those gloves here when you arrived?" Alfano asked.

The man in the suit answered, "Who the hell are you?"

Again, Alfano flashed his badge. "Were those gloves here?" he repeated.

"No, we always bring our own," the suit answered. "Don't trust no one."

"Were there any others in the room when you arrived?"

"No."

Alfano shut the door behind him and crossed the hall. Like the first room, there were four people. Alfano asked the same questions. The answers were almost the same. He was beginning to think he was on a fool's errand. He checked the last two rooms; they were empty. But the card on the door read "Schwartz." The other, across the hall, read "Jones," the name of the boxer Sammy was in the ring with now. Alfano pushed open the door to Sammy's ready room and looked around. Sitting on a shelf filled with towels and rolls of tape were a pair of boxing gloves. He felt the gloves and found the harder pad in the nose of both mitts. He slipped the tip of his pocket-knife near the seam edge of the right-hand glove, cut through the leather and stitching, and then pulled out the pouch. It looked identical to the ones they'd recovered earlier. He stuck the pouch in his pocket and tied the gloves together. When he crossed the hall and found another pair of gloves in Jones's prep room, he was surprised and then alarmed. The gloves were normal, no lead shot. Shit.

He sprinted down the hall and back to where McDunnah waited. He heard the bell ring, and the roar of the crowd. Above him, the two boxers were pummeling each other. Jones seemed to have the upper hand.

"We need to stop the fight," Alfano said to McDunnah as he handed the sergeant the gloves he'd taken from Sammy's room. "Jones's gloves are loaded."

They both looked up as Sammy was staggered by a blow to the left side of his face. He stumbled backward. Jones pressed in.

Alfano ran to the timekeeper and reached past him to the leather thong that was secured to the striker for the bell.

"What the hell are you doing? There's still a minute and a half left," the timekeeper said, looking at the timer on the table.

"Not anymore."

Alfano pulled the thong and jerked it repeatedly, looking up as he did so. The referee was waving his hands to stop the fight. The ref then began pulling Jones away from Sammy. Sammy collapsed to the canvas.

McDunnah was directly behind Alfano. "What do you want me to do?"

"Get Jones out of the ring and bag his gloves," Alfano said. "And find out all you can about the gloves! Any information would be helpful."

With the help of his trainer and cut man, Sammy was getting to his knees. A vial of smelling salts administered by his trainer snapped him back, his eyes cleared. He looked across the canvas to Alfano and meekly smiled. Alfano climbed into the ring.

"You okay?" he asked.

Sammy was up, balancing gingerly on his rubbery legs. He said, "Did you get my signal?"

"Got it, Sammy. I checked out the rooms. They laced up Jones with the loaded ones. Whoever left them there was targeting you. Why the hell didn't you tell Jones's manager?"

"And be a chicken shit? I knew I could take the kid, loaded or not. That's why the loaded ones is still in the room. I didn't even tell the trainer."

"Sammy, that was stupid. That's why he almost killed you, tough guy."

The announcer walked up to Alfano.

"I don't know what the hell just went on, but are you two going to leave? I need the ring," he said. "The next fight is in ten minutes."

While Alfano had been talking to Sammy, the referee had

declared Jones the winner.

"This fight was fixed," Alfano told the emcee. "And I'll make sure the commission knows, get it?"

"Okay, but I still have another bout." He glanced at Sammy. "We will deal with all that shit later."

Two groups, with the fighters in the lead, were working their way through the crowd. Alfano understood that the matches had to go on—it seemed heartless. He scanned the crowd; most were on their feet, trying to see what had happened. At the far end of the seats stood two familiar figures, watching. From behind Alfano came the sharp report of an exploding firework; the faces of the crowd glowed yellow. Debbie Tillerman and Isaac Solomon's faces lit up red with the next explosion.

The fireworks were early. Alfano quickly climbed down from the ring and found McDunnah cutting away the laces of Jones's gloves. More pops and detonations filled the black sky above the fountain. Green and red light washed over the lagoon and the stage.

"I didn't know there was something wrong, Officer," Jones said as he held his arms out. "Honest to God, I didn't. They was in the room when we got there. So's we assumed they were for us. I never boxed with brand-new gloves. It was kind of special. You get that?"

"We get it, kid—you are not in trouble," McDunnah said. "Detective?"

"I need to chase down the Solomons. They were here a minute ago. You okay?"

"Aces," McDunnah said with a grimace.

"Get Sammy to the hospital and have them give him a going-over. He might have a concussion. I'll find you later."

Alfano headed to where he'd last seen Debbie and her father and then jogged along the waterfront, weaving in and out of the throngs of fairgoers watching the fireworks. Just past a group of children putting gobs of cotton candy in their mouths, and others with handfuls of stuffed animals, he spotted the father and daughter walking hurriedly away from the stage and the lagoon. He caught up to them as they reached the restaurant that extended out over the lagoon.

Seeing Alfano, Debbie stopped and took hold of her father's arm. "Stay right there, Tony," Debbie said. "Don't come any closer."

In her right hand she held a chrome revolver; with her left she held her father.

"This is not how this has to end," he said, yelling over the cannonade of explosions that filled the night sky.

For Tony, this was not how it would end, not again, not here, not tonight.

"Just give me the gun, Debbie. We can work this out." The crowd, eyes to the heavens, surged in and around them. In the chaos, he pulled his pistol and held it to his side.

"Father," Debbie said as Isaac Solomon stopped and was now holding onto the railing, breathing hard, a pained expression on his red face.

"Sit, Father. You have to sit," Debbie said, trying to draw her father away from the railing.

Alfano started to move toward them.

"Stop, no further, just go. Leave us alone."

"You know I can't. You know what needs to be done," Alfano said as he watched Isaac Solomon collapse onto a bench. He went to Debbie's side.

More fiery bursts filled the air; the Sky-Ride gondolas above them glowed in the reflection of the man-made lightning.

"Your pills? Did you bring your pills?" Debbie was asking.

Solomon took a long, ragged breath before reaching over and clutching at his left arm. His pain-racked body shuddered.

Alfano saw a security guard near the rail watching the fireworks. He ran to him.

"Get medical personnel here immediately. That man is having a heart attack." He flashed his badge and looked at the man's identification badge. "Al, did you hear me? Get them now! It's a matter of life or death. And get me fair security."

Alfano went back to the Solomons. He could see that Isaac was in serious trouble.

"He's had heart trouble?" he asked.

"Yes, for years. He's had two heart attacks. I've told him he needed to slow down. Get away from all this. But he wouldn't."

Solomon looked up at his daughter, his face twisting with pain. He held her hand, almost crushing it. Then he whispered that he loved her. When he suddenly relaxed, his eyes were still open and tears ran down his cheeks. He slumped over onto his daughter.

36

THE FIRST LIGHT of the morning sun glowed through the high window of Interview One. It was very early; the streets were quiet for a Saturday. The room, with its one light dangling from the ceiling, was almost silent. The only sound was the whimpering of Deborah Tillerman. She held a damp handkerchief to her face. A glass of water sat half-empty on the table. Detective Tony Alfano stood in the corner, leaning against the edge of the one-way mirror.

"I'm sorry about your father, Debbie," he said.

They had just returned from the hospital, where Isaac Solomon had been pronounced dead from a heart attack. Alfano had placed Debbie under arrest as they left the hospital. She offered no resistance.

Now she looked up at him.

"My father was a wonderful and inspiring man. This was all his idea."

"What was all his idea?"

"To stop boxing in Chicago, to stop the inhumane exploitation of our young men."

"By having them beat the brains out of other kids?"

"It would show the brutality of the sport, the lack of morality, the utter callous viciousness of those involved."

"But young men died because of what you did—others have been injured. You are complicit in assault, manslaughter, even murder."

"That wasn't supposed to happen. It was all a way to show what the effect of boxing can be."

"A stupid and brutal way to show it," Alfano said.

"It had to happen; people need to be shocked . . . see the brutality. The politicians had to be made to care."

"So, why this way? There had to be a better means."

"We tried. We held meetings, we met with the boxing commission, we even talked with the mayor and the governor—nothing. Now more young men, our children, will die. A few must be sacrificed for the many and the good."

"Good God, do you hear yourself?"

A tap-tap came from the door. Alfano opened it to Sergeant McDunnah, who held a bag in one hand and a cup of coffee in the other.

"Thanks, did they check out?" he asked the sergeant.

"Yes, just as you thought." McDunnah closed the door as he left.

Alfano placed the bag and the coffee on the table. The coffee was for him. Debbie had wanted only water when they placed her in the room. Alfano pulled up one of the other chairs, removed a pair of boxing gloves from the bag, and took a sip of the coffee. For once, it didn't taste like asphalt.

He then removed the small pouch of leather from his pocket.

"Mrs. Tillerman, these are gloves that were recovered from the ready rooms at the fair last night. This small pouch, filled with twelve-gauge lead shot, was sewn into the right-hand glove. Another similar pouch is still in the other. These were one of two pairs of loaded gloves found. The method of tampering matches other altered gloves retrieved from other fights. What do you know about them?"

Tillerman dabbed her eyes with her handkerchief and stared for a long time at the glove with the slashed-open nose.

"I've never seen these gloves. I have no idea what you are talking about."

"This pair of gloves was used by one of the fighters last night. He came very close to permanently injuring Samuel Schwartz, the brother of a friend of yours, Linda Gottschalk, and the son of Mrs. Ruth Schwartz."

"So?"

"You are the one who sewed these leaded pouches inside these boxing gloves. And with your father's help have put them into other fights held around the city."

"There is no way you can prove that. I've never seen them before." She looked at Alfano and crossed her arms over her chest.

"We have your fingerprints on the gloves," Alfano continued. "We have a blood sample that I assume will match your blood type. And, I believe, after we search your home—which we are doing right now with a warrant—we will find thread that matches the stitching on the gloves. We have confirmed your father's fingerprints, and yours, on many of the gloves."

"My father is a moral and honorable man."

She turned away from the table and the gloves.

"He is trying . . . was trying . . . to stop this slaughter and waste. No one would listen. Too many were making money. I told you it is all about greed. I told you that."

"Yes, you did. But it also is about revenge."

"For what? It is all about the young men who are dying, the children."

"I think it's all about one man dying."

She looked at him, surprise registering on her face. "My father's gone, my heart's broken."

"This is not about your father's death, but your uncle's."

"What?"

"Your uncle," he said softly. "Your father's brother, who died after a fight thirty-five years ago. It was in the newspaper. My sergeant found it. You told me a few days ago that your uncle David died after a fight. Club and bar fights where both brothers, your uncle and your father, fought to make extra money. Your uncle died after one of those fights. His opponent—a Russian immigrant kid the same age as David—was a tough fighter, and after fifteen rounds, he put your uncle to the canvas. David never regained consciousness. Is that right?"

"Yes, it was all before I was born. It was tragic and senseless, and also the reason my father dropped his gloves and took up the cause."

"Did you know that that boxer, that opponent, all of twenty-four years old like David, was Tevye Schwartzman?"

"So?" Debbie glared up at Alfano.

"Tevye was the father of Benjamin and Samuel, as well as Linda and Rebecca Schwartz. Ruth and Tevye shortened their name to Schwartz when they married."

Debbie turned away from Alfano, looked at her hands resting on the table.

"You knew this . . . the Bible declares an eye for an eye, a tooth for a tooth . . ."

"Are you implying that this all was for revenge for my uncle's death, a man I never knew? Really? This is all beneath you."

"In fact, this is exactly what I'm saying. Tevye died before your father could get his revenge. You and your father's intentions were to have the children of Tevye Schwartz suffer the same fate as your uncle—an eye for an eye."

"Vengeance is mine, sayeth the Lord."

"Yes, and you and your father wanted to give it a little kick in the ass," Alfano said. "Your families knew each other in the Ukraine. Did your father tell you that? Rabbi Harris told me that your families have fought for two hundred years over the theft of a cow."

In any other interrogation, Alfano might have sounded almost cocky when delivering such a line. This time, however, his heart wasn't in it. He simply had to push through and finish the job.

"The real reason Tevye Schwartzman fled the Ukraine was that someone had killed his father during a street brawl. It was during a political demonstration," he continued. "The police were after Tevye; they blamed him for his own father's death. But Tevye knew the killer. He knew it was your grandfather, Artem Zalman, the father of Isaac and David. Then your grandfather also fled the Ukraine and came to Chicago, where he changed his name to Solomon."

Like so many guilty people Alfano had interrogated, he knew when it was over for Debbie Tillerman. She didn't so much slump in her chair as seem to wilt in it.

"So what? Everyone Anglicized their names. Zalman, Schwartzman—I know dozens," she whispered. "And besides, this is all a Ukrainian fairy tale. It's been told a hundred times, each time blaming something or someone: it was the pogroms, it was the nationalists, it was the socialists, the czar. We Jews took sides, sometimes opposite sides, but it was when Czar Alexander III died that the hate really exploded and the pogroms left hundreds dead in the Ukraine. During one of those anti-Russian demonstrations is when Tevye Schwartzman's father died. It was an accident."

Alfano shook his head.

"No, Rabbi Harris knew it all. He's the one who told me the history. It was your grandfather who killed Tevye's father—that was almost forty years ago. The feud was already more than two hundred years old. He said that your father and Tevye accidentally met in a gym in the 1890s, and from there the vendetta was renewed. Rabbi Harris hoped that you and Linda Schwartz had come to your senses and left this all in the past in the Ukraine. It's obvious you couldn't; now two more innocents are dead. You are all that is left."

Debbie Tillerman had nothing left to say. She stared downward, twisting the handkerchief in her hand. At last, she looked up at the detective, her eyes pleading for forgiveness.

He could let this all go. Isaac Solomon paid the debt—he was the state's pound of flesh. He, Tony Alfano, was its sword of justice. He could go to her, hold her tight, tell her it would all be over. He could . . . but he couldn't.

"Someone has to pay the debt owed Daisy O'Shea and Ruth Schwartz," he said. "Someone has to take the fall."

"Is this all I mean to you? Is this what it's all come to? Is there no forgiveness?"

When she looked, there was none in Alfano's eyes.

Reviews Please

Today authors rely heavily on the reviews posted by our readers. As an independent self-publisher this is even more important than traditionally published books. If you have enjoyed this book, please take a few minutes and post a review on Goodreads and Amazon.

About the Author

Gregory C. Randall

Mr. Randall is Michigan born, Chicago raised and Californian by choice. He makes his home in Northern California.

Mr. Randall is the author of fiction and non-fiction works available through the usual outlets and the Windsor Hill Publishing website.

For more on future Tony Alfano thrillers and information on the Sharon O'Mara Chronicles and planned sequels, please visit and connect with Greg online:

http://www.gregorycrandall.info
Read his blog:
http://www.writing4death.blogspot.com

Other books by Mr. Randall available both in print and as ebooks:

Fiction
The Cherry Pickers

The Alex Polonia Thrillers
Venice Black
Saigon Red

The Tony Alfano Thrillers
Chicago Swing
Chicago Jazz
Chicago Fix

The Sharon O'Mara Chronicles
Land Swap For Death
Containers For Death
Toulouse For Death
12th Man For Death
Diamonds For Death
Limerick For Death

Non-fiction
America's Original GI Town, Park Forest, Illinois

These books can be purchased in paperback through all bookstores.

I hope you enjoyed this story!